# SONGS FOR DARKNESS

# SONGS FOR DARKNESS

**by Iman Humaydan**

**translated by Michelle Hartman**

Interlink Books

An imprint of Interlink Publishing Group, Inc.
Northampton, Massachusetts

First published in 2026 by

INTERLINK BOOKS
An imprint of Interlink Publishing Group, Inc.
46 Crosby Street, Northampton, MA 01060
www.interlinkbooks.com


Cover art by Aya Ghanameh

Originally published in Arabic in 2024 as *Oghniyat lil-atma* (أغنيات للعتمة),
by Dar Al Saqi, Lebanon



Library of Congress Cataloging-in-Publication data available
ISBN-13: 978-1-62371-562-5

Printed and bound in the United States of America

To Marwan, Rola, and Mira, who light up my soul

*In the dark times*
*Will there also be singing?*
*Yes, there will also be singing.*
*About the dark times.*
—Bertolt Brecht

# The Letter

New York
December 18, 1982

Dearest Ouida,

You know that you've been my best friend since childhood. You were there all throughout my teen years. And now it's my turn to pack. I'll pack up my clothes—and my daughter's clothes—in a suitcase and leave.

It was really difficult to get everything together in just a few days, walk all the way to East Beirut, and get on a boat to Larnaca.

But the most difficult thing was getting over my fear. And not just that but also pursuing the desire I'd suppressed for so long out of that fear. Fear of doing something, anything. Fear that Mazen would be able to stop me from traveling with Lama at the last minute. Fear of confrontation, fear of making decisions—to move, to travel, to live in exile.

On the day of my son's seventh birthday, I began to feel I was a stranger in my own country. Mazen came and ripped him from my arms that day. And there was nothing to protect me—not my family, not my education, not the law, not all my knowledge of the way the world works. None of those things could protect me from male privilege supported by religion, enforced by law. Nothing at all could protect me or defend me as a mother.

In Beirut, I feel both nostalgic and estranged. I'm afraid to leave the city. I don't know how to live anywhere else. But at the same time, I know all too well that I'm not protected there. Conflicting emotions. Perhaps they're a subconscious coping mechanism to keep me from going mad—they'll help me adapt to this place, which is so changed that I no longer recognize it.

Loss structures my life now. Every moment is loss. Loss informs everything—the roads filled with militiamen who prevent me from moving freely, lonely children, hungry cats, houses destroyed by bombardment, desiccated trees, mountains with their guts spilling out, dark streets, deadly news reports, corpses displayed heartlessly on television screens. Pictures of martyred teenagers, their bodies used to fuel the fires of war, line the walls of Beirut's streets.

Despite all of this, I stayed in Beirut. And every morning, I searched for a reason to get out of bed, only to say, "Good morning, world. Good morning, misery." I found comfort in writing. I did what my mother couldn't.

But eventually I could stay no longer. My fear of traveling made me lose my son. His father took him without batting an eyelash, weaponizing religious law though he'd always been secular. I don't want my fear of traveling to make me lose my daughter too.

I left Beirut behind: sad, destroyed, defeated. It had lost its people, its youth, and its spirit. Beirut is my past that I no longer understand. But I do need to understand it for my departure to feel real. Moving from one place to another is not the same as actually leaving. Truly leaving a place must first take place inside your heart and your soul. Inside your body.

The soul can dry up. Just like how streets dry up. There is no more water, then no more trees, no more birds. They lose the breath of life, familiar touch, the kind of love that smiles back at you through the looking glass. The sounds of friends' voices are gone, simply gone. I didn't believe you all those years ago when you told me there was no place left to live. You were wracked with the pain of your brother's suicide. Now it's my turn. Reading my letter now you'll say that I'm always late with everything—I make decisions later than everyone else. I was late to get married and late to get a divorce. Yes, I'm also late in writing to you. I never imagined that one day I'd be leaving Beirut. It was equally impossible to imagine that one day I'd be writing you a letter from New York and slipping a book manuscript into the envelope. I wrote the last chapter of the book here; it took years to complete.

When I looked down at Beirut from the airplane window, I saw how the past devoured it. The past turned the city into a stranger who expels the people who love it, staring at them heartlessly and telling stories I do not understand. I started thinking about my great-grandmother Shahira, who passed away five years ago. And my grandmother Yasmine, who lived a life as short as a flower. She was a spring butterfly, always fluttering around dreams of happiness without ever catching one. Then there's my mother, who was swallowed up by the sea. Or at least that's how my father insisted on explaining her absence. Perhaps she just wanted to disappear and live in peace.

Each of these women, in her own way, wanted to create a glimmer of light from within herself to brighten up her life. To make it possible to carry on. Shahira managed to do some of that, despite everything. Helplessness and an early marriage killed Grandma Yasmine. My mother is a different story all together. She lived in a world far removed from reality. Perhaps she was struggling under its weight and was rejecting it in her own way by escaping.

I'm sending this to you because most of what I have written is for you to read. You've witnessed much of it. I'm writing to you after collecting so many scattered bits of our lives. Writing is the only way I can bring them all together. We, the women of the family, our stories are bound together by an invisible ribbon that can only be cut by death. The death of words.

If I don't write it down, I will be lost, just as Beirut was lost and Mona was lost. Just as my mother was lost before both of them. I wrote all of this so that my daughter can know what I know. So that I can protect myself and her from being lost.

Shahira died.
Yasmine died.
My mother's fate is unknown.

You'll tell me that I'm writing for the dead and not for the living.

But in our lives, the dead *are* the living. They often lead us towards choices about our existence, without us even realizing it.

I told myself that if I didn't write about them, you, and me, I would die as well. Words from the heart are the only words that matter. If I don't allow them to fill my life, I will have died twice.

I'll tell you all about Shahira as I see her—as I saw her—and about the world that she built singlehandedly. I'll tell you about Yasmine too, her dream of owning a tailoring shop, which never came true. She didn't manage to design and sew dresses for the ladies from the city who summered in the mountains as she'd once hoped to. I'll tell you about Layla, who lived her life through novels; she'd dream, feel sad, or fall asleep every time she read a book.

Shahira chose to outsmart fate. Yasmine never struggled against it, and Layla didn't acknowledge fate—or even the passage of time—at all. Love is an illusion, Shahira used to say. My mother always said that time was an illusion. The women in my family differ on many things; the only thing that they shared was a deep yearning for true love.

Life didn't give Grandma Yasmine space to say much. Motherhood killed her. As for me, I was deluded enough to believe that my life would be different from the lives of the women who came before me. I spent many years at university; I thought that this would shield me, make me equal. I thought it would defend my inherent human rights from the violence of law and tradition. Somehow I believed that my professional work would make me stronger in the face of this violence and that my individual, personal freedom wasn't simply an illusion. I thought that we could change things by taking action. But I discovered that nothing has really changed.

I inherited my olive-green eyes and lush honey-hued brown hair from my grandmother Yasmine. I got my love of books and literature from my mother. But sometimes I've simply had enough, I'm finished with all these things that have been passed down to me. I now want to save myself from madness, from illusions and delusions—the yearning for true love and the oppressiveness of motherhood. But to what end?

Shahira died, asking, "What if war breaks out again? What if the locusts come back, raid our provisions, eat our food, and kill our children?" And they did come back, Ouida! In fact, they never even left to be able to come back. They were always here, weevils in the ground. We invented ways to keep on going each and every day. But eventually we could do nothing more.

I found writing about my mother very difficult. My hand trembled every time I tried to put pen to paper. I thought a lot about what I would write. Where would I start? Should I begin with my perpetual longing for the complicity we once shared and that I figured was lost? Or with her unspoken attachment to my brother? Or the world of novels that she never was able to emerge from? Or should I begin by writing about Salem's brutality towards her? Every time I sat down to write, my body ached so much that I worried my heart would stop.

Many words will simply stay lost. I won't be able to write them down. I'll keep them in my memory, so I can't feel their pain. A day will come when the words will be stronger than me. They'll emerge carrying their own wounds, they won't need me to find the light of day. I will become the subject. I know that time hardens the heart, but it also makes us forget our pain.

There are some complex issues that we must leave to time, that time alone can solve.

When this manuscript reaches you, you'll read it through my eyes rather than your own, through my heart not yours. You'll see that I'm trying to recall childhood images from Ksoura, to hear once again the roar of the wind wrapping itself around our house, to experience the sound of winter rattling the windows, to inhale the scent of damp October soil. I'm conjuring how morning brings a fresh sunbeam crawling across the floor of the room, as if nature hadn't lost its mind the night before. As if nothing had happened. We always used to wait for the morning and never worry, because we knew morning would inevitably come. But today, we've started to worry that it won't come at all.

You'll read about Shahira. And Yasmine and Layla. The violence of our lives and the questions we have. Is it possible to build a nation and a future surrounded by so much destructive male power? By so much physical, religious, legal, and psychological violence? Or should we leave?

Leave? Yes!

Women always leave. Or they shut up. Or they go mad. Or they simply wither away and die before their time, like cherry blossoms.

Why am I writing so much in this letter, when you're about to read the manuscript that I finished just today? It seems to me that you already know everything, and that despite the distance, you know what happened to us.

It's snowy outside. Lama is sound asleep in the bedroom. From the window of our living room, on the top floor of the old brownstone in the middle of Harlem, I can see the northern edge of Central Park, I can see snow on the treetops. The snow is starting to fall harder and cover the cars, muffling the noisy streets. Everyone is home now enjoying the warmth I am missing tonight.

Hugs and kisses,
Asmahan

# Ajmat, Western Beqaa

It is the spring of 1908, the morning of her fourteenth birthday. Shahira stands naked in the big tub, shivering despite the hot water her mother is pouring over her head that runs down her body. She scrubs her back with a loofah and soap, tipping hot water over her again and again. Confused, Shahira crosses her arms over her flat chest as her mother keeps pouring water over her head. She lathers soap onto a coarse loofah and points to her daughter's private parts, saying, "Scrub there, scrub well, get right between your thighs." The girl takes the warm loofah and scrubs herself vigorously, wondering how she'll find a way to tell Yazid about this, since he won't come to Ajmat until June. Her mother keeps repeating herself, as if Shahira isn't doing it well enough. "Let's go, scrub. More . . . more. A girl has nothing if she's not clean. Don't do it like that, my girl, come on. You're a girl not a boy."

Shahira doesn't reply. She stifles the yelp of pain she was about to let out. She speeds up her scrubbing with the loofah—between her thighs right up around her vagina, as if taking revenge on her body. She carries on nervously, more vigorously, until her skin turns red and she all but draws blood. Hasna repeats herself mechanically. Shahira continues scrubbing until it really hurts. She can no longer see anything because so much steam is rising from the large copper pot resting on the fire.

Her uncle's wife, Ikhlas, knocks on the door. She really loves Shahira—she's raised her like her own daughter. She's sad about the arranged marriage that broke the girl's heart, but she feels she can't object. Shahira's older sister Safaa had died of a strange illness that ravaged her body. Her color changed. She stopped eating. She could no longer stand, even to cook for her sons Fayez and Kamal or help them change their clothes. In her final days, she needed someone to steady her so she could sit and wash, as well as help her to the bathroom. Her mother traveled from Ajmat to Ksoura to be by her side. One month later, she passed away.

Near the end, her body was no more than a plank of wood; the blue veins in her neck and arms turned black. She could no longer sit upright. She just lay on the mattress, eyes fixed to the ceiling. Every Thursday evening, Hasna went out into the courtyard, raised her palms to heaven, and prayed. She asked God to grant her daughter some comfort, to take her soul into his eternal embrace. She was living death, alive with her body wasting away.

Safaa was married to Nayif Dahli, a distant relative on her mother's side, from a village in the valley to the west of the mountains. He owned a lot of land filled with stone pines, orchards full of fruit trees, and fields of seasonal vegetables. Safaa was married off to him when her sister Shahira was still a child. She bore him two children and only rarely visited their village after her marriage. Life was hard in Ksoura. Everyone had to work. The distance between Ksoura and Ajmat felt immense, the roads connecting them were narrow dirt paths, only passable by mules and donkeys.

Ikhlas knocks on the door a second time: "Open up, let me in!" Hasna opens the bathroom door and in a whisper orders Ikhlas to hide her feelings. She mustn't oppose God's will. She should be encouraging with Shahira and give her appropriate advice, not add to her worries. Hasna dries her hands, picks up the long white scarf she'd hung on a nail on the wall, puts in on her head, and ties it around her neck. Before leaving, she asks Ikhlas to help her daughter, the bride, get ready—the Dahli family will be there soon. The marriage contract will be signed and then the groom, Nayif, will take Shahira to her new home. Standing at the bathroom door, Hasna shakes her head, sighs, and points at her daughter's body. "Look how the devil makes girls curvy, in the blink of an eye their bodies change. All glory to God, the Creator."

And thus went Shahira's fourteenth birthday—the day she was married off. No one seemed to have noticed this coincidence except her. The men of the family had agreed upon everything ahead of time—the dowry, the terms of the marriage, how the ceremony would go, and that she would move into to her new husband's house on the day that the official marriage papers were signed. There were many reasons for accelerating the ceremony and wedding formalities, especially the distance between the bride's and groom's houses. For Nayif and his family, it was important to avoid another trip to Ajmat because of the distance and rough roads. Also, the wheat harvest in Ajmat would begin less than months later, and Shahira's family would have to devote themselves to the work needing to be done. That part of the season was devoted to the final irrigation of the wheat fields, and they wouldn't have time organize the wedding reception.

Very little wheat was grown in Nayif's town, Ksoura. People might grow some for household use, but most people had none at all. The family did own a vast stone pine forest, however, and the pine nut harvesting season was also coming soon. The first stage of the pine nut harvest is most difficult. That's when they need the help of the village youth who climb the trees and pick the cones, collecting them in giant burlap sacks. Then they take the sacks to the rooftops, empty them, and spread the pine cones out to dry in the sun. When they're dried out, they can be opened. The olive harvest follows a few months later.

Shahira went silent when she learned about her upcoming marriage. She stopped singing all together. Marriage meant that she would leave her town, Ajmat. Hasna knew that nothing could change what had already been agreed upon and she cried. Her eldest daughter, Safaa, had died, and the two families had to raise her grandchildren. Who could possibly love and care for them better than their auntie? Both families knew that focusing on the children would also relieve the financial pressure of the wedding contract. In this type of situation, the groom has the right not to pay a dowry to the bride's family because the deceased woman's dowry would automatically be passed on to her sister, the new bride. This offers emotional and financial relief to both families.

Hasna stood there sobbing as Ikhlas helped Shahira into a long brown silk caftan, colorful flowers and leaves worked onto its edges with needle and thread. It was the very same caftan that her uncle's wife had worn on her own wedding day. Sorrow had hung over the house since Safaa's death. It was unusual for a wedding celebration to be held after less than the full year's mourning period. But necessity dictated new rules and people in town had to accept them. In this case, necessity meant that Nayif—a widower for only a few months—needed to find someone to look after his two young children at home in Ksoura.

Hasna knew that what had happened was unexpected, and she didn't want to marry her daughter off in such circumstances. But she also knew that refusing this marriage would carry a specific implication—that her daughter wasn't good enough to take the place of her late sister, because of some kind of congenital, or worse yet, mental defect. Moreover, such a refusal would affect her as a mother even before it impacted her daughter's reputation. People's tongues would wag with made-up tales about her behaviour and her character.

Hasna was not unaware of Shahira's visits to the cellar in the garden behind the house, where she secretly met a boy. Yazid spent summers with his family in Ajmat. They shared a childish romance for two summers in a row. He wept that third summer, when he learned that she'd gotten married and moved from Ajmat to faraway Ksoura. He would never see her again, never inhale the scent of her skin or recite poetry to her. She would never sing to him.

Shahira was twelve when she met Yazid; he was three years older than her. His mother suffered from asthma and her doctors had advised her to leave the coast to avoid the summer heat. The family stayed in a small house next to her uncle's, and Shahira began visiting Yazid's mother daily to learn to read and write. She already had a basic knowledge of the alphabet, but she started reading every letter and number her eyes fell upon. One day, she looked up from the page of a book she'd read aloud with no mistakes, and announced to Yazid's mother proudly, "I want to be a teacher like you."

Shahira started meeting Yazid in secret. She'd visit her uncle's house as usual, and then go out back behind the house to the dark cellar where they stored provisions and animal feed. She'd bring her cat Limouna with her so if someone happened to question her about being there, she could reply that the cat had been hiding in the cellar, and she was bringing her back home.

They whisper and embrace, with no one to hear them but Limouna. She gazes at them for a while, then curls up and falls asleep. They stretch out on the straw-covered ground hugging, discovering the meaning of being in love for the very first time. Their scent fills this dark space. She sings him songs learned from her mother and uncle's wife. She tells him about the roads that she walked on to reach an area reserved for threshing, where they spread out sheaves of wheat. She sings again, asking him to repeat after her, but he doesn't know the words. One day he brings books he loves and recites poems he's memorized from them. Antara, Omar bin Abi Rabiha, the Rubaiyat of Omar Khayyam—this last one became dear to her heart.

Yazid was perhaps the first city boy Shahira had ever spoken to. When he first arrived, she laughed at his coastal accent. She asked him what his name was and what he did for fun. She started questioning him: Do they grow wheat in the city? How do they protect it from thieves and animals after it's harvested? Do he and his friends take midnight walks together? Do they count stars and gaze at the shimmering moon resting above them in the sky?

She told him all about her long nighttime walks with her girlfriends, counting stars, waiting for one to fall onto her finger. Mothers always warned their daughters that counting the stars at night would leave permanent scars on their skin. But Shahira wasn't scared. After such a long time, she'd never caught one in any case. She told him about springtime evenings when Ajmat's roads were overgrown with fragrant jasmine bushes, their scent enveloping all the houses. She would talk and sing, his eyes wide open listening to her stories. "You are Shahrazad, not Shahira!" he exclaimed one day. At first, she wondered why he called her this, but she found out why when she discovered *One Thousand and One Nights* among his mother's books.

Perhaps it was Yazid's absentmindedness that first attracted Shahira to him. Or perhaps it was his habit of always carrying a notebook around with him to write down the poems he found in notebooks and magazines. Or maybe it was that he listened to her and her funny stories. He told her that in the city they had neither wheat nor areas set aside for threshing. They had instead a small garden with orange and pomegranate trees. He told her that he was going to be a poet.

She began imagining his house, the one surrounded by palm trees and orange trees that he'd described to her. It was located on a street where horse-drawn carriages passed. She enjoyed the way he spoke about himself. It piqued her curiosity and made her want to get to know him better. In the beginning she saw him every day at his house, next to her uncle's place. He told her about his school, the classroom where you could see ships anchored at sea through the window. He talked to her all about the sea—how its mood changes from one season to the next. She told him that she'd hardly ever seen it, at most maybe once a year, but that when you look at sheaves of wheat from a distance, rippling and shining golden in the sun, they look just like the sea.

She started meeting him in secret, away from her family. When they got together, she'd rush over to him, hug him passionately, and lick his face and neck. He'd laugh at her boldness, saying, "Your cat taught you how to lick!" She was amused by the accent he'd brought with him from the coast, and often imitated it. He put his hand over her mouth, whispering poems to her from a book he'd brought with him.

Then she'd start singing. She closed her olive-green eyes and sang songs she'd learned from the women in her family. They sang during the wheat harvest, on the threshing room floor, at weddings, and while doing housework. Sometimes they also sang the same songs during mourning periods, but they cleverly would change the melody, rhythm, and tone to suit the occasion. They used their knowledge of rhythm and lyricism to craft songs for different occasions.

Shahira loved singing and knew that she had a beautiful voice. She used to go with her uncle's wife to weddings just so she could sing. After a while, she began adding things she'd learned from Yazid and his mother's collection of books. Shahira rarely sat at home with her mother; she was constantly on the move between her house and her uncle's. She liked to accompany him to his simple local shop and also went with him to help him buy the products he sold.

People grew accustomed to seeing Shahira walking up and down the roads in town, delivering things from her uncle's shop to people's homes, always greeting the elders who sat on the bench outside the door. Looking at her you would've thought that she was raised on the road, with gravel and stones. She walked toward the valley singing. At times, she walked with her eyes closed, assuring herself that she knew the road by its scents. If she ever got tired, she would curl up under the oak trees and take a nap.

She would also go with her father and uncle to inspect the wheat fields and assess their maturity. The seeds are planted about six months before the end of summer, and then it's harvest time. The farmers stop watering the fields in the final month to help the sheaves dry out and grow as much as possible in the summer sun. When harvest day comes, everyone is ready. It's a day to celebrate hard work in Ajmat. Not one person stays home. Shahira would go with her parents and siblings to the fields, where they'd meet up with her uncle, his wife, and all the women and men in town. Everyone has their own sickle, and they work all day.

You can see them cutting down the yellowed sheaves of

wheat, the color of sunbeams. They tie them into giant bundles and gather them all in one central place to make it easier to load them on the backs of the animals to transport them to the area used for threshing. Shahira would walk behind the harvesters to pick up the fallen sheaves of wheat, moving them to the side so they could later be gathered up into smaller bundles.

Animals are tethered to machines in the huge space used for threshing. They prepared the equipment for this and set it up in this area well ahead of time. Shahira's father then pushes the animals around in a circle. Other people use special tools to winnow the chaff away and shake it off to separate it from the wheat. They also lift the tools up so the wind can help blow the chaff off away from the wheat sheaves. Women help men to work the harvest, foreheads burnt by the sun. Laughter and giggles fill the air as wheat flies all around, sticking to their dresses. Their voices ring out in song. The women all work together to make hay to store and use as animal fodder in the winter.

~

In Ksoura, the passage of time made Shahira forget what she'd learned from Yazid in two long, consecutive summers of her young life. She almost forgot him as well. She hardly remembered any songs, except the harvesting ones. The harvest seasons were deeply ingrained in her memory. So too were images of winnowing the wheat and cleaning away the chaff stuck to the sheaves before the wind changed directions in mid-August. That was always an important day. She used to spend the whole day in the threshing area with all the girls of her age from Ajmat. They collected all the stray, scattered pieces of straw into burlap sacks. Shahira would then take hers to Ikhlas, who crafted it into little dolls she dressed in colorful outfits.

Shahira took many of the threshing songs with her to her new life. Seasons were different there, since there was no wheat harvest in Ksoura. But nonetheless she'd sing these songs when she was working at home or up on the roof, picking olives and pine nuts, or spreading the beans and legumes out on the rooftop to dry.

Reem al-Falla, Wild Gazelle
Beauty of beauties
Delight of lovers, past and present
If only you and me were alone
We would enjoy the melodies of the rebaba

Reem al-Falla, Wild Gazelle
Hello and welcome,
    a hundred, a thousand times
You with your kohl-lined eyes
Prancing by in a velvet dress
Your sweet gaze is too beautiful
Your scent is beyond compare

She stands up, shaking dust and grain off her clothes, dizzy from the summer heat. The thin scarf covering her head doesn't protect her from the scorching sun. She walks slowly down the wooden ladder, holding on tightly as she descends rung by rung. She's always a bit scared to fall from a ladder. She knows that this is how her grandma in Ajmat died—falling from a ladder onto a stone floor. Though she is both curious and brave, many things still frighten Shahira.

She enters the house, still feeling like the top of her head is burning. She pours water into a deep basin, dips her hands in it, and wets her forehead, then the top of her head, several times. She dries her hands on the edge of her dress and lets the cool water dribble down her face and neck. Euphoria washes over her as she shakes her head from side to side like a happy child.

Sitting on a wooden chair in the garden, a sudden longing for Ajmat overcomes her. She recalls walking along its fragrant roads on spring evenings. Her eyes roam over to the young jasmine plants from Ajmat. Ikhlas had sent her some saplings, wrapped in a damp towel. But the scent of jasmine was different in Ksoura. No one was going to believe her when she told them that she'd planted Ajmat jasmine; its scent was different when it matured and blossomed in Ksoura. She takes a needle and thread out of her wooden sewing box and starts mending the ripped trousers belonging to her late sister's sons, Fayez and Kamal. She pricks the tip of her finger with the needle and a drop of blood pools. She licks it . . . then puts her finger in her mouth and clenches it between her lips.

A faint, long-buried memory passes through her mind. She remembers his name—Yazid. But it's difficult to recall his facial features. She begins singing, repeating the verses in a steady voice, pausing to look around the living room that transforms into a bedroom at night. She sees the details of her real life, here in Ksoura. She tries to remember Yazid's face, his eyes, his scent that filled her every time he hugged and kissed her, and when she ran her tongue over his neck. She really wants to recall his scent, but she can't manage it. She wonders if their love was just an illusion and that's why she's forgotten how he looked and smelled, or if every love is one day consumed by amnesia.

On her first night in Ksoura, she was fairly well-prepared for what to expect. Her uncle's wife had taught her everything, or so she believed. She'd been told to close her eyes and wait for it to be over. But Shahira's curiosity was stronger than her five senses. She wanted to know. She wanted to feel. She didn't want to just look and hear and smell. She wanted to experience it all at the same time. That's why she kept the lantern lit and watched him take off his clothes, then come over to her fully naked, as she lay on the bed made up on the cement floor. She was exhausted after the long journey from Ajmat to Ksoura, but she kept her eyes open. She was frightened when he bent over her, stark naked, and quickly mounted her. She hadn't expected that. The scent of his body filled her nose. She didn't like his smell, and she wasn't prepared for another scent, that of his desire.

What she herself would have desired was for him to sit with her, so they could rest after the long and tiring journey. She would have wanted to sing, her mother's songs and Ikhlas's songs. Perhaps in that moment she would have wanted to begin to make the place her own, to tame it, to get to know the man better so that he would become hers. The songs were the only thing she possessed, and she wanted to reassure herself that she would still be able to sing. She tried to make her voice heard, but his body on top of hers stifled her ability to breathe freely, let alone sing.

She examined his face. Faint shadows of the lantern's light were dancing on it. He seemed even more strange in this heavy silence, interrupted only by a persistent hum emanating from his chest. She turned her face away and closed her eyes. She began reliving the long journey from Ajmat to Ksoura. It smelled of wheat mixed with horse dung. She'd dozed off a bit in the little horse-drawn carriage that Nayif had rented from a stableman in Bdadoun. When she woke up, the carriage felt as small as a doll's house, that she was stuffed into cuddling with Limouna. Through a crack in the reed-wall of the carriage, she could see the sun starting to set over the Mediterranean. She began humming, her voice barely audible over the din of hooves clattering along the rough dirt roads between the two towns.

Her body shuddered due to a sudden pain in her vagina; the images of her journey to Ksoura dispersed. She bit her hand to stifle a scream as Nayif spread her thighs and entered her.

She started to get used to his lack of attention to her as a woman—her feelings, her issues. She gathered fragmented memories of her childhood town and her time in the cellar with Yazid and made them into a fortress where she could seek refuge from ignorance and harm. Whenever she was sad and down, she would sing. She wanted to weep, but tears never found their way to her eyes. Her soul wept; only singing can wipe away the soul's tears. Singing helped her deal with her unexpected life in Ksoura. She now had two young boys who needed her, and a man who left her to figure out this new life all on her own. His family saw her as nothing more than a younger extension of another woman who had been there and gone. Quite some time passed before people stopped calling her Safaa. So as not keep repeating the same mistake, they started calling her simply Imm Fayez.

It was hard for her to get used to wearing her late sister's clothes. "Wash these and wear them," her mother-in-law Imm Nayif told her, as she threw the clothes she was holding into a bucket of soapy water. She then went back to hanging the woolen blankets and covers outside in the sun to prepare for winter. How could she wear her sister Safaa's clothes when they still smelled like her? How would she look in them? And how would Nayif see her? Would he think of Safaa when he looked at her? How would the boys, the family, the rest of the town react to her?

When the second month of autumn came, the sting of the coming winter started to make itself felt. Shahira began to feel cold in the thin clothes she'd brought with her and been wearing since her wedding day. There was no other solution. Safaa was taller than her and fuller figured. But Shahira no longer cared about how it felt to inherit her dead sister's clothes or what others would see or think. At that point she was only concerned about how to make them fit her smaller, thinner body. She solved the shoe problem by folding pieces of cloth and stuffing them inside her sister's shoes so they would fit her narrow feet.

~

Shahira's life was different in Ksoura. In Ajmat, she was the youngest in the whole family. She was raised between two houses. Her uncle who'd never had his own children was her next-door neighbor. Her parents had Safaa, then two boys, and finally said that was enough. But after many intervening years, they were blessed with Shahira. They never expected to have another child and left her to grow up on her own, like an untamed weed. Perhaps this was lucky for her, since she experienced a freedom none of her siblings ever did. She spent most of her childhood playing outside on the roads and open spaces in their town, waiting for moonrise. When the adults were napping in the middle of the day, she and her girlfriends roamed through the fields where the natural springs were.

She often slept over at her uncle's place, spending time with his wife Ikhlas, who hadn't been blessed with children. She loved Shahira and treated her as if she were her own daughter. On weekends, she'd go with her uncle to his shop. He sold things like flour, loose tobacco, and animal feed. She helped him at the cash register and with his bookkeeping as well.

She was raised almost as if she were a boy; she enjoyed a degree of freedom rarely experienced by girls of her generation. During the wheat harvesting season, she sang. She also composed lyrics to songs that she then taught to the other girls.

As a child, Shahira only left Ajmat once a year, at the beginning of spring. That's when she'd accompany her uncle's wife Ikhlas to Saida, where her sister lived. They spent a few days there each year. Ikhlas would come back with colorful leftover fabrics that she bought from a fabric shop. She made little dolls out of the cloth and put them on display to sell in her husband's shop.

Shahira's life totally changed after her marriage, when she came to this place where she knew no one, which was nothing like her town. Her cat Limouna, who she'd insisted on bringing with her, was the only thing in her life that remained somewhat familiar. Her accent and way of speaking was unlike the women in Ksoura; her life in Ajmat was nothing at all like the confined life she had to live in this new town. She was married to a man she didn't know and whose habits she was unfamiliar with—even if he was her late sister Safaa's husband. After their marriage, she found out that he couldn't even count from one to ten and "couldn't tell the difference between a stick and the letter I," as the saying goes.

She had to employ her own basic reading and math skills to look after their land and their household affairs. She managed the olive harvest and the produce from their pine forest. She recorded how much they sold. She also kept track of the accounts of their seasonal renters. At first, Nayif was wary of letting Shahira take care of responsibilities that he himself was never up to and had left to his father to deal with. But his father passed away only months after they were married. Nayif was unable, or in the best-case scenario, unwilling, to do it.

His total ignorance of accounting came as a surprise to Shahira, as did his long absences from home. But his deep expertise in meteorological conditions, flood-prone areas, and the movement of the stars amazed her. On clear days, he'd show her the stars and explain them. "This is the Big Dipper, and over here is the Little Dipper." Every evening, he would search for Sirius, the Shepard's Star, which guides them and helps them find their way. As for the morning star, he laughingly said that it guides drunks home after a night of partying. He chose clear autumn days to go out and hunt birds at dawn, deep in the heart of the area surrounding Ksoura.

He also loved to collect small colorful finches and built large cages for them. He made a sort of glue out of gum tree bark and used it to attract the birds who'd get stuck and be unable to fly. He was accompanied on these outings by Garabet, their Armenian neighbor, who'd come to Lebanon and settled in their town.

Garabet had been discharged by the Turkish Army after the Young Turks took power. Their arrival fueled Turkish nationalism and hostility toward the minorities living there. After this period, Armenians became strangers in their own country, and even enemies to supporters of Turkish nationalism. Garabet was dismissed from the army with no compensation. He was forced to sell off all his possessions in order to leave his village and travel—first to Syria and then to Lebanon.

He arrived with his wife Anahid and their two daughters at the beginning of 1914. World War I was imminent. They lived next door to Nayif; only a large staircase separated the two houses. At first, the family didn't mix with anyone except Shahira and Nayif, who had welcomed them and provided them with provisions.

Sometimes Nayif would be away for two days or even more. He and his brother Said would take their seasonal produce to sell on the coast. The number of children at home kept increasing. Shahira stayed home to look after them with the help of Nayif's mother. When Nayif did come home, she'd have gotten used to him being away. She organized her life and the whole family's life, including tending to the fields, around his absences. She preferred this. Arranging things when he was around threw her off. She felt almost glad when he was away, because she had more time to do things that he put off day after day. Years of Shahira's life passed like this. She devoted herself to improving the lives of everyone in her family. All of this, however, prevented her from forming friendships with other women living nearby, in town or the surrounding areas.

Shahira forged her first connection to the outside world through an English school run by a Protestant missionary woman. She insisted on educating the children there, though the school fees were "back-breaking," as she put it. Education was her compass—she let her commitment to education orient her and guide her in everything she did on a daily basis. It was her only remaining link to her life as a young woman back in Ajmat—the passion of her brief relationship with Yazid and her friendship with his mother who was a schoolteacher in Beirut. She still dreamed of having a life like Yazid's mother. She was now pursuing this dream through her children.

She wanted them to go to school, study, and have the life that she and Nayif never could. But how would she be able to keep paying their tuition fees? Even though it was a missionary school, each family had to pay fees based on their economic circumstances. The school administration usually calculated families' ability to pay based on the amount of land they owned, even if most of the land owned by villagers produced no revenue.

Despite knowing how missionaries kept strict records based on their own calculations, Shahira kept thinking about ways to keep the children in the school. One evening, when Nayif came back home, the two of them sat down to dinner together after the children had gone to bed. As if reading her mind, he said, "Fayez is a young man now, and it seems that he's not really all that clever or suited to learning. Kamal does better than him in school and knows how to read and write. That'll do."

"What do you mean?" she asked.

"I can't keep paying fees for all the children. The ones who can't make it will have to leave school," he replied loudly.

"That would be such a pity! The boy's lived through so much already. He saw his mother melt away before his very eyes . . . it's a miracle he's able even to recognize letters after that," Shahira pleaded.

"I want him to come with me to the fields. I'm all alone and getting tired."

"But you're not alone. I'm with you. And Garabet was hoping to work with you, if you'd hire him."

"It's not enough though. I want my son to know his land and his legacy. I want him to learn how to sow and plant as well as keep track of harvests."

"He's so young still, though."

"Shut up! When I was his age, I used to sow the fields, plant the seeds, and help my father sell the produce from the harvest."

"Bou Tannous's children and his brothers' children are all going to school. Why shouldn't your children?"

"Good for Bou Tannous's children. Let them study all they want."

"The world is changing, Nayif."

He retorted sharply, "It's changing for poor people. We have enough land for Fayez not to need to go to school. Let poor people study!"

Shahira went silent, eyes filled with worry. She knew that arguing with Nayif wouldn't yield results, in fact the opposite. It would only make him more stubborn. It occurred to her that he perhaps had come this conclusion because he himself was illiterate and not at all interested in education. She wanted to let him know what she was thinking, to tell him that he shouldn't repeat his father's mistakes with his own children. But she brushed this idea from her mind like you protect a moth from hovering too close to a flame.

She didn't sleep at all that night. How would she keep Fayez in school without a major fight erupting between her and Nayif? When angry, he turned into a raging bull.

She tossed and turned. She knew that if Nayif succeeded in keeping Fayez out of school this year, his brother Kamal would meet the same fate the following year, and their daughter Yasmine the year after. This would continue year by year until all of the children were out of school. She knew that Kamal was the cleverest of them all and that he had overtaken his brother academically. She figured that what Nayif was saying was probably true. But she still couldn't bear the thought of taking the child out of school when his siblings were going every day.

Shahira felt her temples throbbing. She got up, tied a cloth around her head, and hoped she could fall back asleep. At dawn, everyone else was still sleeping. She got up quietly and put on a heavy coat. She crept silently into the pantry, feeling her way in the dim darkness. She lit the lantern and stayed there for a while.

Morning light guided her path home from the pantry. She woke the children to get them ready for school. She left the youngest, Tawfiq, asleep next to his grandmother. She was afraid of what she was about to do. She knew deep down that it was the only solution, but that didn't quell her fear. She packed up the children's school bags and sat watching Nayif drink his coffee. She waited silently for him to go out to the fields.

She hurried the children off to school. Fayez carried a burlap bag she'd sewn for him, in which she'd put a bottle of olive oil and bars of soap. She gave Kamal a metal bucket full of olives and covered it tightly with a lid. Yasmine carried the rest of the supplies—enough zaatar and olive oil for everyone, as well as a bag Shahira had filled with pine nuts. Fayez, Kamal, and Yasmine set off to school, Shahira walking behind them holding Nadim's hand.

Before the children went to their classrooms, Shahira collected everything they'd been carrying. She walked up the wooden staircase that led up to the second floor of the building, where the principal had her office and lodgings. The door was ajar. Shahira knocked and pushed on it gently. It opened on a large hallway, with a giant sofa and a table surrounded by burgundy-colored chairs. In the center of the wall facing her, a large stone fireplace crackled and roared. On the wall hung portraits of bearded men wearing hats. Not one portrait of a woman hung on that wall.

No one was in the entryway. She walked through toward the room overlooking the playground on the other side. It was a cold day. She found Miss Stewart sitting near a small iron stove, a pile of papers in front of her and a notebook in her hand. She was busy with the school's administrative work. She wore a green sweater and a navy-blue knee-length skirt. Her bare feet were clad in flat shoes.

Shahira just stood there. She was suddenly struck by fear and forgot how to speak. What would she say? How would she begin? A huge cream-colored cat, curled up on the carpet near the fireplace, captured her attention. At that same moment, the principal raised her head and saw Shahira standing there. In formal Arabic, she said, "Welcome, how can I help you?"

Mute, Shahira stuttered, pointing at the sleeping cat, "She looks just like my cat, ma'am. They could be twins." Hearing Shahira's voice, the cat woke with a start. She stretched out and leapt up the wooden steps leading to the top floor.

Shahira came closer and spoke quickly as if she were afraid her words would somehow escape her. "I brought these gifts for you, madame principal. I came here because my husband wants to take the children out of school . . . we're having financial difficulties."

"I'm sorry to hear that," the principal said, in accented Arabic. Then she looked back down at the papers in her hands.

"I came today to offer you a proposal that I hope you'll accept. I want the children to stay in school and I'll pay you in kind every year with food we produce."

"What?" Shock was written all over the principal's face.

"Yes indeed. I can bring you all the olives, olive oil, pine nuts, and fresh bread that you need, happily."

"No, no, impossible. This is a strange request. It's difficult, much too difficult, Mrs. Dahli." Shaking her head left and right, the principal added, "We teach children gratis only in the first and second year. Then the family must contribute so that we can continue our mission. You have four children. Do you know what four means?" the principal asked, raising her voice.

Shahira nodded her head to indicate that she did. But she thought about her son Tawfiq, who would need to start school in two years. She suddenly found herself adding, "OK. Add to this all of the winter provisions I prepare every year, and we'll divide them in half between the two of us."

"It's tricky, difficult. Too difficult." The principal hesitated as she adjusted her glasses and looked back down at her papers.

"Alright, Miss Stewart, I'll tell you what. I'll throw in fruits and vegetables too. Consider our garden your garden. Our chickens and their eggs are your chickens and your eggs." Shahira said this last word, secretly smiling to herself and looking down at the principal's unshaven legs full of freckles.

It wasn't easy to get the principal to accept such an offer. But after quite some back and forth, Shahira was able to convince her. Shahira couldn't count the number of times that the orientalist

British school principal repeated over the course of their conversation in formal Arabic, "This is difficult, very difficult, Mrs. Dahli."

What Shahira managed to do isn't easy to describe. Was it an offer to facilitate the payment of the fees in installments? Or a way to appease the principal? Or something else entirely? Shahira herself didn't even know. She didn't know how, but she left the principal's office certain that her children would be able to remain in school beyond that year and that Tawfiq would have a place there when he was school-age in two years.

Shahira knew that the school administration didn't have a unified fee structure for all the students. She also knew that the fees were fixed in relation to families' individual situations. Many of the children in Ksoura studied for free. The Dahli family were landowners, though, which prompted the administration to demand fees that the family couldn't afford.

She returned home, mentally calculating how much she'd have to give Miss Stewart each semester to keep the children in school. She felt that she'd made a mistake and given in too much, made too many concessions. She believed that most families in town wouldn't give the school administration anything near what she would have to. But she then quickly shook these frustrating thoughts from her mind. She told herself that she would find some way to manage. Despite all this, she started wondering as she was scattering leftover vegetables around the chicken coop, "We sorted out the children's education, but now how will we manage to keep them fed?"

~

Singing was the only thing that gave Shahira some relief from her daily struggles. It wasn't only physical struggle but also the mental exertion of having to think about so many things related to managing the children and their studies. She had to also ensure that they had warm clothes for the winter and enough firewood for them to keep warm. This all exhausted her, as did her constant feeling that she was fighting on several fronts. However, what exhausted her the most was the time she spent convincing Nayif of things she wanted to do. Perhaps this had to do with the very considerable age difference between them, or to their differing ways of thinking about family and the future. With time, she learned to resort to whatever solution required the least amount of talking.

She started what she thought was right quietly, telling herself that the day would come that she'd let Nayif know everything. That's when it all would be out in the open. But this wasn't a good solution and she often felt frustrated. It was in her nature to talk about what she was doing. She walked the children to school in the morning with the things she had to give to the principal—olives, pine nuts, fresh eggs, and cookies she'd made herself with flour and carob molasses. She stood there waiting for the children to go into their classrooms, Yasmine on the girls' side and the others on the boys' side. All the children played together in a shared courtyard at recess.

Shahira personally delivered what she brought to the principal. Then she stayed a little to talk to her about her plans. She needed to share this with someone. If she couldn't, she'd feel as if she were choking. She liked to talk to the women in the family while they were planting crops out in the fields, or even to the woman selling fabric who came once a month to collect money from Anahid, the Armenian seamstress, and other women in town. She even spoke to Fayez, who she always insisted help her with whatever she was doing. After her persistent promises, he'd agree. They'd sit together on the roof, him helping her to empty the pine cones, taking the dried seeds out by hitting them on the floor to break them open.

She told him about her dream of building an olive press in the fields. If this dream came true, she could earn enough money to pay for all their school fees and even for further education through middle school. Fayez didn't care about any of this. He'd been withdrawn and silent since he'd lost his mother. She knew that he'd watched Safaa fall ill and pass away. Kamal joined them and sat near Shahira. He actively accepted her invitation to help her and started asking questions about her life in Ajmat. He was curious, totally different to Fayez. He grew attached to Shahira from the moment that she'd arrived in Ksoura.

Nayif heard about Shahira's dreams again and again. They passed through many people, adults and children, like a game of telephone wending their way back to him. This gave rise to many quarrels that were difficult for Shahira to avoid.

"More school?" he shouted angrily. "What do they need more school for? Where is this middle school? Where do you want to send them?"

Many mouths to feed, many school fees—Shahira tried to face up to this poverty in her large family, especially after her sister's two children were joined by three more of her own. She gave birth to each of them while keeping up with her agricultural work, work on the house, and housework inside. She worked and labored, gave birth, and then went back to work.

Labor pains with Yasmine surprised her when she was in the pantry behind the house with Adla, Nayif's brother Said's wife. Shahira didn't find Adla particularly comforting; in fact she found her rather naïve and boring. But this didn't stop them from spending many hours together on the roof during the pine nut harvesting season, washing and drying the pine cones, then breaking them open and cleaning them. She complained to Shahira about how hard her life was while prising apart the pine cones, "This is our destiny. It's what fate has written for us."

Shahira would reply, "If we can't face up to our fate, we can try to outsmart it."

Adla thought she understood what Shahira meant and responded in her simple way, "Every day I pray and ask God to take Said by the hand and grant my children success so I can rest." Shahira would wave her hand at Adla as if to implore her to stop saying nonsense. "Pray away, but prayer alone isn't enough. If prayers could fill our water jugs, we wouldn't have to walk all the way to the spring every day to fill them up."

Deep down, Shahira was truly convinced that fate had been unfair to her and the women she knew. But she also believed that she could mitigate its harshness by outwitting it. Despite all her best efforts, however, labor pains surprised her, and the amniotic fluid that gushed out from between her thighs frightened her. She sat down on the pantry floor, because she could no longer manage to get herself back to the house. Adla ran to the midwife Imm Geryes's house. She arrived just in time to catch the baby at the last minute, cut the umbilical cord, wash the newborn, and help change the new mother's clothes. Shahira might have lost the baby had Imm Geryes not appeared, because she briefly fainted and lost consciousness and Adla didn't know what to do.

"I swear on the Virgin Mary, that woman would have died if it weren't for me," Imm Geryes repeats every time she remembers Yasmine's birth. Wrapped up in white swaddling clothes by Imm Geryes, the baby belted out a cry that echoed through the pantry. Shahira's female neighbors all came over and gathered around her. Despite her pain, Shahira put the newborn to her breast and nursed her. Then, after a while, she slowly walked back, holding her baby in her arms while Adla supported her shoulders.

Back at the house, Umm Geryes brewed an herbal tea made from local flowers, cinnamon, and ginger, telling her, "Go get some sleep." Shahira sat on the bed, low to the floor, and started slowly, absentmindedly to drink her hot tisane, as if emerging from a long tunnel. After preparing a healthy lentil soup for her, Umm Geryes said goodbye, advising her to stay in bed and rest until the next day. Shahira however got up right away to help Adla wash the sheets filled with sweat and blood, boiling them in a big pot on the stove, adding soap and laurel leaves to the water.

At fifteen, Shahira became mother to a baby girl. She felt she was already a mother to two boys, Fayez and Kamal, as well. Motherhood was a deep pleasure for her and gave her great satisfaction. Shahira didn't know the meaning of sexual pleasure in bed with Nayif though. She saw intercourse as a duty that she had to fulfil in the shortest possible amount of time. She sometimes lost her patience and bit her lips until he was finished, the taste of blood filling her mouth. He would get off her, turn onto his side, and fall into a deep sleep. That's when she could breathe a sigh of relief, go into the bathroom and start scrubbing her belly and vagina with a rough loofah. She put her finger inside herself, closed her eyes, and conjured up images of Yazid in Ajmat. This made her feel so good she would almost faint. Her body shuddered multiple times. And she was just there sitting on the wet wooden chair, slowly pouring water over her body, producing a nearly soundless sigh. Shahira's desire was always somewhere else, not in the marital bed. And she didn't care. Just as she was satisfied by motherhood, she was aroused by her own body, alone with herself.

Life in Ksoura carried on even with poverty and war surrounding them. However, the year locusts invaded Lebanon during World War I, leading to the great famine, left an unforgettable impact on people's lives. Shahira would never forget the day when the insects crawled into town and people panicked, trying to get rid of them however they could.

The locusts arrived in the spring of 1915. It was less than a year after the outbreak of the war. People began collecting dry wood from the forests and lighting fires around their seasonal crops, cellars, and pantries near their homes, in order to drive the insects away. Their attempts failed, however, and larger political forces bore a responsibility for this too. The locust invasion preceded a major siege of the mountain.

Remembering all this Shahira, used to say, "The War of 1914 besieged our mountain—by land and sea, everywhere. Everyone became enemies of everyone else, but they were all against us," continuing, "Wars don't end, they never end."

The mountain was trapped in the jaws of these forces and paid the price for these conflicts. People kept passing the news among themselves, saying if it weren't for the Ottoman alliance with Germany, and their oppression—especially the policies of safarbarlik, forced conscription—thousands of Lebanese wouldn't have died. People would have been able to bring food and supplies in from Syria by land. The naval blockade imposed by the Allies caused the death of thousands who were deprived of access to food and medicine. It wasn't the first time that locusts had infested Lebanon. It had happened before, and people had lived their lives without thousands dying. But the land and sea blockade definitively caused the great famine in Lebanon. And the mountain fell victim to it. That famine led to new waves of emigration from Mount Lebanon to the Americas, as well as other countries. Ships carrying people on the verge of starvation landed on their shores. These migrations weren't only the result of famine, but also the persecution suffered by people living in Mount Lebanon throughout different stages of its history.

Shahira would never forget the day the locusts attacked the town—it was the same day her son Tawfiq was born. He was the third child she delivered, after Yasmine and Nadim. She used to say that without Adla, the town's midwife, Imm Geryes, would never have reached her. Imm Geryes was afraid not only of the locusts but also the hot khamsin winds that hit the region that day, causing a frightening drought that affected the fragile seasonal crops.

Shahira was lying on the low wooden bed in the little room, writhing in pain. Umm Geryes steadied a large bowl of hot water on the ground next to the bed. Nayif's mother stood above her head, with white towels she'd sterilized in boiling water. Adla had brought a bottle of orange blossom water as well and kept it nearby to sprinkle on Shahira's face in case she fainted. Though her second birth, when she welcomed Nadim into the world, had gone smoothly, Adla would never forget how Shahira had lost consciousness when she was giving birth to Yasmine. She recalled how Imm Geryes, who'd just arrived when it happened, had been also afraid that Shahira would stop pushing the fetus out, and it would suffocate at her cervix. She remembered how she had to splash cold water on the new mother's face and chest while shaking her and slapping her cheeks repeatedly to wake her up, tensely repeating, "Push . . . push, just a bit more. Put your faith in God and push a little more, push until you hear your baby's voice, yellah."

This birth was easy, much like Nadim's was. But panic about the locust attack prevailed. There had been news from many nearby villages and towns about the locust infestation—how they ate everything, fresh and green or dried up. In the morning, people started sealing up windows with old rags, burlap bags, and spare cloth. They locked the doors tight to preserve food and prevent locusts from getting in. Shahira hid all the remaining foodstuffs they had in locked cupboards. Famine had started to spread amongst the population and no one in the mountain was spared. After the birth, Imm Geryes departed with a small jar of olives that Adla had given her for her family. Imm Geryes shook her head disapprovingly at the jar. "If Nayif were home he would've given me more."

"May God bring him home safely. As soon as he's back, you can come and take what he owes you," Adla responded, showing her annoyance and gently guiding her to the door.

Weeks before Shahira gave birth to her third child, Nayif snuck over the border to Soueida in Syria to bring wheat home to the mountain, far from the watchful eyes of the Ottoman Army. They had forbidden the export of wheat from Syria and allocated everything produced to the German and Ottoman armies. From the beginning of the war, the Ottomans brought in a German unit for combat training.

It was a dangerous journey for Nayif and his brother, who feared being arrested on their way to Soueida. At that time, Mount Lebanon was suffering from the increased influence of Jamal Pasha, who limited the power of the Ottoman mutasarrifite. He passed coercive laws with the goal of abolishing the mutasarrifite system in Mount Lebanon. In addition, the army was searching for wanted young men in the mountain.

It was in this frightening atmosphere that Nayif and Said left Ksoura to catch the train that stopped in Aley on the way to Damascus. They disguised themselves on their journey, working on board cleaning and selling newspapers. They feared being randomly arrested. With the increasing power of Jamal Pasha during World War I, men who left their homes in the mountain regularly disguised themselves to hide from informants.

They disembarked at the station in Damascus and hired a mule to take them to Soueida. They bought wheat from relatives there, who provided them with two mules and mule drivers to carry the bags of smuggled wheat back across the mountains and from there to Ksoura. It was a long, difficult journey over rough road. They had to walk all night and hide during the day.

One night, two guards at an Ottoman army checkpoint stopped them. They held everyone in front of the tent, waiting for the light of day which would bring with it orders from the leadership about what the two soldiers should do with the confiscated items. Nayif had two unopened bottles of arak in his possession. He'd brought them to treat any possible sores or blisters that might develop on their feet on such a long walk over so many days. Immediately after halting their caravan, the two soldiers retreated to their tent to play cards and drink tea. Nayif got friendly with the soldiers, proposing that they could divide up and share the things they were carrying so they could resume their journey to the mountain.

Neither of them responded. They carried on playing cards and asked Said to make them a pot of tea. While it was boiling on the fire, one of them mentioned that he liked his tea dark. Said prepared the tea and laid out two cups. Before he took the tea into the two soldiers, Nayif took the pot from him, saying, "Give it here, I'm gonna take care of it!"

Nayif put the metal pot back on the stove. He spilled out a bit of tea onto the floor, and opened the bottle of arak, pouring about half of it into the kettle. He then put it back on the fire to heat it up again. He looked inside the teapot and noticed the liquid had turned from black to dark brown. He was afraid that the soldiers might discover what he had done.

He had a small bag of pine nuts amongst his things, which Shahira had prepared for him to take with him on the road. He took the kettle in to the two soldiers and opened the bag of pine nuts, handing it to them and saying that the most delicious tea is boiled with aniseed and has pine nuts sprinkled on the top. Still fearful that they would discover his secret, he painted a friendly smile on his face. He walked over, placed the kettle on the nearby table, filled his hand with pine nuts, and quickly added them to the tea.

His face betrayed his anxiety. He feared they'd notice the change in taste or color. He nervously reminded them again that he'd added aniseed and pine nuts to the tea. As they poured their tea into the cups, Nayif looked up and attempted to distract them by talking about stars and constellations. Gesturing at the clear night sky, he pointed out the group of stars that made up the Big Dipper. We waved his hand and he continued, "And this is the Little Dipper."

He kept on talking, telling stories about weather change, the movement of the tides. The soldiers were drinking their tea all the while, gazing up at the shining stars. They refilled their cups while Nayif reinvented stories about how one day he used the morning star to find his way home when he was lost. Everyone knows that fear can make people lose the ability to speak. But the opposite happened to Nayif. He realized quickly that he had no other way out; talking was his only chance to save himself and those around him.

So he didn't stop talking. And the soldiers didn't stop drinking. They enjoyed the taste. They asked for a second pot and then a third. Just before midnight, when the first bottle was empty, they seemed suddenly tired. That's when the third pot of tea was finished. Nayif looked at them, about to open a second bottle of arak, but by then he was sure that they'd drunk enough to keep them in a deep sleep until morning.

Their heads flopped down onto the table and they both started snoring. Meanwhile, Nayif gestured to Said and the mule drivers to creep away slowly. They then continued their journey by mule toward the path leading down to Aley in the Matn mountain range. Before leaving to catch them up, Nayif gathered up all the food left in the soldiers' tent and emptied their pockets, taking whatever might be useful for their return journey. They arrived at a natural spring; the mules were clearly exhausted. They all drank and filled their empty containers with water. They entered the forest of oak and sycamore trees waiting for a new evening that would conceal them and allow them to continue their journey.

The light of dawn broke over Ksoura as Nayif arrived home. He asked the mule drivers to unload the cargo and wait so they could have breakfast together. The cry of a newborn reached his ears and he entered the room where Shahira was resting. He kissed her forehead and then stood near her to gaze at his infant son.

"God blessed us and brought us back. And now we have a new mouth to feed and child to educate," he said, staring at the infant suckling at his mother's breast.

"Your son has been without a name for seven days," she told him, without raising her eyes from her newborn son's face.

"We named him Tawfiq!" he replied proudly.

# Between Two Blockades

People's hunger worsened during the era of the locusts between 1915 and 1916. There was also a naval blockade of the coastline of Lebanon, Syria, and Palestine by the Allied powers, preventing the Ottoman Army from reaching the Suez Canal. This was compounded by the Ottoman Empire's persecution of the people of Mount Lebanon. Jamal Pasha, nicknamed The Butcher, also imposed a second blockade—this one by land—preventing the entry of flour and grain from Syria. In addition to the blockade, the Ottoman troops confiscated livestock and tracked young activists to either imprison or forcibly conscript them. Like all of the towns in Mount Lebanon, Ksoura suffered from Jamal Pasha's oppression. He was eventually assassinated by an Armenian after the events of 1922 and his unjust, criminal persecution of the Armenians.

The safarbarlik was a dark period in the history of Lebanon. The mountains were held hostage between the two blockades, which mercilessly murdered the people living there. Few people were able to extend a helping hand to someone in need. They would take what grain they had to relatives and family, by walking with their livestock at night and moving from town to town on rough roads.

The two families based in Ajmat and Ksoura rarely visited each other. However, Shahira's brothers did bring wheat and grain to Ksoura by mule on one arduous journey from their village in the Western Beqaa. Through extraordinary effort, families there were able to save some provisions by hiding them underground, away from both locusts and people. They struggled hard to save their livestock—to feed their animals so they could stay alive. But many perished even before their owners could eat them. The animals that managed to survive most successfully were chickens, because they fed on the locusts. During the Great Famine, chickens became an enemy of the locusts and a great friend to human beings. They allowed people to eat their eggs. The many natural springs in Ksoura also contributed to saving some of the seasonal crops, and thus saving the village from the worst of the famine, compared to others in Mount Lebanon, where a huge number of people died of hunger.

The famine sowed fear. Fear in turn sowed violence. Some wheat arrived to fill Nayif's cellar, and he had to think about how to distribute it in a way that wouldn't lead to grudges and conflict in his family. He had so many relatives in his extended family, his brother and his brother's family as well as his own family, which was growing year after year, more and more mouths to feed, hungry for bread.

In a trembling voice, Shahira told tales of people who she couldn't save, who'd died of hunger. She had to focus on rationing the food she had to save her family and the people closest to her. Most people didn't have the means or resources to save anyone; the few people who could were the rich, and they weren't suffering from hunger. Some of those people could have saved others but didn't. They sold grain and flour at prices far exceeding what any normal farmer could afford to pay. Poor people suffered and went hungry, especially itinerant farmers who didn't own land. They did wage labor in nearby towns. Some landowning people also went hungry because locusts ate all the seeds they'd prepared for the sowing season. The land remained unproductive for more than two years—until the end of the World War I.

Every town had to pay taxes to the mutasarrifate. This put economic pressure on mountain dwellers. They were lean years. Shahira started eating tiny amounts, depriving herself of food to save it for her children. Most of what they'd planted yielded very little. This added to the mountain region's poverty and the number of famine victims. Syria and the Beqaa Valley provided enough wheat to feed Europe. They called it the "breadbasket," as Shahira always reminded people. But it couldn't feed the mountain.

What happened to the predominately Christian mountains was devastating and tragic. The death toll was less destructive in other regions in Lebanon where people were able to avoid the famine more easily. Merchants continued to sell their goods and hired mules to transport wheat and grain through hills and valleys, bringing them in from Palestine and selling them at exorbitant prices. Some merchants from Beirut and other places on the Lebanese coast kept grain to sell at prices that ordinary citizens couldn't possibly afford. Some charitable organizations founded by the country's elite didn't live up to their mandate of distributing donations they received to the people. Instead, they operated according to market logic, or even at times corruption.

The famine didn't end until the First World War ended. It created the memories that shaped Shahira's personality. Her fear of poverty and hunger marked her. A second world war came and went and the first stayed with her.

Decades passed. Shahira kept remembering and reliving her

memories of the war and hunger, as if they were ever present. Layla's daughter Asmahan studied journalism and wanted to write a book about the women in her family. One day, she spoke to Shahira and asked how she'd lived her life during those wars, noting down everything she said.

> "They knew we were starving, and no one helped us—not the Germans, not the Turks, not the Allies. Not even the businessmen of our own country! They sold us and didn't buy us back, my girl . . . But we didn't die. The war taught us rely on ourselves. On ourselves and our land—not on strangers. But you know, people forget the lessons we learned."

Asmahan wrote everything Shahira said down in her notebook. She though that corruption here is as endemic as earthworms, and as old as the Phoenicians. She believed that what is happening today is merely a repetition of what happened in the past—that fear has taken root in the land here and goes together with corruption.

> "My girl, it's such a pity that this country doesn't support its own people. Look at Kamal! Look at Majd, Fayez's son, your brother Walid, or your friend Ouida. Where are they ? Half the village has left . . . and there are so many like them." She followed up, "We stayed here. Where could we go? God should put an end to politics and war. My son Kamal went abroad because of this. We're still here, but a third of us emigrated, and a third of us died!"
>
> "But how, Grandma? How were people in the World

War I able to get out when Lebanon was blockaded?" Fayez's daughter Mona asked, listening to the conversation between her grandmother and Asmahan.

"My darling girl, they found a way and they left. The ships blockading us always needed people to work on them. People left with them. They worked the decks and never came back. Quite a few who left on those ships may have drowned or died at sea. But some people did arrive alive. It's the same as people leaving to live abroad today. New people leave every day, dear. Your life ends but war never does."

Shahira said all this with the painful memories etched onto her face.

~

After the end of World War I, it became difficult for Shahira to let go of things she didn't need. But she managed to make use of this obsession. She used everything she could put her hands on to improve life for herself and her family. She got to know the families who lived in the villages around Ksoura. Most of them came from the coast and rented or built houses to spend the summer in. Women started buying provisions and homemade bread from her. Adla and other women in the family helped her. She sent oil, olives, and rosewater to these families by mule. She added to these bundles good-quality pine nuts, homemade local soap, fig jam, seasonal fruits and vegetables. She would set a price, and if she didn't get the amount she asked for, she'd ask them to give her old clothes or scraps of fabric that they didn't need, as well as pots and pans, kitchen supplies, and furniture.

Shahira sorted through everything she received to decide what she needed and wanted for her house. Then she stored what she'd chosen in the cellar where she kept her household provisions and olive oil so they wouldn't spoil. With the help of Anahid the seamstress, she used the various fabric scraps to fashion colorful blankets, pillows, and curtains. She also made them into clothes for her children and all the children of the family to gift them on Eid al-Adha. She gave the used kitchen supplies and dishes to the neighborhood women who helped her process the pine cones on her rooftop during the harvest.

Every Easter she made cookies and sent them to the women living in the Christian quarter of Ksoura as a gift for their children. Nayif was forced to grant Shahira powers that no other women in the town enjoyed. She'd come to a town where she was the only woman who could read and write. Even if some women in Ksoura could read a little bit, Shahira stood out because she also knew basic arithmetic. She never managed to realize her dream of opening a classroom in her house to teach girls to read and write, because the housework and agricultural work she shouldered left her no extra room to think about anything else. Her interests shifted to different matters, things she never expected she'd be involved in.

She was no longer sad that she hadn't become a teacher like Yazid's mom, who spent every summer in Ajmat. With time, her old interests, dreams, and desires faded. Every night, she laid her head down on her pillow and thought about the next day and what she could do to improve her family's life as much as possible.

More than any dream she'd had back in Ajmat, her mind was now preoccupied with olives. She was concerned about giving a substantial part of their olive harvest to the owner of the press in the next town over. She worried they'd mix Nayif's olives with others. She often expressed her unwavering conviction that their land produced the best olives in Mount Lebanon and that when the owner of the press mixed them with others, they lost their flavor and their value. Shahira replaced her modest dreams, once close to her heart, with bigger ones, far beyond her imagination as a young person. Her dreams grew to be as vast as the land she looked, after, and now they included her whole extended family.

After the First World War, Lebanon entered a new phase. Its borders were drawn by the French. Slowly, and with some difficulty, the mountain began to regain its former life. Shahira tried to amass some savings, but it was impossible in a big family with five children. The difficult economic situation spared no one, and poverty continued for quite some time after the end of the war. The people who were still living there hadn't forgotten the great famine they'd suffered from, so fear ruled their thought process and behavior. Nonetheless, Shahira began laying aside small amounts of money from the proceeds of her sales in a small cloth bag stuffed with cotton. Each time she added some, she sewed the bag back up again and hid it among the pillows and blankets folded away in the house's liwan.

After a few seasons, when Fayez had grown up and come of age, she counted what she'd laid aside. She found that she'd saved almost enough to buy a stone for an olive press and build a well near the natural spring in the field. She sat with the pillow in her hands. She told herself that she could pay for the cost of the press from what she produced.

She thought about how she might be able to entice Fayez into working with her. She'd taught him arithmetic when he was young. He could help her run the olive press during school holidays; she knew that with encouragement and praise he could do it. The olive press might be able to guarantee him a steady job when he was older. She also knew that she'd have no problems with Kamal. He was the closest to her and most affectionate of her children. For sure he'd help her with the olives, by removing the leaves and in other ways too. Likewise, Yasmine was almost twelve years old and could help look after her two younger brothers so that Shahira could devote herself to managing both the press itself and the business side of things.

She wanted to locate the olive press in town to make it easier on people who had to travel more than twenty kilometers from Ksoura to get to one. Every year they struggled to transport their olives on mule or donkey backs. Having the olive press under her own supervision would ensure the quality of the oil she used in her house—and that it was not mixed with the lower quality oil used to make soap. She thought that they could also benefit from the olive pomace, the solid remains of the olives left over after they are pressed. After letting it dry for a month, it could be used as fuel for heating, cooking, and baking bread. In this way, they could maximize the olives' benefits and sell the rest of the harvest to the merchants who came from Beirut each year to buy their crops. This project had been one of Shahira's dreams and she acted as if it were a reality she lived on the daily, though she hadn't managed to achieve any part of it yet.

She wanted to build an olive press, but she knew she couldn't get started without informing Nayif. He'd make a huge fuss about it if she embarked on such a big project without telling him first. One night, she tossed and turned and didn't sleep a wink. She got up the next morning, insomnia still visible on her face. Everyone else was still asleep. She put the pot on the wood-burning stove, inside which the embers had been burning all night long. She planned to make his favorite breakfast: ful mudammas with oil and garlic, and with parsley and mint on top.

The children woke up to go to their respective schools.

Yasmine only had one year left at primary school. Every morning, she walked to school with her two younger brothers. Fayez and Kamal had already begun attending the middle school in the village next to Ksoura.

"God willing, we'll soon have an olive press here," she told Nayif as he dipped his fresh bread into the ful, eating heartily. She sat right across from him, cutting burlap sacks that she'd washed and dried so she could fashion them into mattress covers and children's underwear. She said this without lifting her eyes from her work, as if just floating words into the air, hoping that he'd catch them by chance and not make a fuss. She didn't even look at his face to see if it registered any sort of reaction. She kept on doing what she was doing, feigning a sense of calm, though her heart was pounding from fear. Her hand was trembling so much that she pricked her finger with the needle more than once. She ignored the pain in her chest, wiped away the drops of blood with her right hand, then continued her work.

She knew exactly how this man thought. She'd learned how to avoid tension between them, because he could become violent quickly and then lose all ability to have a conversation. Once that happened, there was no use in even trying to speak to him. Her mother had told her that he beat her sister Safaa when she was pregnant the first time. She'd bled a lot afterward and had a miscarriage. Her own life had hung in the balance for days. She only fell pregnant with Fayez more than two years after healing from that incident. Nayif never raised his hand against Safaa again after that. Shahira remembered her mother talking about it and was afraid whenever she saw signs of anger creeping onto his face. She always hid her fear, however. She stood up to him, straight as an arrow, as if to remind him of what had happened to her sister and to say that this miscarried fetus could have been here today—a young man, as tall as he was, helping him with whatever he needed!

Shahira used her shrewd intelligence to tame Nayif, to make him a less vicious, aggressive person. She may have succeeded many times, but she still was careful to avoid quarrels. She knew when to keep quiet about things she intended to do. He'd mercilessly scolded her more than once, discouraging her and breaking her resolve.

She was secretly happy that he didn't respond at all when she mentioned the olive press. At first blush, it seemed that the idea appealed to him. "Go make me tea," he said abruptly, as soon as he'd finished his breakfast, as if to remind her who was boss and that he made the decisions. He was showing her that her role as a woman was to respond to his commands, and that was it. "And put a spoonful of molasses in too," he added, in an even brusquer tone. She went into the kitchen as he stared at her from his seat near the stove.

Deep in his heart he admired her. But it was admiration mixed with fear. He felt vaguely threatened by her and feared her boundless courage. He could neither explain nor understand this feeling. Nevertheless, he turned the idea round and round in his head silently, stirring the spoon of molasses into his mug of hot tea. He nearly burned his finger before quickly placing the cup on the low wooden table next to him. He smiled inwardly, imagining himself standing in front of this large olive press that all the farmers in town and from the surrounding areas flocked to.

He suddenly shook his head, expelling this image from his mind, and heard himself say in a low voice, "From where?" He then picked up his mug again, blowing on it, and then slowly stirring it. He began thinking about where the two of them could get the money to pay for a press. He would also need to buy a donkey to move the stone. He currently had only one donkey, and he needed that one to transport provisions and sell things after the harvest in the nearby towns and villages. He started shaking his head, as if he was speaking to someone else. He finished drinking his tea, put on his field shoes, and started getting ready to go out. Without looking at her, he repeated over and over, "Allahu karim, God is good."

Every suggestion Shahira made he'd always say would be answered by the will of God. It was a somewhat malicious way to convey to her that she was free to dream but her dreams would never come true. She followed him around, explaining all the benefits of building an olive press in their field, how much it could change the life of the entire family. But he carried on getting ready to go out. She stood in doorway watching him disappear down the dusty path to the field, noticing that he'd lost nearly all the hair on the back of his head. He was almost bald. She thought that perhaps he was afraid to try to improve his life for fear of failure—he'd never had to work hard to become the owner of this land, because he'd inherited it from his father. But she told herself that he was a good man. She was sure deep in her heart that if any danger befell her and the family that he'd be right there by her side, doing everything he could to save his family.

The two of them now had a big family. Their land couldn't produce enough to assure a decent living and new clothes every year for their children, especially because the school principal was consuming a large share of the olive and pine nut harvest each season.

But after she put a serious plan in place to procure an olive press, it was difficult for Shahira's dreams not to come true. She sought out the help of Said's son, her nephew Ghassan, as well as Fayez and Kamal. Building an olive press is difficult and time-consuming. She had to go to the workshop to inspect it every morning. They built a large room out in the field with a broad, raised platform, atop which they placed a large stone with a hole in the middle. They also had to install spouts leading into a stone trough, one for oil mixed with water and another for pure oil to run into after floating atop the water. They had to wait until the ground was totally dry before they could even start building.

Some time passed before Nayif visited the building site. When he saw how seriously and enthusiastically his nephew was working, he lent a hand in building a large storeroom for the olives and the oil to protect them from the vagaries of weather, animals, and people.

The olive press's grand opening was an unforgettable day for Ksoura. It was particularly memorable for Shahira. She stood watching the oil mixed with water flowing under the stone being turned by the animals and then the pure oil floating atop the water as it spilled into another basin. The local people all hurried to help Shahira and her family. Every person who harvested olives was expected to come and work pressing olives, "Those who bring their cows will be rewarded with garlic," she'd say, repeating the local saying meaning diligence is the mother of good fortune. She'd say this while pointing to the huge, nearly full trough.

The farmers put their olives in big burlap sacks to carry them to the press. Usually, they pressed them on the same day they came, or the next day at the latest. They didn't like to leave them for more than one day without pressing them into cooking oil. They collected, sorted, and cleaned them, plucking off their leaves. They took the best ones to eat or make oil from. Then they put the ones that were too small or infested with weevils into another bag to be pressed separately, so their oil could be used for making soap.

They no longer had to spend so much time on the road

between their lands and the faraway olive press. They could meet around the local press, share stories, and sing songs until nightfall. People could make their way home after that. One day, Shahira unleashed her singing voice that had been trapped in her throat for so long. She started singing loudly, filled with a joy she'd not felt since the faraway days of the wheat harvests and women singing in Ajmat. Her voice helped her regain the memory of songs and poems that she thought she'd forgotten.

She sang:

> Say hello and welcome, my love,
> The arrow launched by her fluttering kohl-lined eyes
> struck my heart,
> Wave your hand in welcome,
> the arrow struck my heart

That afternoon, they gathered up firewood and lit the wood-burning stove to roast potatoes and acorns on it. Shahira passed around fig jam sandwiches for everyone present. She patted Ghassan on the shoulder. He'd been there right beside her since the very beginning of the project. "I never would have been able to do it were it not for you, Fayez, and Kamal." Ghassan smiled and stared down at the ground shyly. He took a taste of the fig jam and swallowed his sandwich in one bite. After a few minutes, he turned to her suddenly and quietly asked, "When will I be allowed to marry Yasmine?"

# Yasmine

Shahira had waited for this question. At the same time, she avoided it. She didn't want her daughter to marry without having finished her studies or at least before having learned sewing and tailoring. It is true that she'd outwitted fate, but she couldn't change the customs of the people of Ksoura. This marriage was expected by the families. Ghassan was waiting for Yasmine to come of age and be ready for motherhood.

Just as Shahira herself married young, Yasmine would be married to Ghassan—her father's brother's son—when she was not yet fifteen years old. It was almost like a marriage between the two brothers Nayif and Said. This type of marriage prevented outsiders from infiltrating both the bloodline and the inheritance. It would help the family stick together through good times and bad. They'd keep their land holdings, crops, and houses in the family, and their children would all remain in one place. Even if there were disagreements, the family's power would be preserved. Everyone expected this marriage to take place as soon as Yasmine came of age, when her small chest started to bud. She blushed with embarrassment when Adla came over and referred to her as her daughter-in-law. She asked her to do household tasks as if training her, making her practice for the predetermined role she had in a life waiting for her there.

At first, Yasmine was enthusiastic. She thought that perhaps this would herald the beginning of a better life, in which she could realize her own personal dreams and also start a family. She was a dreamer; it wasn't difficult for her to believe in this illusion. She'd been raised with the notion that Ghassan would one day be her husband. She knew that he was kind. On her wedding day, she was ready to be a beautiful bride, the center of attention, and for everyone to throw rice at her and sprinkle her with rosewater. People would dance and sing while she walked through town flanked by her father and brothers all the way down to the groom's house—which would soon be her home. The singing and dancing framed the portrait she'd drawn of this new life. In any case, there was no way that either Yasmine or the men of the family would reject the idea of this marriage. Shahira had managed to find a way to outwit her fate when she found it oppressive, but Yasmine was actually a carbon copy of her father. She believed that you couldn't change what fate sent your way—you simply had to accept it.

Yasmine and her mother were very different in terms of both stubbornness and perseverance. These were two qualities Yasmine lacked. Were it not for her slender build and green eyes, no one would have believed that this gentle, good-natured girl was Shahira's daughter. Marrying paternal first cousins was a norm in Ksoura. It was difficult to ask for a beautiful young girl's hand in marriage if she had an unmarried male cousin.

Yasmine discontinued her education after primary school. There were no schools for girls beyond that level in their town or any neighboring towns, only for boys. If Yasmine had wanted to continue her studies at a middle school, she would have had to travel far from Ksoura every day. This was impossible for a girl. So, she woke up each morning, and instead of getting ready to go to school, she helped her mother prepare breakfast for her siblings before they went to school. Thus, rather than dreaming of continuing her studies—what Nayif called an impossible dream—she replaced it with an acceptable dream. This was a reality check that girls of her time were used to. She learned sewing and tailoring from their Armenian neighbor Anahid, who lived nearby with her husband Garabet and their two young daughters.

The moment Ghassan and his parents came to Nayif and Shahira's house on Yasmine's wedding day to walk her to her marital home, Shahira let her deep, enchanting singing voice soar. Anxiety danced in her eyes as she lifted her voice in song. She was singing of joy, though afraid of the future she'd let her daughter Yasmine drift into.

> We bade the new bride farewell, and tucked her into bed
> under rose petals
> We dressed her in her wedding gown,
> and in her mother's eyes
> a joy of sorrow flickers
> to eyes that don't speak, but we still hear them.

Time passed quickly. Yasmine had just begun learning how to sew when she married Ghassan. She was still a few months away from being able to cut and tailor a dress for clients. But her wedding couldn't wait for the realization of her personal dream, because Ghassan didn't want to work in the fields like his father and uncle. He wanted to leave Ksoura and move far away to work on the coast. But he also wanted to get married before leaving the village and embarking on this adventure, as he also wanted to insulate himself any future unknowns.

He began his married life resentful of the family and constantly quarreling with his father. They all lived in the same house with him and his new wife. In the period just after the wedding, he fought with his father daily. Shahira thought that things would regulate themselves as soon as he started working, managing the olive press. She thought that it would settle him and make him calmer. This would then help put Yasmine at ease, as the tension between her husband and his father sapped her energy. However, Ghassan barely worked with the olive press for two weeks. He told Shahira that he didn't want to do this work, he wanted to leave the family house—and their town—to look for work elsewhere.

Not even one day passed without some kind of fight between him and his father. Said started to worry about his behavior. "You have land! Who are you going to leave it to?" he'd repeat angrily. They'd raise their voices at each other and Ghassan would storm out of the house. Yasmine never knew where he spent his days. He'd come back only at nightfall.

Yasmine listened in on their arguments from the little room that they shared. She felt that she was stuck in a hole that she'd dug for herself and that there was no hope she'd ever escape. She was overwhelmed by a sorrow she didn't completely understand. A strong desire tugged at her—a desire to go back home to her own room, to flee into Shahira's embrace and stay there with her all night. She wanted to just leave and return to her parents' house, but she didn't want to walk alone late at night. She wondered if the dream of a better life had to be this difficult. Her life had changed; she had to scale back her dreams.

She wanted to complete her sewing and tailoring lessons, and to move into a house with her husband. Their house would have one large room just for her to work in. She'd receive women there who wanted to have clothes tailored for them. It was difficult to do this in a small house that had three whole families living in it, the third being Ghassan's brother, Maher, and his pregnant wife. Yasmine started insisting that they move out of his family's house. But how would they do it? Where would they go? She started spending most of her days between Shahira's and her sewing lessons at Anahid's house.

Ghassan's family didn't like Yasmine's nearly daily trips to see her mother. It caused a lot of tension between the two families. "Enough with this back and forth, you're married now. It's your duty to help your husband's family. This is your house now," Adla told her bluntly.

Life for the couple wasn't easy or full of promise. It wasn't just the ever-increasing tension between Ghassan and his father, but all of this did lead to issues between the couple.

One day Ghassan dropped Yasmine off at Shahira's house. "You're the only one I can count on, mother-in-law," Ghassan said to Shahira while drinking tea, adding, "I can't go on like this. Can you speak to the school principal, Miss Stuart? She's helped a lot of the guys find work. Maybe she could help find me a job. I need to leave this town!"

Ghassan went to Beirut a month later and took a bus to Haifa in Palestine. Miss Stewart had found him a job in a railway company, after Shahira had begged her for help. He went to Palestine with the idea that Yasmine would follow him after he'd found a house for them. He was gone for months without Yasmine hearing from him at all. Four months later, a letter arrived. In it, he told Yasmine to stay in Ksoura and that he'd come back during the holidays at the end of the year. Yasmine stayed with Shahira and finished her sewing and tailoring lessons. Then she started working with Anahid, helping her and practicing her craft in preparation for opening her own independent shop.

Yasmine wanted to move to Palestine where Ghassan was working. She could open a tailoring business in their apartment there. While she waited for this dream to come true, she started sleeping over at her parents' house because it was closer to work. At the time, this decision seemed reasonable to Ghassan's family because his brother Maher's wife had given birth to twins and they needed room for the new babies.

Ghassan was settling into his job, living in a flat with four other employees who'd come from Syria and Egypt to work for the railway company. He thought it was better for Yasmine to stay in Ksoura so he could save as much money as possible. If Yasmine moved there to live with him, he'd have to rent a house and furnish it, which would cost a lot—he wouldn't be able to save a penny.

At first, he came back to Ksoura every season. Then his visits got further and further apart. He'd stay with his family for a week and travel back once again. He always brought gifts for the family. He'd give Yasmine hers when they were alone in their room in her family's house. She was as excited as a child when she got her gifts; they helped her forget the long stretches of loneliness she experienced when he was away.

Life was confusing for Yasmine. She was married but she lived with her parents. Her things were scattered between her parents' house and Ghassan's family's house. When Ghassan came home, her life got even more confusing, since him being there made the gravity of their situation more apparent. They had no house, no family of their own, no children.

"How are you going to have children if he's in one place and you're in another?" Adla said, clapping her hands together in protest. They'd been married for a year and Yasmine wasn't pregnant yet! To Adla, this seemed too a long a time. She asked Shahira to go with her to a sheikh to ask him for a talisman that would help

Yasmine get pregnant and have a large family. Impatient with Adla as usual, Shahira said, "Don't be silly. If you want to go to a sheikh, go yourself!"

In the end, Yasmine got pregnant without needing a talisman or magic spell. Shahira was right to insist that all her daughter needed was Ghassan to stay there for a while, and not keep flitting off when he'd barely just arrived.

During her pregnancy, Yasmine liked to leave the house and walk to the fields. She'd walk slowly, feeling her pregnant belly growing heavier each day. She dreamed of having a girl, despite constantly hearing the prayers of everyone around her hoping for a boy. She wanted a girl who'd resemble her mother—not her. She knew deep down that she lacked courage. She also knew that some character traits were inherited, passed down through the generations, and that she hadn't inherited much from her mother, not enough to be a brave and strong mother herself. She felt safe near Shahira, and she knew that it was a good idea to stay in Ksoura and not to go live in Palestine. She asked herself, Who would help her take care of the baby there? Who would stop her and say, "Good morning, Yasmine" when she went out for a walk? Perhaps they don't have fields there. Or even flowers.

These were her interior monologues, convincing herself that not following Ghassan and staying in Ksoura was the right thing to do. On one of his visits home, Ghassan brought a book with maps and pictures of the cities in Palestine. She opened it and started looking at the photos. He pointed out where Yaffa and Haifa were located. He put his finger on the spot where he thought the railway office was located. From the map, she thought it looked like where he worked was right on the seaside. But Ghassan told her that where he worked wasn't actually that close to the sea and that it was more than half an hour's walk to the beach.

He was away from Ksoura for six months, so he wasn't there to see Yasmine's belly swell in the early months of her pregnancy. When he returned, Yasmine was due to deliver within a few weeks. He decided to stay put and wait to see his firstborn child. One day, the two of them were alone in their room at Shahira's house. He caressed the mountain that was her belly, then leaned over to kiss her right on her mouth, her lips, and her big round belly many times. Yasmine blushed with embarrassment. A stifled laugh escaped her as she shyly wrapped a sheet tightly around herself.

The weather was hot; no breeze slipped through the window. The stifling weather exhausted her, but she remained wrapped up in her sheet. Though they'd been married for nearly two years, Yasmine still hadn't really gotten used to Ghassan. She couldn't understand how a woman could get undressed in front of a man. They'd never lived together for more than a few months because he was always away.

Their marriage ended in tragedy after the birth of their daughter Layla. Yasmine died that night. Severe internal bleeding left her lifeless. They found her when everyone woke the following morning. None of them had felt her pain or suffering from the extreme bleeding. The famished cries of the newborn had awoken Shahira. She was in her swaddling clothes lying next to Yasmine on the blood-soaked bed.

Both the family and other townspeople held Imm Geryes responsible. She'd aged, her eyesight had gone, and her hands were no longer capable. But she didn't give in or quit. She kept working tirelessly in Ksoura and other nearby villages. However, young families—especially those with family members who'd studied on the coast—started bringing in trained, certified midwives or taking pregnant family members to the hospital to deliver their babies.

~

Death goes right along with life in Ksoura. It is the people's daily bread. Death comes suddenly; it snatches people who love life. Famine, wars, and locust attacks are not alone in bringing death to mountain folk. Ignorance and insufficient precautions also lead to disease. Sometimes a lack of means can also lead to premature death. Women gather around the bodies of the dead to mourn together. Grief cannot be expressed by tears until the professional mourner comes from a nearby village with a group of other women who repeat the funeral incantations after her. The sounds of wailing and sobbing rise after these women arrive, having walked the whole distance from their village. On warm days in early spring, many of them walk barefoot. Each woman carries her shoes in one hand and a little black handbag in the other. They put their shoes back on when they approach the mourning site.

It was very hot in Ksoura on the day Yasmine was buried. There was no wind, not even a light breeze. The courtyard overlooking the stone pine forest was filled with men. They sat under a large white tent that had been erected the previous morning. Large jars had been filled with cold spring water that the children of the town were pouring into clay pitchers for people to drink from.

Ghassan sat with his father, uncle, and Yasmine's brothers to receive condolences. He was disoriented and could barely choke out thanks to the people who'd come to mourn his wife. He'd arrived in Ksoura two weeks ago to celebrate the birth of his baby with Yasmine. Intense guilt ate away at him because he hadn't slept in their shared bedroom on the night of the birth. He'd stretched out on the sofa in the living room and fallen asleep there. Perhaps if he'd slept next to her, he'd have felt her pain, or she would have called out to him, said his name, asked for his help. If he'd slept next to her, he would have rushed to get Imm Geryes or carried her to the hospital—he would have saved her.

He looked inside the house where her body was. Women from his family and other townswomen gathered around her as women from neighboring towns and villages continued arriving. As they reached the doorstep, the women all stopped, and the one leading them started to wail. The women inside stood to welcome them and started crying loudly too. All the women's voices joined in various rhythms. None of them could hear her own individual voice in the sea of black and white.

The men were outside talking and receiving mourners while this was happening inside. Conversations mainly about politics and war were mixed with people exchanging news about their crops and harvests, how scarce productivity was that year. Ghassan went inside from time to time, bent over Yasmine's body, and cried—the men of the family never leaving his side or letting him be in the hall alone. They would then quickly leave, accompanied by the mourning chants of women, which rose up every time the men from the dearly departed's family would enter.

Shahira couldn't see anyone, even if they were standing right in front of her. Grief left her unable to communicate. She just stayed seated, right next to her daughter, who was laid out on a wooden bed. From time to time, she stroked her daughter's shoulder and face. Yasmine was covered with a white sheet so only her head was showing. A white mandeel was draped over her head and neck.

Distressed, Shahira bent forward, bringing her head right up close to her daughter's face, whispering to her as if there were some life still inside her. It's true that death had snatched her daughter away, but to Shahira it seemed to be merely an illusion. Yasmine looked as if she were simply sleeping and would soon wake up. It was as if life and death were reconciled in her peaceful presence.

Women from the family had been delegated to sit with her—Fayez's wife and Maher's wife comforted her as she rocked back and forth in a slow rhythmic motion, blaming herself for having left her daughter alone that evening. She'd gone back to her own room, where she'd taken her medication for the joint pain that had recently plagued her. It plunged her into a deep sleep.

She leaned her body back and swayed her head to the rhythm of the women's mourning chants. She wanted to cry but couldn't. She felt the tears stop right at the surface of her eyes; they wouldn't fall. She never cried. Not even on the day she married Nayif did she cry. She felt herself choking. She let out a low moan and then was silent. She went back to stroking her daughter's face. She leaned over again and brought her face right up to Yasmine's, whispering, "Why did I leave you?" She said this loudly enough that all the women around her could hear.

"How could I have left you? I let you die all alone!" One of the women came over, hugged her tightly, and said to her while crying, "Death comes to us all, it's God will." Adla was sitting right behind Shahira and interrupted, "Cry Shahira, it's good to cry." But Shahira couldn't cry. She'd never shed a tear. She simply shook her head, protesting in her choked-up voice, "How is it God's will to deprive me of my daughter? Why?"

When the time came to move the body to its final resting place, Shahira stood up. She started circling Yasmine's bed. She still half-believed that her daughter was asleep and would wake up soon. She started walking around and around the bed like a moth fluttering around a flame in its final dance before self-immolation. Her face showed a mix of inexplicable and contradictory emotions:

happiness mixed with tragedy, as if joy had become another face of sorrow.

The family held Imm Geryes responsible for Yasmine's death, it's true. But there were whispers amongst the women in the family that cast some doubt upon this. One day Imm Geryes told Shahira that Adla had been going around the family saying again and again that Shahira was the cause of Yasmine's death, and it was nothing to do with Imm Geryes.

That day, she heard Adla say that Shahira hadn't listened to her and never went to speak to the sheikh as she'd asked her to. Her lack of faith must have led to her losing her daughter. The curse of the evil eye was strong, and Shahira hadn't done what was necessary to protect her daughter. After Adla finished talking, Imm Geryes got up and left without even drinking her coffee. She felt that she'd been relieved of a heavy burden that had weighed on her since the young woman's death. She felt liberated from an accusation she'd heard over and over again.

But what Adla said reopened Shahira's wound. She hadn't forgotten this wound, nor would she ever. But she tried to cheat her way out of feeling sorrow and grief, consoling herself and compensating for her loss by lavishing limitless love on her granddaughter Layla. She tried to heal her wound with silence. But wounds don't heal when words turn silent. Shahira secluded herself in her room, mourning her daughter with her plaintive singing:

> Oh my child, the jasmine asked about you
>         I told her you were asleep
> Don't be angry, don't blame me
> My tears are hidden
>         in my soul

The house is closed, no one can enter
all the doors are locked
If perhaps Yasmine could return
joy would return too

After those years in which Shahira had taken Adla to be naïve and helpless, the day had now come for Adla to settle her scores with Shahira and take her revenge. "You've been weak of faith your whole life. If you'd had faith, if you'd believed, you'd have made the talisman. This is the wrath of God," Adla told her.

Sometimes, death hardens people's hearts instead of softening them, leading them to see others as the cause of their loss. Relations between the two families worsened day after day, year after year. If that short marriage had never taken place, the families probably would still be dreaming of a day when they could be more cohesive and closely knit. That dream would have been more solid than reality, which is full of surprises and can contradict predictions.

The two women, who both married into the Dahli family, still talked, worked together, and exchanged information about their lives. But they no longer visited each other's homes, and the little girl Layla became central to the ensuing struggle between the families. Once when Adla came to take Layla, just five years old, she cried and hid behind Shahira's skirt. She refused to go with her Grandma Adla. Ghassan used all the wisdom he could muster up to ask Shahira—in front of everyone—to look after his daughter, Layla. He wanted her to keep living at Shahira's house. This forced his family to stay silent and stop insisting that the little girl come and live with her grandparents Adla and Said.

Shahira experienced Yasmine's death as the most terrible tragedy she'd lived through. It broke her heart. Yes, her daughter had grown up and married, but she'd always remained her little girl.

And she was really still a child when she passed away. She'd called her Yasmine, the family's jasmine flower, the only girl amongst four brothers. She had a special, unique, and different character.

Her daughter's death accelerated Shahira's acceptance of fate. "We all die one day," she said, choked-up, adding, "But it's harsh to live with and difficult to bear." She ate less and less; her joints and limbs hurt more and more. But despite the aches and pains and difficulty getting out of bed in the morning, she felt that she still had a lot to do, especially raising her little granddaughter.

Layla was born practically an orphan, and Shahira clung to her. She slept next to her grandmother in bed at night. She grew up with her grandmother as her mother, with the nearly constant absence of her father. Her mother's brothers were also mostly living in Beirut or on the coast somewhere, so they were absent too. When Ghassan visited Ksoura to take Layla for the day to his family's house and to play with his brother Maher's children, she always wanted to leave in the evening. She wanted to go back home to her own house, as she referred to Shahira's.

"I want to go home to my house," she told Ghassan in the evening. "This is your house too," Adla answered, offering for her to sleep at their place when her father was in town. But Layla refused and insisted on eating her supper with Shahira.

"She's stubborn and wrong-headed like her Grandma Shahira," Adla said angrily, eyes fixed on Ghassan and Layla leaving to go back to Shahira's. Feelings of guilt pervaded him since his wife's demise. This got worse with time and was manifested in his constant silence and sadness.

Despite her difficult life, before Yasmine died, Shahira had faith that time couldn't break her, that she could overcome whatever life threw at her no matter how harsh. She believed that the effort she and Nayif had expended as parents meant that they produced successful children who grew up, studied, and matured. Some of them already had built their own lives, futures, and families of their own. Fayez married and had children; Nadim did as well. But even though Shahira had more family members, Yasmine's death changed her outlook on herself and her life.

"Death has broken me," Shahira said, and frequently repeated. Then World War II erupted. This made Shahira relive her terrible fear of poverty and hunger. After Yasmine's death, her fear of famine had already increased, for no obvious reason.

Perhaps it was because she'd lost faith in life and her own power to outwit fate, as she always used to say. Her fear was accompanied by overwhelming sorrow, and now there was the added impact of Nayif's deteriorating mind and the onset of dementia. Forgetfulness slowly began to devour his memory. It was no longer a repository for the past; he couldn't remember names or places. He couldn't even recall the names of his children or grandchildren. Sometimes his memory would return to him in a flash, then just as quickly die out and fade away. He started losing things—he couldn't remember where he'd put his glasses or the medicine he took every day.

Shahira looks over at him while stirring the tomato sauce on the fire. She sees him sitting as usual, in his spot next to her, helping by adding firewood to keep the fire alive in the stove, his mind wandering off from time to time. He forgets what he's doing. He listens to the neighborhood children playing in the town square next to the house. He calls out to them to come inside, thinking they're his children. Then just as quickly he closes his eyes and drifts off in his chair, motionless.

She'd always known that he was a good man. But she never experienced herself as a woman with him. She didn't know her feminine side except for the two summers before her marriage. She remembers that day when he and the men of the family arrived by mule in Ajmat to ask for her hand in marriage. It was a Saturday. She was sitting on the stone bench in front of her uncle's shop near their house, enjoying the warm spring sun. He came to town with his father and brother. She saw them get off the mules looking tired. One of them was carrying a small cloth bag that Nayif's mother had filled with food. Nayif lifted a box off the mule's back with a gallon container of oil and another of olives, as well as a second box filled with bars of soap. A vague feeling washed over her as she observed them from afar. She suddenly felt cold and hurried into the shop, hiding inside.

~

After Yasmine's death, Shahira rarely left the house. She stayed home. Anyone who came over would have thought no one was home. Layla being there with her was a comfort and helped her forget her sorrows. She was told that Yasmine certainly had been reborn somewhere, and that she now has a new face and name. This newborn would someday remember her past and visit Shahira, her mother in a previous incarnation. Hearing things like this helped calm her nerves, though she kept visiting the cemetery.

Sometimes, she would ask Fayez's wife Mufida to take Layla to play with her cousins Mona and Majd. Then she'd walk to Yasmine's grave down in the valley near town. Often Anahid would come with her, carrying a candle and a bouquet of flowers in a vase. Anahid would light the candle and leave it slowly burning on the ground next to the flowers. Anahid believed that the soul of the deceased would be able to feel who loved her and came to visit her. On those days, Shahira sits in front of the cemetery gate speaking to Yasmine in a trembling voice. She wants to cry but she can't. She doesn't bring candles or flowers when she visits her daughter. It isn't part of her family's customs. But she does sing to her.

Who can she entrust the management of the olive press to? Who will work the land, look after the fields, and harvest the crops? Shahira wonders about this while slowly climbing back up out of the valley towards home. She knows only too well that none of the children want to work in the fields. They left agricultural life, attracted by freelance professions and salaried work in teaching or government administration; they were still ruled by French mandate at the time.

In the end, she left the management of the olive press and sales from their harvests to Ghassan's brother Maher. She started doing work that allowed her to stay home and avoid going out at all. One Sunday afternoon, when she and Nayif were eating lunch alone at home, he had a rare moment of mental clarity. He told her that their current situation was the result of her insistence on educating the children—none of them were left to help harvest the crops and work with the olive press.

He asked her if she would have insisted on educating them if she'd known that their education would push them to emigrate and build lives far away from the family and Ksoura. She looked up at him and nodded her head. This is the circle of life. No generation is like the one before. All she'd wanted was for them to be happy with the life they chose. But deep down she didn't know if what she told Nayif was really what she would have wanted deep down.

She felt as if there was always something heavy pressing down on her chest and she carried it with her permanently. She stopped eating. She would go out into the garden on the pretext of looking for the little kitten that Layla had found by the door one day and kept. She'd just stand there and stare at the sea far off in the distance. Her body shivered. She felt that fate, which had defeated her with Yasmine's death, was pursuing her.

Shahira's pains increased until she could no longer pinpoint their exact location. She felt them early in the morning when she couldn't get out of bed. Or she felt them at other times when she lost the ability to move her arms, even to change her clothes. She started to worry about dropping things she was holding in her hands—a plate of food or even a cup of coffee. Her fingers were all twisted up. She complained of stiff joints and difficulty walking in the morning. One day, she finally agreed to let Fayez take her to see a specialist in Beirut. It was one of the few times that she ever rode in a car. She'd always hated these strange machines that made such a lot of noise and left you feeling dizzy. She preferred riding on a cart pulled by horses or even sitting atop a donkey that walked slowly and silently. Fayez had to stop more than once along the way because Shahira suffered from motion sickness and had to throw up on the side of the road. From the time she'd arrived in Ksoura, she'd never felt so broken, weak, and truly helpless as that day when Fayez took her to the doctor in Beirut.

It was as if Shahira's illness that winter destroyed a sort of hidden bond that held her family together. With her energy and vitality, Shahira was the key to the family's ability to communicate. Of her children, Kamal remained the closest to her. He'd pop by her place randomly, sit and chat for a while, and then go back to work. He'd found a job as a court clerk in Aley. One day he brought a newly married teenage couple from the Beqaa home with him. He thought Mahmoud and Hajar could help Shahira around the house and also work in the fields.

Kamal helped them to settle into a small place he'd built for them out in the field. It was difficult at first for Shahira to agree to have a woman she didn't know in the house sweeping, washing, and picking vegetables from her garden. Hajar couldn't help but notice Yasmine's pictures positioned all around the house. She stood in front of one and wept openly, crying and wailing as if she knew Yasmine, as if she were a member of her own family. Hajar could do many things that Shahira could not. She cried hot tears, her sobs wracking her entire body.

All coincidences are destined. Shahira had faced off with fate her whole life and now it has sent a woman to help soothe her soul, dry her tears, and rejoin the world. Shahira got used to having Hajar around; she adopted her in a way. Hajar shared her own story—when she was no more than five years old, her father murdered her mother. That fateful day, her mother had gone to the natural spring in their town in the Beqaa. A strange man was passing and stopped her to ask how to get to the main road leading to Chtoura. She walked with him to show him where the road was. Someone who had seen her started wagging their tongue, telling a different story. This gossip quickly made its way to her husband, who accused her of cheating on him. He stormed into the house like a madman; she was sitting in front of the copper basin, washing everyone's clothes. He snatched a kitchen knife off the table and attacked her. "You've brought shame on us all, you whore! You've brought shame on us." Afterwards, he walked to the police station and turned himself in, saying that he'd washed away his family's shame. And he sat down calmly. He was imprisoned for one month and then walked free.

~

Fayez moved to Beirut after he got married. He only came back to Ksoura on holidays. He'd married a young woman from Ksoura whose family had moved to Beirut when she was a young girl and her father had found work as a security guard at the Serail downtown. Fayez opened a little stationery shop right next to their flat in Jal al-Bahr, selling notebooks and paper products to students at the nearby schools and university.

Unlike Fayez, Nadim and Kamal didn't migrate to the coast but to the very heart of the mountain. Nadim worked as a teacher in Broummana. Kamal managed to find a job as a court clerk. Work kept them from visiting Ksoura. Their political activity in the party sapped any free time they had left.

Winter weekends changed at Shahira's; the house was nearly empty. The only one left was her youngest child, Tawfiq. If you visited, you'd hardly know he was there. He stuck to his studio and had no interest in social life or the lives of the townspeople.

Nayif started losing his memory more and more. Sometimes he woke up in the morning and asked Shahira to sing to him. She sat next to him and started singing as she fed him. He asked her where his mother was. He'd get up, saying that he had to go home to see her. "This is your home. Your mother passed away years ago," Shahira would gently inform him. His eyes would fill with tears as she hugged him and patted his shoulders to try to calm him down.

With the coming of spring, Shahira went back to sitting in the sun in front of the house on Sunday mornings, waiting for her children to visit. The family got together on Sundays. After Yasmine died, her waiting took on more urgency; she missed them and asked them to come over. Nadim came with his family. Sometimes he'd bring Kamal along too. Fayez started arriving later and later, sometimes even after the family had finished eating lunch. He bet on the horses and kept losing his money. His gambling addiction became another challenge Shahira had to deal with after Yasmine's death. When she found out, she bemoaned her bad luck. "Why,

God? Why did my son turn out like this? I raised him and educated him just like the others, late nights and all."

Secrets never stay secret in Ksoura. Everyone heard Shahira cursing her luck the day she found out Fayez was betting on the horses at the newly opened racetrack. "It's haram . . . haram. If you lose it's haram, if you win it's haram. It's just wrong. Do you know where this money is going? Or how you got it? And who from?" She said all this angrily when he walked into to the garden where the family was gathered. "Mom, please, calm down and lower your voice," Fayez said, hugging her. "We've gone a few times, it's not a crime."

She was upset when Fayez told his brothers about what he'd been doing at the racetrack and which horse he'd bet on. She saw his story as corrupting them and encouraging them to join in. Then he mentioned people from the Abdel-Nour family, explaining that they'd been asked to build the racetrack at the request of the French. Shahira moved closer and sat right next to him. She started listening closely to what he was saying and interrupted, with obvious displeasure, "The French want a racetrack?"

Fayez looked at her, nodded, and kept on talking. Shahira got up, annoyance written all over her face, and walked away, saying that she felt cold. She went back inside, as her joint pain had started bothering her again. She sat in her usual spot in the living room near the window looking out on the garden. She contemplated her sons sitting together outside, muttering to herself angrily, "The French want horseraces? It's not enough that they destroy everything, now they want to ruin young men's minds? Inshallah the Abdel-Nours' projects won't see the light of day."

She was leaning forward, her head bent over her knees when Kamal walked in. He kissed her hand and asked her to come out and sit with them in the garden. He hugged her, telling her not to worry about Fayez, that he's stubborn and hardheaded by nature.

Like his brother Nadim, Kamal was a member of the SSNP and he didn't get on well with Fayez. They disagreed about a lot of things—from public, political positions to their private, personal lives. The issue of betting on horse races added one more thing not to agree on.

Shahira didn't like taking any medicine for her joints. At first, she refused to follow the doctor's advice. However, Layla, who'd now reached the age of ten, started reminding her when to take her pills, handing them to her with a glass of water. She'd stand right in front of her grandmother to see with her own eyes that she'd swallowed them, "I don't want you to leave me like my mother did. Take your medicine . . . for me."

Shahira pulled Layla toward her and hugged her tight. She answered with a laugh, "I'm like the devil—I never die. Tomorrow we'll go for a walk in the fields together and pick acadinia fruit and almonds."

Layla loved nothing more than those nature walks with Shahira. They'd wait for winter to end and the weather to warm up a bit, and then head out together toward the valley. Layla would describe everything to her grandmother as if she were totally blind: the tree branches, the stone path, the spring flowers, the sunlight peeking out and then disappearing behind the trees. Shahira reveled in these descriptions and felt as if she were seeing everything anew—as if she'd never seen any of it before.

Layla searched for rocks with unusual shapes that she could collect and take home in her skirt pocket. She picked up colorful cicadas and put them in a paper bag. She gathered the flowers she'd picked into a bouquet. When they got back home, she marked the date and the place she'd found them on each stone she'd collected. She put the bouquet of flowers into a vase with water and set it on a table near her grandfather Nayif, who'd lost his memory. He sits on his chair daydreaming all day, every day. "These are flowers for you, Grandpa!" she exclaims. He turns toward her, smiling and nodding his head a little. Then he goes back to his daydreams.

Often, she sits down on the sofa and tries to record everything she saw during their walk in her notebook. She sometimes changes the colors in her descriptions. For example, she might record that she saw a tree with orange branches, or pink grass growing in the fields. She delighted in her ability to change the picture with just words. She liked coloring on the pages where she'd written these sentences. Not long afterward, she'd fall asleep on the sofa where she'd been sitting.

Layla being in the house was both a source of happiness and a way of keeping active for Shahira, especially after her boys left home and Tawfiq isolated himself in the studio he'd built for himself behind the house. Shahira would have hot soup waiting for Layla every day after school. She'd ask Hajar to set the table and then would lead Nayif by the hand so he could eat supper with them. She'd also call out to Tawfiq, inviting him to join them, but he rarely responded.

Unlike his parents, Tawfiq remained untamed. He ate and slept at all hours. Layla loved him the best. They took walks together in the fields on weekends. He liked to bring his art supplies with him, find a place to sit, and start drawing. He gave Layla colored pencils and told her to draw the things she liked to talk about. But she used them for writing instead of drawing.

When summer came that year, Shahira felt young again. She no longer noticed her aches and pains; the medicines had cured them. The doctor had told her that the pain she was suffering from would afflict her on cold winter days. She started reducing her medicines and living a nearly normal life.

That summer passed peacefully. But World War II was at their doorstep. The world was tense.

Nazism was on the rise in Germany and the Europeans feared Hitler. People in Ksoura believed that they were safe from the wars happening out in the world. They thought if the wars stayed far away, they wouldn't suffer the way they had in World War I. But radios began invading homes. With them, the globe shrank. It started to be difficult for people in town to isolate themselves from what was happening, especially Nadim and Kamal, who'd started hosting SSNP meetings that attracted young people from Ksoura. They wanted Lebanon to be independent and liberated from the French Mandate.

Though World War I was long past, the specter of famine and poverty hung over the lives of people in the mountains for years. The time between the two world wars wasn't enough for people to have forgotten their suffering. They remembered what it was like to be hungry and poor, to lose loved ones. During this inter-war period of only twenty years, life changed in Ksoura. Many young people fled unemployment and poverty after the First World War. They emigrated to North and South America. Those who didn't emigrate left for coastal towns and cities looking for work.

One day at noon, Tawfiq was painting in the garden behind the house. Hajar ran up to him, sobbing loudly. "Grandpa's dead," she wailed. Tawfiq dropped his paintbrush and rushed into the house. His father Nayif was sitting on the sofa as usual, his head resting on the left side of a large pillow, placed there to prop him up into a sitting position. There was an untouched tray of food in front of him. Hajar had wanted to give him lunch. She went over and thought he was sleeping. She shook him gently, but when she touched his hand, she found it cold as ice.

Shahira returned only a few moments later. She hadn't finished her visit to Anahid or cut the cloth for the dress she was working on because she'd had a sort of premonition. She felt something heavy in her heart and insisted on rushing back home. She could hear Hajar's sobbing before she walked through the door and knew deep down what had happened before even seeing Nayif on the sofa in his final rest. The day of his burial and funeral ceremony, she told her children, "I knew it in my heart. He just wanted to leave this world."

# Layla

Layla always felt that memory consisted of a borrowed life that she hadn't really lived. Memory meant stories she'd heard as a little girl and couldn't deal with. She'd grown into a young woman with an overwhelming feeling that she'd been cut off from what had come before her, that there was a missing link between the present and the past. She felt that her memory didn't connect her to anything. It was the memory of a life she hadn't lived. It was lost time that she didn't know how to cope with losing. It was an adopted, illusory memory, and not hers.

From the time she was born, she'd only seen one photograph of her mother. It was from a few days before her wedding. The bride and groom had gone to a studio in Beirut to have their picture taken. In the photo, Yasmine sits on a chair holding a bouquet of artificial flowers. Ghassan stands to her right, his hand on her shoulder. It's a black-and-white photo, but over time it's faded to gray, obscuring the details of Yasmine's face. People spoke about her mother, Yasmine, a lot, and Layla invented pictures in her mind from these stories.

At first, Layla only imagined her as a version of her grandma

Shahira—same face, same scent. But with the passing of time, she heard more and more stories about her mother, helping her to invent a face and a scent, as well as the color of her hair and eyes. The first writing she ever did was a description of Yasmine, conveying what she'd picked up about her from the women in the family. She'd write and rewrite, incorporating little details that she'd been searching for that were missing from previous descriptions. Each time, she invented an image that she hoped resembled her.

She used a piece of charcoal to write her mother's name on the walls outside the house. She drew circles and eyes, saying that they were her mother's face. She wrote "Yasmine" dozens of times on the wall encircling the house and the door to the house itself. She also sketched out flowers and the sun near them. Shahira observed her from afar, rocking in her chair and calling out . . . Layla!

She wanted to tell her to stop writing on the walls and not get all dirty with charcoal, but suddenly she thought of Yasmine, and the little girl who'd been gifted to her just before her mother passed away. That was enough to make her fall silent, saying to herself that she should be able to write whatever she wants, whenever she wants. The winter rains would come anyway and wash it all away.

With time, Layla discovered that there were many things she didn't know. She learned that she'd grown up in a house that was permeated by a haunting sense of loss. It was a house with no women except the two of them—her and Grandma Shahira. Even Hajar, the woman who helped with housework and agricultural work, never stayed the night. Hajar's husband Mahmoud came every evening to take her home to their lodging in the fields. None of the women who'd brought Shahira into their family when she got married still lived in the house. They lived in areas where Shahira wouldn't want to live or even visit. She deeply believed that all places were the same and the only thing differentiating one place from another are the people living there.

But Layla herself used to dream of being near the sea in Beirut. She could see it from the second-floor flat that her Uncle Fayez had started building but had not finished. One bedroom was completed and furnished and he stayed there with his family when he came to Ksoura, waiting for the money to finish it. Layla loved the balcony attached to that big room looking out over the sea. She started begging her grandmother to let her sleep over there. She sat outside on the balcony and watched darkness fill the sky and fall over the sea, the lights of the city reflecting off it. At night, she watched the stars dance, bouncing from place to place. She liked to wake up in the morning and track the movement of the clouds through the day. When night falls, the clouds stretch out into thin wisps throughout the sky. Layla can only see shadows of the stars, as if they've covered their faces with a diaphanous veil.

Sometimes she gets sleepy, but she insists on waiting for the full moonrise. She likes to stay out on the balcony where the shadows of trees in the garden play in a pantomime of silence only interrupted by the nonstop purring of the cat on her lap. Shahira allowed Layla to spend time up there by herself during the school exam period. Layla said that she wanted to study in peace, removed from the hustle and bustle of family visits. Shahira assented and let her be. When Layla finished studying, she read poetry and other Arabic literary texts. She enjoyed poems by Umar ibn Abi Rabih, al-Mutanabbi, and Ahmad Shawqi. She discovered short stories by Mikhail Nuaimy, Maroun Abboud, and Kahlil Gibran. She lay down and stared out at the distant sea. She thought that it seemed far away, but it wasn't all that far if she really wanted to go there!

Layla finished the school year and was thrilled when her father got an official letter from the school informing him that she could get a university scholarship if she maintained her high marks in physics and mathematics in the final three years of school. Ghassan wasn't in Ksoura to receive this letter because he was still working in Palestine. Fayez read it and congratulated Layla on her hard work. That year, summer flew by. Layla spent the happiest days of her life with Rose, her classmate and childhood best friend. They spent most weekends together, usually reading and chatting in Layla's room. Time raced by when they were together.

One Saturday, Rose started reading Kahlil Gibran's *The Prophet*—she'd found it on a shelf in the library. She was totally immersed and kept reading until she heard her brother calling her to come home. The next morning was a Sunday. Joy visible on her face, Rose told Layla that Halim Bou Tannous had visited the family. He was the young man who'd seen her at one of her cousins' weddings in Ksoura. She'd told Layla about him at the time. He'd come with his family to their house the day before to ask for her hand in marriage.

~

Just before summer drew to a close, Layla attended her friend's wedding at the church in Ksoura. After she was married, Rose moved to her new house—the flat above Halim's family home. It was a small apartment, with just one bedroom, a living room, kitchen, and bathroom. Halim built it and then looked for a bride to furnish and live in it. He promised her that he'd build a bigger house before they had children. He worked with his uncle in the wholesale trade in Beirut, clearing goods through customs at the port and organizing their transport to the warehouse. After the wedding, weeks passed before Layla saw Rose. She went over to say goodbye before moving to Beirut for her studies. They promised to always meet up when Layla was back at her grandma's house for visits. Rose wept while hugging her.

Layla's move from her school in the mountains to the Evangelical School in Ras Beirut was sudden. She lived at her uncle Fayez's house in Jal al-Bahr with him, his wife, and her cousins Majd and Mona. According to Fayez, the move was so that Layla could successfully complete her last three years of school and win a university scholarship. He reminded her of this all the time. He wanted his niece to finish her education and become an engineer to fulfil the dream he'd originally had for his daughter Mona. That dream had not come true.

In Beirut, Layla met Miss Helen, who taught her English literature. This meeting changed her life and showed her that her love for literature, rather than physics, wasn't a bad thing. In Miss Helen's class, she found herself not caring about improving her science and math grades as she was expected to do.

Sudden rain took fifteen-year-old Layla by surprise on her first day of school in Beirut. She got to class late that day in September 1941. Everything was new to her, and she was all turned around—the city, her uncle's house, the streets, the school, even the food seemed different.

As she opened the classroom door, she spotted the teacher standing near a big window. She was a tall woman, holding a book in her hand. Layla entered, apologetic and out of breath. Her clothes were soaking wet. Miss Helen smiled at her, told her to take off her jacket to let it dry, then carried on reading from Charlotte Bronte's *Jane Eyre*. Layla looked like a drowned cat who'd been pulled out of a well, but quickly forgot what a miserable state she was in. She forgot all about her soaking wet clothes and dripping wet hair. She was enraptured by how the teacher was reading the novel aloud, as if reciting a poem.

There was something magical about those moments when a hush fell over the twenty-student class. Layla hadn't experienced such reading sessions at school before. Miss Helen read a long chapter and explained it, placing the characters and the narrative in their historical and social contexts. English literature classes with her meant not only studying language but also history, geography, and different civilizations.

Before the end of the lesson that day, the sky opened up and sunshine streamed through the window, bouncing off her desk and graying hair. A rainbow formed. The students started whispering to each other gesturing to the bit of sky they could see. Miss Helen stopped reading and asked the students what a rainbow meant to them: How did they see it? The lesson transformed on the spot. It became a conversation about rainbows, with each student sharing what they thought about them. When she posed the question to Layla, she responded that she didn't know how rainbows were formed but she always dreamed that she could hold the two ends of a rainbow in her hands and never let it go.

Their beautiful relationship grew stronger. Helen would loan her a book every now and then and Layla would devour it quickly, in just a few days. Each book helped her build a warm, cozy world that protected her from feeling orphaned, lost. Books even helped her accept those feelings as a part of her life.

Helen asked Layla to teach her Arabic. At first, Layla found this a strange request. Hadn't Helen been living in Beirut for years and never thought of learning Arabic before? They started meeting on Friday afternoons at Helen's house near the school in Ras Beirut. They sat on the big sofa in the office and studied. Layla gave her words to copy down and then figure out the meaning. All the while they listened to the music coming from the living room. Occasionally, Helen changed the record, or put on the Ella

Fitzgerald record on repeat, singing along to "Little White Lies."

One Saturday morning, Helen passed by to see Layla's family in Ksoura, when Fayez happened to be there. He'd expressed his admiration for Helen, who sometimes visited them on weekends and had even stayed over at their place. She went into the kitchen and helped Shahira prepare lunch. After lunch, Shahira served tea and found Helen sitting on the ground trying to turn on the radio that rested on a low table. She wanted to hear the news program that gave an overview of world affairs, with the escalation of the Second World War in Europe. Sometimes when she was there, Layla go out and see Rose, leaving Helen to talk to Fayez.

Her semiweekly visits with Rose were charged with emotions that Layla didn't experience in Beirut. Rose was content in her new life and about to give birth to her first child. She started telling Layla all the details of her daily life, about her house, who visited her, her husband, and their intimate relationship. She laughed when she got to sharing news from their bedroom. Layla asked her if she was happy. She nodded her head yes and stayed silent.

Layla added on a follow-up question about whether she wanted to finish her studies and get her baccalaureate. Rose stared back at her. But she didn't reply. They carried on talking about family affairs and things related to the house that took up all her time. Deep down, Layla wondered what it meant that Rose was giving up everything she'd ever dreamt of doing. She was afraid that she too might give up on her dreams one day, like her friend had. Before saying goodbye, Layla gave Rose her copy of *The Prophet*, which she had so moved her. She told her that she already had a copy and didn't need this one.

Soon after, Rose lost her newborn baby only one week after he was born. His death came as a huge blow, as this had been her first pregnancy. She fell pregnant again shortly after, which helped to mitigate the tragedy. She gave birth to her daughter Ouida only one year after losing her first baby.

~

Fayez took responsibility for Layla in her own father's absence. He saw how intelligent his sister's daughter was and expected her to go to university and graduate as an engineer. But he soon learned how passionate she was about literature. After getting to know Miss Helen better, he began to imagine her as an important professor of literature. In the beginning, Shahira had mixed feelings. How could she let her granddaughter go back and forth to Beirut? She'd looked after her since birth and raised her as a daughter. But at the same time, she knew how important it was for Layla to continue her studies, so she could qualify for a scholarship to get a university degree.

Layla's father Ghassan was still working for the railway company in Palestine. Layla had grown used to his absence from her earliest childhood. Yasmine's death had increased his feeling of alienation from his family and after she died, he preferred to stay and work in Palestine, far from Ksoura.

From the time she was small, Layla dreamed of getting to know Beirut. She wanted to walk the city streets and discover their secrets. Despite being homesick, she enjoyed the move. She could spend the whole evening reading short stories, novels, and poems. Shahira could no longer barge into her room and nag her about studying if she noticed her reading something other than her schoolbooks or listening to Asmahan on the big wooden radio.

Layla reminds Shahira of herself when she used to let her voice soar, singing on the roadside in Ajmat with other girls her age. Her eyes shone as she recalled those memories. But even so, she heard herself saying to Layla, "Now is not the time for poetry and songs." In those moments Shahira felt like a stranger to herself, estranged from her voice and the songs she loved to sing. Perhaps she was afraid that her granddaughter would lose her drive to study, afraid that she would grow sad as Shahira herself had. She feared that Layla's dream of studying at the university would fade away. Shahira knew very well that they were similar people. She also knew that she would do anything to make Layla's dreams come true.

At the time, Layla's main concern was that her grandmother would simply leave her in peace. She wanted her grandmother to get out of her room and close the door behind her. To avoid her grandmother's commentary, she would open a history or geography book and hide poetry between the pages. Then she would read poems, reciting them over and over, until she fell asleep.

In Beirut, Layla lost herself in books. Though she wasn't at the top of the class, she felt that spending time in Miss Helen's library was reward enough. She was obsessed with everything connected to literature and literary texts. Her first year in the city passed at record speed. The second began with Layla greedily devouring English and Arabic literature. She felt that she could achieve anything. However, Helen's sudden decision to return to England came as a surprise. It made her feel newly orphaned once again, and she experienced a different kind of sadness.

Before Miss Helen said goodbye to the class at school and returned to her country, she gave Layla many of her books—novels, short stories, poetry collections. On her last visit to Helen's office, Layla saw piles of packed boxes stacked up on the floor. Many were filled with books, others with small paintings that she'd done herself. She told Layla that she was taking Lebanon's natural beauty—the mountains, the sea, the mountain houses—with her in her suitcase.

She said she'd come back when she missed her friends in Lebanon. She'd lived in Beirut for more than twenty-five years and gave birth to her daughter there. Then her daughter left to study at a British university, and so she went to the UK, where her parents were originally from. She met a boy there and decided to stay. Helen remained in Beirut, as did her husband who taught at the Syrian Protestant College, later known as the American University in Beirut. Layla had never met him, but she'd seen a couple of pictures of him in the living room and the home office. As soon as she heard she was going to be a grandma, Helen decided to return to Britain. She didn't want to be far away when her first grandchild was born or miss out on the child's early years. She was also anxious about her daughter being so far away when a world war was raging.

Miss Helen's decision to leave Lebanon was a great loss for Layla. She learned the true meaning of reading with her, how it can change a person's life and worldview. She provided her with books to read and fill her growing little library. One of the reasons she'd grown so attached to Helen was surely that her mother had passed away giving birth to her. Her father's prolonged absence only added to this. Every year when Ghassan visited Lebanon for the summer, he promised he'd return for good soon. But from a very young age, Layla discovered that the meaning of the word "soon" actually meant it might take a very long time to come true.

Layla's grandma Shahira was always very affectionate, which meant a lot to her, but she couldn't express her innermost feelings to her or tell her everything she was thinking. But she could talk to Miss Helen. She felt that her grandmother had a split personality. On the one hand, she was ready to stand up and fight for anything. But on the other, she tried to stay aligned with social expectations of conformity. Layla grew up walking the tightrope between these two grandmas, not leaning too close to either one. This had to change though; living in the city had opened her up to the whole wide world. Her balancing act had become a barrier to her mind, body, and soul.

Layla had built a little library she was immensely proud of. It reminded her of Helen. She kept buying books using the allowance her father sent her from Palestine. She read *Spirits Rebellious* by Khalil Gibran. The end of Warda and Hani's love affair left her with a heavy heart. She tried to figure out how she could save more of her allowance to buy more books. At the end of her second year of school in the city, she wrote to Miss Helen. Waiting for Miss Helen to reply took longer than she could bear.

When she moved into her Uncle Fayez's house in Beirut, Layla shared a room with her cousin. Mona became her confidante. Layla told her everything. For her, Beirut was the biggest world a person could ever imagine living in. She walked around, discovering the streets in Jal al-Bahr where they lived. Taking walks was her favorite pasttime, as was writing down everything she saw on her long rambles around the city. On these excursions, she'd look at the doors and balconies, trees and building walls. It felt like mere seconds before she was walking through Marfaa, sometimes pausing to watch the waves rise quickly, then fade and recede, only to rise up suddenly once again.

She noticed that the same sea she'd seen from the balcony at home seemed so savage up close. She started trying to capture in writing how the sea looked in its different phases. She walked up the hill through neighborhoods lined with residential buildings, their balconies filled with plants and flowers. During a break at school, she sat down, took out her notebook, and looked up at the clouds. Her words were a camera. They could capture images—the journeys taken by clouds, how they moved through the sky's own sea.

In the evening, she read aloud to Mona, sharing her descriptions of the different faces of clouds. Mona commented that all clouds look alike. Layla didn't care and continued reading from her notebook. Mona laughed when she heard her talk about what she observed on her walk—the strange plants hanging on a balcony near Wadi Abu Jamil and her classmate who chewed gum, imitating the principal's loud voice and awkward way of speaking. Layla affectionately nicknamed Mona Duckie because of how she walked with a waddle, moving in an almost circular motion. This may have been caused by a childhood accident. She fell from a low balcony at school, landing on a mound of dirt in a corner of the playground. She was fortunate. The dirt saved her life.

~

One afternoon, Layla came home from school and found Yusuf, the physics teacher, tutoring her cousin Majd in the dining room. That's how they met for the first time. She said hello and rushed into her room.

She met him again the following week. Then the next one as well. Each time, they exchanged only a few words. But warm and promising words, nonetheless. They both felt that words were not enough. They shared a growing desire to discover each other further.

One particular day, after arriving and greeting him, Layla sat down to read in a corner of the dining room where Majd was working with Yusuf. She stole a glance in their direction from time to time. Yusuf stared at the cover of the book she was reading. He then said to her with a confident smile, as if following up on a previous conversation with someone he knew well, "I'm going to bring you a better book than that one you have there."

She looked up, as if waiting for him to keep speaking. "How

do you know what kind of books I like?"

"Taste in books isn't something you're born with, it develops over time."

She shook her head and pursed her lips ironically. Mischievous eyes fixed on the book in her hands, she remarked without looking up, "It seems, professor, that you have a lot of self-confidence."

His words had provoked her. But there was something in him that made her want to understand him better. Perhaps it was his confidence. She wondered how a young man his age had so much self-esteem. He appeared to be very worldly. It could be that simple curiosity compelled her to get to know him better. At times, she felt curiosity ruled her life.

"A lot?" he replied smiling. Then he went back to working with Majd.

"Let's see . . ." she retorted, challenging him. Then she got up and went into the kitchen to get something to eat.

Yusuf kept his promise. The next time she saw him he gave her a book on Marxism, translated into Arabic. "What do you think?" he asked, handing it to her. Smiling, he presented his own challenge, "I'm going to ask you about it when I see you next."

They started to meet more frequently. She always made sure she was home when he was there. He also increased the amount of time he spent tutoring Majd, so he could see her.

They became friends. And this soon developed into attraction. They saw each other more and more. He regularly supplied her with books about communism all over the world. She read about Lenin and the Bolshevik revolution. He also gave her a book about Rosa Luxemburg.

Layla had so much to discover in Beirut. People, city streets, nightlife—it was all there. Now she also had Yusuf, who lived in the city and knew it like the back of his hand. He became her guide to this vast place that felt to her like it was the whole world. They met up outside her house, at times when he wouldn't mind her being out. Eventually, they started meeting in his apartment.

His two-bedroom apartment seemed empty. The living room had only basic furniture: a sofa, a bookcase, and a table. A few paintings hung on the walls. They depicted a beach, a café, a bustling market, and people whose eyes were filled with sadness. She liked the way he'd organized his few things on his bedside table and wooden bookshelf in his bedroom. She turned her gaze away from a painting of a naked woman. A beautiful woman. Layla felt a little jealous. But she told herself that it was only a painting.

Yusuf shared the apartment with a roommate. Its north-facing windows gave on the sea, looking out at its wide expanse. The view of its vastness was blocked only by red-tiled rooftops and the hangars lining Beirut's port. From the little kitchen window, Layla could see the ships in the port; she heard their whistles as they came into to dock. There were white French ships as well as others painted all kinds of colors, flying countless different flags.

It was a calm, residential neighbourhood. The building was flanked by the Collège des Frères and Mar Maroun Church. From the living room balcony, she could see the school's green-tinted windows. Though the street was quiet, she could still hear some noise—street vendors, children playing in the alley, and the honking horns of cars passing through downtown. Church bells resonated through the narrow streets several times a day. Layla would go on foot to Yusuf's place from her uncle's house in Jal al-Bahr. When she was with him, she felt like she never wanted to go home ever again. She used to hate weekends because she had to go back up to Ksoura, only coming back to the city every Monday.

Even though she was so close to her grandmother and really loved her friend Rose, she preferred being with Yusuf. With him, it was like she became a grown-up all at once. He made her feel like a woman. And not only because sex had become a part of their relationship. It was also because of how she discovered Beirut through him. Walking through the city with him at all different times of the day imbued it with new meaning.

She didn't go to all the political organizing meetings that he pushed her to attend. Sometimes she simply stayed at his apartment, relaxing on the sofa, listening to the raised voices of the people gathered in the next room. These heated political discussions seemed pointless to her. If they'd recited beautiful poetry, it would have been easier on her ears.

Despite everything, she still preferred to stay there, on Yusuf's sofa, his scent preserved deep within its pillows. When she's on that sofa, she forgets herself, reading or listening to songs she loves broadcast on the Voice of Cairo radio show. She later discovered Radio Orient in Beirut, which broadcast Fairouz's first songs a few years later. She also listened to programs on Al-Quds Arabic Radio. From the time she could choose what music to listen to herself, Asmahan's songs were her favorites. She didn't have enough money to buy records. She recorded the lyrics in her little notebook to memorize them. Miss Helen had gifted her a new notebook before she left, and she recopied the words to all of Asmahan's songs in it.

Her life was full in Beirut. She no longer spent as much time with Rose in Ksoura as she used to. But she needed to talk about her new experiences—the cinema, discovering the city, love and intimacy with Yusuf. Mona was the person closest to her in the city. They would stay up late at night together sharing their news of the day. Mona didn't think much of Yusuf, however. So she refused to collude with Layla and help her protect their relationship.

Nor did Mona share Layla's love of novels. She preferred sports magazines and books on politics. But she wanted to hear

Layla retell stories from the books she was reading and enjoyed listening to the details. This made Layla happy since she cared about what Mona thought about the things she shared with her. Mona was upset when Layla told her about her relationship with Yusuf. She'd known him for a while and thought that he'd bring Layla nothing but trouble. Layla didn't listen to her. The young man had already filled her heart with love and curiosity. He sparked her desire for exploration, and it had become impossible for her to hold it back.

Layla began to question whether her relationship with Yusuf was fulfilling her desire and curiosity to get to know the city and new places, or her longing to taste delicious, forbidden fruit and experience paradise. Perhaps both. Getting to know him coincided with getting to know this city, which was a microcosm of the universe. When he kisses her neck, and his lips slide over her chest, the thrill of discovery and pleasure comingle. When he caresses her skin, she closes her eyes, wishing these moments of sheer paradise would never end. When the pleasure comes to an end, the desire to relive it remains. Running his fingers through her long, messy chestnut hair, he would stop suddenly and announce, "You'd better get going, it's getting dark out!"

Before she left, he hugged her and said, "I'm working on my application for a university scholarship. I have to finish all the paperwork and send it this week. Everything is going badly right now; a war is looming, and if I don't get it all together, I might not be able to leave the country."

Layla didn't listen to the final bit, or perhaps she didn't want to hear what he was saying, fearing for their relationship. Every time she left his apartment, she felt she was leaving heaven. All that remained was a pain in her lower lip and red splotches on her neck. She would stand in front of the little mirror above the bathroom sink, the lust that continued to course through her body making her wet.

She wrapped her colorful scarf around her neck and took the stairs down to the ground floor of his building. But instead of turning toward the sea road to walk home, she wandered around his neighborhood, as if the space outside his flat was a sort of extension of the intimacy she felt inside it. She felt that, having discovered his apartment and bedroom, she was now taming the streets and neighborhoods around them. A fleeting thought crossed her mind. She recalled Yusuf talking about applying for a scholarship to study abroad. But she told herself that this was in the future; it was too soon to start worrying about it.

Despite the chilly weather, she basked in the last few warm rays of sunshine. Her body was still warm, and the smell of love lingered on her skin and in her hair. A secret smiled played on her lips as she skipped slowly up the road. She crossed one big street before turning down a narrow alley lined with mulberry and acidinia trees, across from the École des Trois Docteurs school. She continued walking up the hill, thinking about how to reach the highest possible spot. She walked until she reached an open square bordered by a few houses with red-tiled roofs.

She was tired. She rested on a boulder on the side of the road. Mulberry, pomegranate, and orange trees lined the little fields around the houses belonging to the Sassine family. The fragrance of sahlab mixed with cinnamon wafted through the air.

At the corner of the square stood the man selling sahlab. He was young, barely a teenager. He walked through the residential streets whenever the weather was nice in the fall. She continued walking toward the Couvent de Nazareth. She was hungry. She bought a roasted ear of corn from a boy standing in front of the big wooden convent gate. She devoured it greedily, paying no notice to the charcoal staining her hands and mouth. She kept walking down little alleyways, as the sunset azan from the Beydoun Mosque resounded through the sky, echoing all around her and the neighborhood.

She felt for the scarf she'd wrapped around her neck and lifted it over her nose to inhale its scent as she continued walking.

She began to really love the new place she was at with Yusuf. She was discovering more of Beirut's secrets every day. She walked until she reached the square and stopped for a moment. She gazed at the cheerful yellow buildings, their windows and balconies decorated with black wrought iron. She thought about the people who lived inside. She imagined happy girls and their mothers. Rain began slowly, gently falling in tiny drops. She tilted her head toward the sky just briefly, smiling. Then she turned right.

She slowed her pace as she crossed the intersection, leaving the Beydoun Mosque and Achrafieh behind her. She took her time. She let herself enjoy the light damp breeze saturated with the scents of autumn. Leaves falling from the trees fluttered around her, mimicked by the edges of the skirt of her school uniform.

The moments that had just passed flooded her mind. She wondered if this was truly what heaven was like, if what she was living was infinite desire. She desired to keep him stuck to her, as if they were one body, his arms encircling her. Or were there yet other realms they'd not yet even entered? She wanted these moments of pleasure and discovery to never end. Discovery had taken on another meaning entirely. Curiosity no longer came with fear, but confronted fear and overcame it.

The first time they had sex, she felt his body relax and then him pull out of her. She experienced a twinge of pain followed by a drop of pink blood that she wiped away with the edge of her panties before putting them back on. She didn't care as she wasn't invested in the notion of virginity. Perhaps she wasn't aware of the importance of what she'd done in that moment and the impact it would have on the rest of her life.

To her, this felt like a little scrape that would heal quickly and soon be forgotten. A long time passed before she discovered that she was not like other people. She didn't care one bit about marriage, setting up a household, or starting a family. Her dreams of going abroad to study might have been the reason. Or maybe it was all her reading, which took her to worlds far from her reality. Or maybe it was the passing of her mother, which had deprived her of a role model for how to build a home and a family. There might have been other reasons that Layla was unaware of. But none of this mattered to her as long as she had her inner happiness discovering new worlds.

Contrary to what Yusuf expected, she was happy in her somewhat shaky belief that she was now fully a woman. She couldn't understand why he'd hugged her at the door and told her not to worry just before she left his place. At that moment, she missed Rose. She wanted to tell her about everything that had happened and what she was thinking. She wondered if Rose's life was still dominated by domesticity and family. She wanted to know if there was still room for their friendship and little shared secrets, especially after Rose gave birth to her daughter Ouida.

Layla gauged people and the world through the lens of her curiosity. Curiosity propelled her to find a way to live out her dreams. This same curiosity led her to flip through every book she found in Yusuf's library at home. It might be an exaggeration to say that she'd read all of them. She was most attracted to the novels that she added to her own collection almost every day. She browsed through Yusuf's books more quickly. She was more interested in being in his flat than she was in reading his books. His little ninety-square-meter apartment was her own secret world that had nothing to do with Ksoura or her uncle's house. The word "communist" frightened her family. Communists were their ideological enemies, especially since members of her family belonged to many other political parties, none of which were communist at all.

Layla's uncles and her cousins felt that she was breaking a sort of unspoken family pact about their political affiliation. But she didn't care at all about political differences; she viewed people in relation to their individual behavior and feelings. Her kind of judgements were more along the lines of, This person is generous and kind, that one is selfish and a liar. Political affiliation was of no importance to her. She only knew her uncles' politics from snippets of conversations in the evening, uttered in front of guests. Her father Ghassan, away in Palestine, never cared about politics either. But he changed in Palestine. With the passing of time, he came to realize that politics had a hand in everything that had happened and was happening around him.

# November 1943

The Second World War had entered its fourth year. Germany still dreamed of expanding its territory and conquering the Allies in the Middle East.

When the war ended, many countries gained their independence. In Lebanon, the taste of independence from the French was in the air. People took to the streets, protesting the French Mandate: "Leave our land. We want independence!" The country was at the boiling point. Beirut's public squares were filled with protesters demanding the French leave Lebanon. Facing the throngs of ordinary Lebanese civilians were dozens of armed French soldiers, posted all throughout central Beirut.

In the morning, Layla walked from Jal al-Bahr to the Burj, downtown. She claimed that she had to take an exam that had been canceled the week before. She was afraid they'd find out from the radio that school had been canceled that day. A short while later, she found herself downtown. The capital city was living through something new. People from all over the country had joined the protests and taken over the heart of the city center.

The women's protest was the most vibrant and active. Layla felt compelled to participate in this demonstration and launched herself right into the crowd of women. She forgot all about meeting Yusuf. She walked in the throng, repeating the chants they were shouting, along with zaghareed, clapping, and songs. She could see the inner strength on the faces of these women as they locked arms and marched downtown to General Spears's office. Layla walked with them to his office at the British Mandate headquarters.

The women had written him a letter. They'd drafted it as a group and Claude Thabet had edited it into its final form. The march unified women from different backgrounds, beliefs, and ideologies. They loved their country and demanded independence. Some of the names Layla heard that day stuck in her mind: Angèle Abdel Messih, Amira Timani, Jamal Nassif, Niam Fakhoury, and many others. These women's words echoed over and over again in Layla's mind.

She felt the great determination shining in the women's eyes as they walked arm in arm. It was determination filled with hope, unshakable so long as they all remained together in the heart of the city. The very sight of these women moved her and suffused her with love and strength. "Beirut has become my whole world," Layla told herself as she joined them. Women's solidarity filled her so full she felt she would burst with joy.

Had her mother Yasmine been alive, she too would have joined this protest march. She would have locked arms with Layla and the other women, shouting their demands for independence and freedom. Layla truly believed this. She'd imagined her missing mother in so many ways over time that it was difficult for her to know which was a realistic image of her.

Clouds began to gather. But they couldn't block out the deep blue November sky. More women from all over Beirut joined in the march and their numbers swelled. These women may have disagreed about many things, but they agreed on two fundamental issues—Lebanese independence and Lebanese sovereignty. Their chants filled Beirut's streets and skies:

> We're Lebanese
> all of us
> we're
> Lebanese
> What do we want?
> Independence!
> What do we want?
> Freedom!

When she reached the Church of Saint George, she didn't find Yusuf. Maybe he'd waited for her and then gone home. That's what she thought at least. She continued her journey to his flat near the Collège des Frères. She walked up to the stairs to the second floor and knocked on the door. No one answered. She left a note saying that she was going to join the next demonstration and would meet him at the same spot tomorrow.

She was late getting back home. Her Uncle Fayez was waiting for her in the living room.

"How are you, Layla? We hardly see you these days."

"The country is being turned upside down, Uncle Fayez!"

"It can be shaken up, but it won't fall apart. Everything in the country will stay the same."

"What do you mean?"

"Nothing is going to change. The French will leave, they'll rule from afar. And if it's not them, someone else will rule from afar," he explained, showing little interest in what was happening in Beirut. Layla appeared not to understand what he meant, or perhaps just didn't want to hear it. She walked over to the window and, gazing out at the street, commented, "This is the first time I've loved Beirut so much. I've become a part of it, and now it's part of me.

He smiled at her indulgently. "What do you think about Salem, who was with me when I visited your school? How did you like him? He's a dear friend, and a distant relative of ours."

Layla shrugged her shoulders to indicate she didn't have an opinion. "I have to go and study now, Uncle. I have exams."

"Of course! No rush at all. When your dad's here next, we'll talk more."

The following afternoon, Yusuf was waiting for her at the Church of Saint George. He was holding a copy of *Al-Tariq* magazine and reading the newspaper. "The French are going to pay a heavy price," he said, pointing at the headline.

After storming his house at dawn and arresting him, the French still hadn't released Bechara El Khoury—along with other men fighting for independence. They were imprisoned in the Rachaya Citadel in South Lebanon.

Layla and Yusuf walked together to the demonstration. This time, women and men were marching together. Yusuf repeated, "The French are going to pay a heavy price," as they walked along with the people in the protest. "We'll stay in the streets until they release them," he added. It was a sunny day, as if Mother Nature was sending them an early spring to welcome Lebanon's independence.

Layla had been in Beirut for nearly two years at that point. While living in Beirut she'd discovered a bigger world. In addition to her daily rambling to discover the city and coastline, she also came across cinemas and bookshops, which she adored.

A year into living there, she met Yusuf, and he became her guide. Curiosity was Layla's only compass in the city she'd loved even before she got there. It helped her to overcome her fear and really try to experience everything freely, not knowing where this would take her or how it would end.

Layla's cousin Mona also came to Martyrs Square and joined the march. She walked with the crowds who were chanting and demanding independence and the liberation of the Lebanese statesmen imprisoned by the French security forces. She chanted right along with them. Suddenly she spotted Layla in the middle of the crowd, walking next to Yusuf. She didn't expect to see Layla with him. She thought that she was at school. When she saw them walking together, her face changed. Mona had repeatedly warned Layla to break off her relationship with him. Yusuf clasped Layla's hand from time to time while they were walking. Seeing them like this upset her.

With some difficulty, Mona managed to cross through the crowd to the other side of the street, muttering under her breath, "She's crazy . . ." She kept on a straight path towards them.

As she approached, she started shouting to them at the top of her lungs until Layla turned around. She looked right at Mona, then turned back around and carried on marching with Yusuf. Mona came right up to her and spoke loudly in her face, "Come on, come home . . . NOW."

"What do you want?"

"They want you to come home," Mona lied.

Layla hesitated before leaving Yusuf and moving toward Mona. But her cousin really insisted. As she moved away from the waves of protesters, she let her resentment show. She gave Yusuf a quick goodbye nod, implying that they would meet the next day or the one after. Then she stepped backward, her eyes fixed on his face. Pointing in his direction, she whispered, "Tomorrow . . ." Still looking at Yusuf, she backed away and soon he was lost in the throng of people. She whipped around and stormed down to the sea road, where she faced off with Mona, who was walking beside her. "Who told you to come after me?" she asked angrily.

"Everyone!"

"Who?"

"Mom, Dad . . . I have nothing to do with it."

"What do they want?"

"I don't know. It's none of my business. Ask them when you get home."

The voices of the protesters grew louder, filling the air. Layla could barely hear what Mona was saying.

"I told them I'd be out."

"Mom thought you meant at school. You said that you were going to school and would be back in an hour. They knew there was no school today. You can't hide the truth."

"Who's thinking about school on a day like today? Aren't you paying attention? Do you even live in this country ?" Layla asked, rage visible on her face. She carried on, "Everything is closed because of the protests. The French don't want to leave and don't want us to be independent. Tomorrow there will be protests, the day after they'll be even bigger, and they won't stop until independence."

"Oh and now you're political?" Mona shouted. "Shouldn't you be finishing your studies rather than out protesting? You still have a year left. One more year and then you're done! You're in line for a university scholarship, maybe even to travel abroad. If you don't get the scholarship, don't even think about college let alone traveling for college. You know your dad won't give you a cent to go to university. The scholarship is your only chance. And you'll only get one if you do well. You have to get good grades, full stop."

This intense conversation took Mona back to a painful incident that made her sad whenever she thought about it. She'd wanted to study architecture. But her destiny changed when she fell off the school balcony and landed in the playground. She remained in a coma for days. When she woke up in the hospital, she couldn't remember what had happened to her. She lost her memory for several weeks. She couldn't remember anyone's name—her family, friends, or classmates, she couldn't even remember her own name. She couldn't recall the name of her school or her address. The only thing she remembered were the toys that she'd left behind in their house on the mountain years before. She also remembered her grandma Shahira's cooking and wanted to go and stay there with her.

Mona stayed with Shahira for months, on the doctor's advice. For the first several months after she fell, she couldn't read. She'd forgotten the alphabet. She couldn't even write her own name. Mona played with her old toys in the attic, where her grandmother stored her grandchildren's old shoes, clothes, toys, and drawings. Months passed before Mona remembered anything. But she totally changed after the accident. She could no longer concentrate. Shahira always said that the medications she was given harmed her, and if she'd been left to her own devices, she would have recovered, regained her memory, and gone back to school like normal.

The accident ended Mona's dream of becoming an architect. But she continued drawing birds, gardens, and houses. She hung pictures of architecturally interesting houses in her room, as well as new drawings of the beach and fishermen in Beirut. At university she studied literature, believing that it would require less intense concentration. What she truly excelled at, however, was volleyball, and she won many awards. Their age difference meant that Mona treated Layla like a little sister. She always nagged Layla to work and study hard. She wanted her to always obey, to do whatever she said. Eventually, Mona went back to playing volleyball. She and her friends founded a volleyball club for girls, and she started training there.

"Hurry up, it's starting to rain" Mona said to Layla, irritated.

Layla was still angry herself. She stared far off into the distance and didn't reply. She either didn't hear what Mona was saying, or didn't want to hear. Then she slowed down a little, no longer walking beside her. She started looking down at the drops of rain moistening the ground.

The rain had started as a gentle drizzle and soon grew stronger. The mulberry trees lining the dirt streets had lost their leaves. The stone pines that the French had planted a few years earlier swayed happily in the sudden wind and rain.

"Hurry up," Mona kept repeating.

"You hurry up and leave me alone," Layla retorted. "Go to volleyball practice or something!" She slowed her pace even more and started taking long drawn out steps, as if searching for something she'd dropped on the street. She kicked at small pebbles as she walked. Four cooing pigeons flew away. She felt the dust swirling around her go up her nose. She lifted her head and saw the pigeons in the sky. A repressed sigh escaped her, then she continued to trudge home. She felt tense and distracted. Negative thoughts flooded her mind, conjuring up familiar feelings of loss. She shook her head as if trying to rid herself of these thoughts. She realized at that moment that she loved walking in the rain, even as it had gotten heavier, soaking her hair and clothes.

She walked slowly, listening to the echoes of voices from the central square downtown. She expected her uncle to once again bring up the subject of her getting married. How would she answer? No, of course! They wanted her to marry a distant cousin of Grandma Shahira's who'd recently returned from America. He'd started buying land and real estate, spending weekends in the countryside hunting, or in Beirut watching racehorses. These hobbies brought Fayez closer to his American-expat relative. They'd become closer friends since he'd returned to Lebanon.

This cousin was obsessed with horses and bird hunting. He also liked young women and wanted to remarry after the death of his American wife in some kind of accident. A week before, he'd shown up at her school with Uncle Fayez. It was lunchtime. He told the principal that he he'd been buying electrical equipment for his house in Ksoura at a shop near the school. He invited her to visit them in the summer. Then he added that he wanted to see his niece. The principal immediately called Layla into her office. She was sitting on a wooden bench in one of the corners of the playground reading a book. Cheeks flushed, Layla hurried to the principal's office. She smiled when she saw her uncle sitting near a man whose face seemed familiar. She remembered that she'd seen him once with her uncle in Ksoura; Fayez had invited him to come up to their flat, which had just been finished at the time.

"Hello," Layla said hesitantly, her voice barely audible. The principal didn't answer but looked at Fayez. She coughed out a short laugh for no reason. "I was near the school, and I wanted to pass by and check on you," her uncle told her. Layla smiled again and didn't reply. Her family rarely came to her school. She hovered near the door, hiding a book behind her back, afraid that the principal might notice the cover. It was a book she'd recently gotten from Miss Helen. She kept her hand over it. Fayez spoke a bit with the man standing beside him; they were both smiling. She felt confused. She wondered where she should put her other hand—in the pocket of her school uniform? Or should she let it swing down at her side? Or should she cross it across her chest and hold her other arm with her hand?

A stray lock of hair fell on her forehead and saved her. It distracted her a bit from her confusion as she started pushing it back. Those few moments felt like an entire year. Meanwhile the eyes of the thirty-something man with her uncle bored right into her. Fayez exchanged a few words with her about her studies before the principal told her to go back to the playground, smiling widely, showing her yellowed teeth.

She later learned that the man wanted to be her groom and had come with her Uncle Fayez so he could see what she looked like. Fayez arranged this for his friend, who was also a relative. She was angry about this. Her uncle, whom she saw almost as a father, had treated her like a stuffed animal—the kind Shahira had made for her when she was a little girl. At that moment she hated her uncle and the school principal too. She stormed back out to the playground angrily, her hair flying behind her. Then she started running in circles as if escaping from the eye that was tracking her.

She really missed her friend Rose. She thought about Rose's life and wondered anxiously if she would meet the same fate as her friend. She thought about Shahira and her mother. She imagined her mother's face, as Tawfiq had described it to her. What if her mother had been here? Would Fayez have dared to do this? She thought about her father, who visited Ksoura so rarely. She thought about Yusuf and how he wasn't a part of her real life. If only she could cry. She stopped and turned, then scurried toward the school building. The bell had rung, announcing the end of the lunch hour.

No one was home when Layla got back from school that day. Mona had returned from the Burj before her, then gone to her volleyball club once she ensured that Layla was home. "Mona lied to me," Layla thought, livid. She went into her room and opened her journal. She wrote about how much she loved and missed two women, Shahira and Rose. A little while later, she heard the apartment door open and her uncle's wife Mufida walk through it.

"Get ready, we're going to Ksoura early tomorrow morning and we're staying until Monday morning," she announced and then left.

That evening, Layla dreamed that she was on a ship with Rose. Then suddenly she couldn't find her friend and didn't know where she was. She'd lost her and grew extremely anxious. She was frightened because she saw warships all around her. Then she glimpsed Miss Helen far away in the distance, waiting for her on the shore. When she landed, Helen embraced her for a long time and started kissing her on the mouth. Then she turned around and saw Rose still standing on the ship. She refused to get off and go with Layla. Instead, she began screaming, demanding to go back where she'd come from.

Her dreams faded with the morning light, and her uncle's voice woke her. Layla rolled out of bed and pulled back the curtains to let the November sunlight in. Rays of sun flooded the beds, walls, and wardrobes despite the fresh chilly air. Mona had woken up before her and already left the room. She had to get ready quickly to go with her uncle and the rest of the family to the mountains for the weekend.

Fayez sang in the car. He loved Farid Al-Atrash and knew all of his songs by heart. He loved to sing even though he couldn't carry a tune. He tirelessly repeated the same songs: "Sunrise and Sunset" (El Shourouq wa El Ghouroub) and "Love Is Great and Here" (El Hobb Ezz wa Hena). Layla was lost in another world. She sat silently in the backseat next to Mona and Majd, staring out the window, contemplating how to escape the trap her family was setting for her, being married off. She told herself that she'd find a way to inform Yusuf. Surely, they could come up with a solution together.

She started to feel like an unwanted guest in her uncle's house. She remembered the joy they'd overwhelmingly expressed when she decided to move to Beirut to study. But it had vanished when Mona made her relationship with Yusuf public. Their joy had been replaced with open doubts about her ability to win a university scholarship. Their doubts may have been unwarranted and exaggerated, but they added to Layla's worries nonetheless.

~

After they arrived up in the mountains that day, Fayez took Layla for a walk in the garden. They strolled around together because he wanted to speak to her about what he called "an important matter." After their walk, she excused herself and went to her uncle Tawfiq's art studio. Not long afterward, Layla and Tawfiq walked out. She helped him carry his painting supplies and a lunch basket. They rambled down the path leading out to the fields. She wanted to express all her anxieties and fears to him. She told him about Yusuf, as well as what Fayez had spoken to her about. She didn't want to marry Shahira's relative. Tawfiq calmly told her that no one could stand in the way of her dreams. She should wait for her father to come back and then tell him about this. Layla felt that this was a surprisingly cold way to respond to her story. She expected him to be more solid about a troubling issue like this proposed marriage.

When they went back at sunset, Layla found her uncle Nadim had arrived. He'd come alone as his pregnant wife was tired and resting at home. Kamal joined them later as well.

That's when what she'd feared actually happened. They kept talking about the relative who'd come from America. Mona tried to convince her, just as her father had. Then Mufida butted in,

"Have you forgotten who you are? You walk down the street holding a strange man's hand in public? Don't you have a father? Don't you have a home and a family?"

Fayez quieted his wife with a wave of his hand. Nadim stayed silent. Shahira was in the kitchen preparing dinner with the help of Hajar. She'd clearly decided to steer clear of a conversation that she knew wouldn't lead to anything good for her granddaughter. Layla looked at Mona, disappointed and exhausted. Mona had betrayed her trust.

Layla was sad and angry. She was overcome by a crushing sense of solitude. She thought about Yusuf. What would he say after she told him what had happened? Their relationship was dominated by her curiosity, and that meeting with him had catapulted her into a whole new world. She'd met people that she'd never have encountered were it not for Yusuf. She read books that she'd not chosen. She attended youth meetings but hadn't joined Yusuf's party, the SSNP. Despite this, she was close to them. Or perhaps her closeness with Yusuf gave her the illusion that she belonged to the group. She believed that being a part of this circle would free her from being trapped by her family. That's why she felt that she might reply to her uncle's wife, "Yes, and this is my life. He's my sweetheart, I love him!" But she didn't say this. Saying the words is one thing and living them out is another. This seventeen-year-old girl couldn't manage to bridge the divide between the two. If she'd been able to, she might have been able to alter the course of her life. But she remained hesitant. Silent. She didn't fully understand everything in the books that Yusuf had given her to read. But reality swallowed up all the theories she'd read and heard Yusuf and his friends talk about.

She sat with her family, looking at them, listening to what they were saying, without participating. The conversation was about convincing her that happiness would be waiting for her just around the corner with the rich American who could make her dreams come true.

She felt like a wild cat that they were trying to tame. She stared back at them one by one. They were all waiting for her to say something. They were waiting for her to say yes, I'll do it. Then they went back to their heated political discussions that she'd heard so many times. Some of them were talking about Greater Syria, and about freedom and independence as well. The others were talking about Arab nationalism or socialism. They debated how best to build a strong state and disagreed on what the identity of that state would be. They would always have heated arguments and disagree. Then they'd insist that life without freedom and independence is no life at all.

She looked at them sitting in a circle around her. She felt as if she were the accused in a courtroom. She thought that their political positions and endless conversations were far removed from her reality. This was so unrelated to what they were asking of her, of all the girls in the family. She wondered: Is this what politics is? Is politics the very absence of a connection between what you say and what you do? Or is the problem with her? Is she naïve for believing what they said? She didn't know the answers to these questions. But she was extremely aware of the fact that she'd lost all faith in Fayez. She no longer wanted to live in his house. She didn't feel that any of her other uncles could do anything either—even Tawfiq. She wondered where she could go. Where could she hide from their words? She leaned forward and crossed her arms over her chest. She folded her legs back under the chair. It was as if she were folding in on herself to protect her body, to protect her desire to remain silent.

What if Yusuf walked into the room at that very moment and announced to everyone that he loved her? What if she stood up and said, I make decisions about my own life, not you? But she remained silent. Her relationship felt like a fantasy happening somewhere else far away. Or like she belonged to two worlds: one is the family she was born into and the other is the world she chose, or that she created and imagined as a space of freedom. This is a parallel world—one in which Layla said phrases she'd learned like "freedom," "self-realization," and "educational equality between men and women." She memorized and repeated these words.

It wasn't clear to her how these concepts that had become a part of her inner life and thought process were lived out in her real life every day. "I won't get married," she nodded, saying to herself, "There's Yusuf and there's also my university studies. The school administration is sure I'll get a scholarship to study literature. I'll write to Miss Helen tonight. I know she'll help me; she promised she would!"

She got up and walked over to the dining table on the other side of the room next to the big clock. She picked up a chair and moved it near the window. She sat down and gazed out into the darkness. Meanwhile she continued listening to them chattering away. Their voices felt far away and faded into the background. Layla may have nodded, letting everyone think that she was leaning towards agreeing with them—or at least that what they'd talked about that evening had left a good impression on her. But her thoughts were another place, far away.

A hush fell over the room at the moment Shahira emerged from the kitchen to announce that dinner was ready. The conversation changed, it became breezier, less contentious. Fayez's wife and daughter got up to set the table and serve the food. There was lentil soup with green chard, a wild hindbeh salad, and country labneh, as well as mashed potatoes flavored with olive oil, salt, and cumin.

It was a miserable Saturday evening for Layla. She sat as far away from her uncles and the rest of the family as possible. After dinner, they all stayed up late huddled around the wood-burning stove, roasting chestnuts and talking about the Second World War, which was coming to them from the Mediterranean coast on one side and the Syrian mainland on the other. They also covered Lebanese independence, which would soon become a reality. As always, an argument started that could only be ended by talking about food. All of this wore Layla out. She felt trapped inside a bottle with no escape.

Shahira looked over at her granddaughter with great concern. She got up and swayed heavily over toward her, encouraging her to sit nearer to the group. But then she saw Layla's eyes brimming with tears. "She's been stubborn since she was a child, just like me, and she'll never show her tears," thought Shahira. She sat close to Layla instead and massaged her shoulder. She stroked Layla's hair, trying to calm her down. Layla didn't lift her head at all, her body a stiff plank of wood, her face locked tighter than a safe.

"What's up, my girl? They're talking about your wedding, and you look like you're at a funeral!"

Layla didn't reply. Her grandmother sat on a chair beside her. Shahira knew better than most what her granddaughter was feeling. She'd raised her after her mother's death, after all. Before he left Lebanon, her father Ghassan said to his mother-in-law, "I'm entrusting Layla to you!"

Layla looked back at her grandmother with no response. She thought to herself, "What good would it do to talk to them after they've already decided to marry me off? I know my uncles. Fayez is the oldest. He decides. Not my father, he's always away. He gave decision-making power to my uncle. My grandmother . . .? I don't understand her silence. She seems to be in agreement too."

That evening Layla went to her room and wrote in her diary:

"Salem asked for your hand in marriage." That's what my uncle Fayez told me, as soon as we got to the house in the mountains. "Of course I'm asking you first. You know how much we love him. He's one of us, like one of the family. But we have to ask you." I knew this is what he was going to say. Now what do I do? Where can I run away to? My dad? He's always away working in Palestine. My grandma? I know she loves me but how can she remain neutral about the question of them marrying me off? Maybe she didn't take my dream seriously. But how could that be? She too was forced to get married and give up her dreams as a young woman. She loves me, yes. But is love the other side of death, the death of dreams? For so many years I imagined that my grandmother would stand up for me against anyone who stood in the way of my ambition. Was I deluded? Is the image I have of my grandmother because I love her so different than the reality? Where can I take refuge? My uncle Nadim who's so immersed in politics, he can't think about anything else? He stayed silent while they were trying to convince me. It was as if he wasn't even there. He spends most of his time reading what the leader of the party writes. And reprinting it and distributing it to his acquaintances. Or can I turn to Uncle Tawfiq? He gets inspiration for his art from family discussions. He makes fun of politics and intense political debates. Can I try Uncle Kamal? He said only one thing, "Let Layla make her own decision." Then just a moment

> before he left, he whispered in my ear as he kissed me goodbye, "You must make your own decision. Don't let anybody mess with your mind." I wanted him to stay and sleep over at our place. I needed him to be there. But he went home. I know how he thinks. But I also know that what he says has no weight when Uncle Fayez is around.

Before she went to sleep that night, Shahira wanted to ask her granddaughter about Yusuf. She waited for Nadim to go upstairs. Fayez and his family too. They'd built the new second floor to make more space. She left her room and went over to Layla's. She was still awake, writing in her diary. She went in and sat beside her on the bed. Layla put her diary down on her bedside table. She said she loved him. Shahira hugged her. She told her to remember that love evaporates like water turns to steam—forgetting this destroys women's lives.

She then opened up to her about her own love story in Ajmat. She shared her secret that she'd never told anyone. Many years ago, before they married her off to a boy who would become Layla's grandfather, she'd loved a boy. He and his family used to spend summers in their village. They met in the cellar behind her uncle's house. It was easy to hide there since it was used to store provisions, animal feed, and stacks of firewood. They'd spend time together alone there until she heard someone calling her home. Before they could spend their third summer together, Shahira was married off. She never saw her love, who was only a bit older than her, ever again. She'd tried to send him a message telling him she'd gotten married. And she never heard anything in response.

Lying in bed the night before her wedding, she felt she was suffocating. She felt her soul was leaving her body and she was going to die of anguish and sorrow. Suspended between sleep and wakefulness, she waited for death to come. But it never came. The sun rose, morning broke, and no one said anything to her.

She blurted out her story to Layla in a hurry, as if it belonged to a forgotten past and she was only recalling it now to convince her granddaughter to get married. It showed how her life was inextricably linked to Layla's, and there was no way for the young woman to escape repeating this experience.

Layla was sitting on her bed, listening to Shahira tell her about her suffering. She realized that she couldn't count on her grandmother this time; she needed to write to her father. Perhaps he'd listen to her and empathize with her pain. Perhaps he'd take her side and support her. How she wished her mother was still alive. Surely, she would've stood by her and challenged anyone who tried to stand in the way of her continuing her studies. But Shahira snapped her out of her reverie, surprising her with a question she asked again and again.

That question was, "Did you get it?" Layla didn't understand right away what her grandmother meant. "What do you mean?" she questioned back. Shahira repeated the same phrase several more times—Did you get it? Layla was dozing off and wanted to sleep. But Shahira wouldn't leave the room until she'd heard the answer from her granddaughter's lips. Layla nodded her head without giving a direct answer. Shaira understood that indeed the answer was yes, she'd gotten it.

Shahira walked out of the room without making eye contact with Layla. She called out to Fayez as she walked through the living room out to the front door. She stood in the garden in front of the house, calling out loudly so that her son could hear her upstairs, where he'd already taken refuge with his family. With firm determination, she announced, "We'll all go down to Beirut tomorrow evening, and Monday morning we'll sign the marriage contract for Layla and Salem."

Layla was half-asleep. She heard the upstairs window open and her uncle's voice. "Salem isn't in Beirut. He's gone hunting and won't be back for two weeks." Then she heard her uncle Nadim on the ground floor shout out of his window, "Let's call it a night . . . This can wait till morning!"

Layla also wondered why her grandmother couldn't wait until morning to announce this to her uncle. It made her mad, and she couldn't understand why her grandmother seemed anxious and in such a hurry.

On Sunday morning, Layla walked over to Rose's house. She found her sitting with her family and her husband's family. She looked happy surrounded by them, fully content. Layla didn't want to stay long; she wanted to go back home. Rose walked with her partway back to Shahira's place. Layla told her about the family's decision, as well as her fear and worries. "You've got two weeks before Salem gets back," Rose counseled her. "There's time to think it over well and then decide."

"I've got two weeks until he gets back, like Rose said," Layla wrote in her diary when she was back at school on Monday morning. She then added, "I'll tell him. I will. Nothing else matters to me. I'll run away with him if I have to. I won't go back home. I'll leave the country with him and finish my studies abroad."

Once she'd confirmed that Mona's position was consistent with everyone else's, and knowing that she'd never liked Yusuf, Layla made a decision. She'd never tell Mona anything ever again.

# The Final Encounter

Layla trembled as Yusuf opened the door. He hugged her without uttering a word. They walked to his room together. It was messy, papers strewn everywhere. She shivered from the cold, and he left her to go close the little window in the kitchen that looked out over the sea and the ships docked in the port. He returned and found her lying on her back, staring at the ceiling. She was fully clothed. He stretched out beside her. "What's up?" he asked, kissing her hair and face. She didn't reply but rolled over toward him. She held him in her arms as if clinging to a log to stay afloat at sea. Her whole body was quivering. He hugged her close and went back to kissing her. She squirmed uncomfortably in his arms. She wanted them to talk, but he didn't stop. Scraps of words escaped her lips. He only heard some of them: "I don't know . . . what do I do . . .?" He looked at her with a slight frown. He'd guessed what she meant. He kissed her again and his lips slid down over her chest, unbuttoning her shirt and running his hand over her body while kissing her on the lips. He kept holding her, as their clothes fell off the sides of the bed and onto the floor.

Their bodies had been aflame with desire and those moments

passed. His body relaxed. They exchanged gentle kisses. Layla asked him where the love they shared was going. He didn't reply. He got off her, turned his back, and sat on the edge of the bed. "Hand me the cigarettes," he said, pointing at the bedside table. He popped a cigarette out of the pack and got out of bed to look for matches in the kitchen. Layla watched his naked body as he walked through the bedroom door. A fleeting question crossed her mind, "What if we're going to break up?" She felt she was choking and so quickly banished this thought from her mind. He lit his cigarette and got back into bed, where Layla was sitting up rigidly, the blue cotton sheet wrapped around her naked body.

They sat in bed, and he listened silently as she told him about Salem. She waited for him to say something, to rescue her from her confusion. He asked her how she met him, what he did, where he lived. He asked general questions to avoid the topic at hand. He was making basic inquiries about a man who'd asked for his girlfriend's hand in marriage! Layla could read no reaction on his face—no resentment, no worry. This only increased her confusion and anxiety. Some time passed before she heard him say that he had something to tell her too. The paperwork for his scholarship to study abroad had come through.

"Take me with you! I'll go with you and finish my studies too. We'll go together."

No reply.

She could sense his hesitation, so she added, "Maybe you don't want to make it official with my family. It's alright, neither do I. I don't care. My mother passed away and my father is out of the country. If you don't want to ask for my hand, I'll come with you without asking my family."

At first, he didn't say anything at all. He fiddled with the edge of the covers, nervously glancing at his watch. She stared at him, waiting for him to say something . . . anything.

After a few moments of total silence, she asked, "So will you go?" He nodded and seemed annoyed. Something was upsetting him, but she couldn't understand what. She searched desperately to conjure up the peace and serenity they'd shared. But she could no longer find them. She was embarrassed and decided it was better to change the subject. She took out a book that Miss Helen had sent her with a letter folded inside.

Then something happened that shocked Layla. It was as if this man whose bed she'd shared was nothing like the Yusuf she knew—or thought she knew.

She tucked Helen's letter into her bag along with the book. She got out of bed and went to the bathroom. She then returned to the bedroom and threw her clothes back on. She felt a weight pressing down on her chest, while he sat calmly reading the newspaper without even glancing up at her. She opened the door and left without saying a word.

She moved in slow motion. She heaved one foot in front of the other with great difficulty. Her heart was a boulder inside her chest. Something inside her had died. She'd lost all her desire in one blow. She didn't know what was wrong with her. And she didn't want to go home.

Her face felt flushed, and she had a terrible headache. But she kept walking, nonetheless. She was overwhelmed by great longing for Shahira; she wished that she could transport herself to Ksoura right away. She just wanted to hug her, to rest her head against her bosom. She slowed her pace even more when she passed in front of the Barakat Building. The workers had started decorating the shops for Christmas, which was coming soon. She stopped for a second to think. She couldn't breathe. And she didn't want to see her uncle or his wife. But she needed to get her worries off her chest, to spill it all out to someone. Who could she talk to? She walked uphill until she reached the Damascus Road intersection. Then she kept walking toward the volleyball club. Mona would be there. Maybe she could sit and chat with her a bit before going back to Jal al-Bahr. Perhaps she could find some relief from the assault she'd felt at Yusuf's place, from the overwhelming feeling that she was sinking into quicksand, being swallowed up by the void.

She walked into the club, exhausted. She heard the voice of Umm Kulthum, Mona's favorite singer, coming from inside the gym. Mona hugged her. When she felt Layla's warm face against hers, she immediately pressed the palm of her hand to her cousin's neck and forehead. "You have a fever—your body's on fire." She took her by the hand and led her to a room at the back of the gym. Layla sat on a sofa, hear head heavy. "Tell me what's wrong," Mona said, worry written all over her face. Eyes closed, she told her that she'd just come from Yusuf's apartment. "When are you going to put an end to that?" Mona demanded. But Layla was too exhausted to answer. A woman outside called out to them, asking about workout times. Mona went to speak to her. Layla stretched out on the sofa and closed her eyes, as loneliness lapped at her slowly and relentlessly.

Mona came back with a glass of lemonade, saying, "Drink some." Layla adjusted herself to sit upright and took the glass. Every time the subject of Yusuf came up, Mona asked Layla to end things with him. Layla asked her directly if she knew anything bad about him.

"No, there's nothing," Mona replied. "But you're still young. Finish your studies first."

"I don't know, I love him," Layla said, resting the glass of lemonade beside her.

"You should see what you look like. Is this a girl happy in love? You don't know what you're doing to yourself. I swear you're a glutton for punishment, a prisoner who loves her chains." Mona was getting angrier as she talked, but then softened, saying, "Try to sleep a little."

Mona left her alone in the room. She closed the door behind her, so Layla was alone with her thoughts. She was still lying on the sofa, staring at the ceiling. The whole world now seemed as small as that room.

Did she love her chains? Was she a glutton for punishment? Layla thought about this phrase. What if Mona was right?

~

It was hard for her to come to terms with what had happened in Yusuf's apartment. They were still naked in bed when Layla had decided to speak about the pressure her family was putting on her to get married. But she hadn't wanted to ruin their time together. She told herself that she'd talk to him about it the next time they were together. Instead, she let him see how happy she was to have received the book and letter from Helen. She began reading the letter aloud. He sighed and stopped her short with a wave of his hand. He didn't want to hear anything about Helen. This woman irritated him, though he'd never even met her. He seized on one line in the letter where Helen encouraged Layla to carry on with her studies, offering to help her with her scholarship application. Without even letting her finish reading the letter, he snapped, "Stop being so naïve. This woman is nothing but a colonialist who wants to make your decisions for you and control your life. She's really gotten into your head. How long will you let her distract you with the nonsense she sends you? When will you ever change?"

She'd never seen him so violent before. She felt his words

lashing into her naked flesh. She wound the sheet around herself a second time as if her nakedness had suddenly transformed into a stain. She wanted to cry but couldn't. She'd inherited her aversion to tears from her grandmother Shahira. She got out of bed, clutching the sheet tightly to her body, and stumbled into the bathroom. She stood there, staring at her face in the mirror. Emptiness was eating her alive. She couldn't understand the anger and enmity in Yusuf's rant. Each word was a swift slap against her face. All while his scent and his juices were still in her body. Where had the lust that had overcome them just moments ago gone? She started to wonder. Was his reaction jealousy? Possessiveness? Simply a lack of love? Or what . . .? It was a moment of true exposure; it left her vulnerable and easily hurt.

"How could he behave like this after we've just had sex?" she asked herself. She couldn't understand his cruelty. She went back to the bedroom, avoiding his gaze, not knowing what his eyes might reveal. She also didn't know how the next words escaped from her own mouth. She promised never to write to Helen again. She stood in front of him, feeling the same way she had on that day when her uncle had visited her school with Salem—shy, confused, and embarrassed.

He was reading the newspaper, paying no attention to her. She was angry with herself for speaking so quickly. Why did she feel guilty? Why did she have a constant need to please him? At that moment, he was a stranger. She felt frustrated and afraid. Looking at herself and the worn sheet, she suddenly thought, "What am I doing here?" She hurried to put her clothes back on and slipped out while he was still reading his newspaper as if nothing at all had happened.

Still lying on the sofa at the gym, Layla wondered if Mona was right. Was she a glutton for punishment, was Yusuf actually the one limiting her freedom?

The last time Layla saw Yusuf, she decided that she'd avoid talking about Helen. In her mind, this might help their relationship go back to how it had been. But she knew deep down that the problem was elsewhere. Not talking about Helen wasn't going to improve their relationship.

He was busy organizing his room when she arrived. She felt a sharp pain in her stomach. She asked him about his plans, if he'd thought about her offer of going with him. She asked if he wanted her to join him later. She reiterated that she was willing to go even without informing her family first. She told him that marrying Salem would crush her dreams.

He continued to pack up the things that he wouldn't need on his journey so he could store them at his family's house outside the city. While packing he finally answered, "It's too big a responsibility for me, I'm not up to it. I can't be responsible for you."

She stood up and inched toward the door, footsteps heavy. Standing on the threshold, she looked at him. "Yusuf, I'm not a child. I can take responsibility for myself. I'm going to study; I'm going to work. All I want to do is travel abroad together."

He lifted his eyes. He came close to her and shook his head. "Stop dreaming. This has been my whole problem with you from day one. You have no grip on reality. Just keep reading your novels!" Then he went back to what he was doing.

She felt she like she might suffocate.

"Who even are you? Who do you think you are? Do I even know you?" she shouted. "If this is how you see me, as someone with no connection to reality, why are you having a relationship with me?" She was so angry that she stormed out of the apartment. He followed her as far as the door, leaning his body against the corner of the entryway, staring at her. His face betrayed no emotion.

She ran down the stairs while Yusuf remained fixed in place. She wished he would call out to her or say even one word. She wanted him to rush out behind her, grab her, hold her in his arms, beg her to stay. She was hoping he'd say he wanted her in his life, that he wouldn't leave the country without her. But he said nothing. All she could hear was the sound of her own shoes hitting the pavement.

She knew that she would never see him again. He'd left her to face her fate alone. He'd travel and make his dreams come true; she would have to abandon hers for an arranged marriage.

Chilly winter air slapped her face. She felt like a worn-out old rag that no one wanted. From the beginning of their relationship, there'd been a lot of things that she hadn't told Yusuf for fear of losing him. She didn't dare tell him that she felt uncomfortable when he spoke to her about politics. In fact, she felt that she was forced to listen to him talk about things that meant nothing to her. Political conversations bored her and made her feel out of place. She didn't tell him that she felt afraid of him when he acted superior to her. She never pointed out that she really enjoyed reading novels and talking to people who'd traveled the world discovering things. She liked people who listened and observed. These things were far more exciting to her than the kind of books he preferred. She didn't tell him that every weekend and holiday she spent in Ksoura, she couldn't even bring herself to finish the books he'd told her to read—she'd always read things she'd chosen instead. Or she'd take her dog Baroud on a walk along the dirt path out to the fields.

Whenever her Uncle Nadim would organize a meeting of his SSNP party comrades at home in the mountains, she'd leave the house. She loved watching the amazing sunsets from atop the road overlooking the valleys and the sea. She never told Yusuf that she no longer saw him in the same way. But she kept quiet for fear they'd break up. With her mother's death and her father being perpetually abroad, the idea of another loss stressed her and made her increasingly afraid of being alone.

Mona came back into her office and heard Layla mumbling in her sleep. She went over to her and felt her forehead, which was even hotter than before. She woke her to give her medicine to bring down the fever. After the gym closed, they slowly walked together back home.

Layla slept for two days straight. Her fever finally went down, but she constantly felt nauseated, like she was about to vomit.

Layla asked her uncle Fayez if she could stay in Beirut rather than go with them up to the mountains on the weekend. She told him that she'd missed two days of school and had to catch up on what she'd missed. Fayez was easy on her, hoping that she had started to come around to the idea of getting married. He was waiting for Ghassan and Salem to come to Beirut so they could arrange the wedding. Ghassan arrived a few days before the ceremony. Salem returned from his hunting trip with his friends a happy man, having shot a significant number of birds.

Everyone else went up to the mountains. Mona offered to stay with Layla, but she said she would be fine alone and was feeling much better health-wise. She would spend all her time studying and no one needed to stay with her.

After they'd all left, Layla went to the clinic at the American University Hospital. A doctor told her that she'd caught a cold, which had caused her fever. He added that nausea and vomiting could be symptoms of pregnancy. He prescribed her vitamins and referred her to a gynecologist to confirm the possibility, since he was a general practitioner and this was not his speciality.

She left the hospital wishing the earth would split open and swallow her whole. Or perhaps she would contract a deadly disease and be gone before anyone in her family knew what was wrong with her. She didn't need to see a gynecologist to know what was happening. She remembered these symptoms in her uncle Nadim's wife. And most important, she hadn't gotten her period that month.

Layla went out for a walk. She didn't know where she was going. Should she tell Mona? Of course not. Should she tell her grandma? Never. Who could she tell? Suddenly, cold December mist turned to rain, her clothes dampened, and she was chilled to the bone. She took the tram, got off in Gemmayzeh, and walked to the Collège des Frères neighborhood.

She walked up the stairs and knocked on the door. Yusuf's roommate Talal opened it. He was surprised to see her and invited her in to dry off. But she stayed in the doorway. He told her that Yusuf wasn't home, he'd gone to visit his family in the countryside and might spend the night there. He added that Yusuf was leaving the country in three days.

"Tell him that I was here and need to see him urgently. It's important," she told Talal, staring ahead of him, eyes fixed on the tiles on the floor behind him. She was too shy to look him in the eye. Talal nodded. He looked at her with compassion, or perhaps pity, as if he knew what was wrong with her. He invited her in a second time. She thanked him, turned around, and inched back down the stairs clutching the handrail. Her shame felt like a weight she could no longer bear. Talal watched her go with silent eyes.

# Layla and Salem's Marriage

Only a few days after Salem returned, Fayez got busy preparing for the wedding, inviting their family and friends. It was like he was the one getting married, not Layla. A few days before, Shahira invited everyone to a pre-wedding lunch, and Salem sat Layla right next to him. He began telling her about what he did and didn't like, as if giving her the key to unlock the secret to a happy marriage. He explained all kinds of things about horses and racing, the types of animals that he'd hunted lately, and how he'd like to raise dogs so he wouldn't always have to borrow his friend's dogs when the two of them went hunting in the country. He said that for him there were two kinds of animals: the kind you raise and the kind you kill. He was hoping to raise and tame horses. He'd picked up this hobby in America, where he'd married a horse breeder called Barbara. Listening to him talk, Layla imagined that his passion for animals was like his passion for young women. She knew that she'd consented to this marriage. And she also knew that she was about to lose her freedom just like the animals he liked to acquire. Busily trying to rub a juice stain off her dress, she unexpectedly found herself asking him sarcastically, "What kind of animal am I to you? The kind you like to collect and raise or the kind you like to hunt?"

Salem laughed at her question for a long time. "Ha ha, you're a smart one, wallah." He called over to Fayez who was sitting across from him on the other side of the table, "Did you hear what your niece said? She's clever, but a little mean-spirited."

Layla listened while he spoke, but didn't look at his face. Tired, she contemplated the various dishes spread out on the table, most of which Salem's brother's wife Hasmik had made. She didn't feel like looking at Salem's face. Or at the table. All she wanted to do was vomit.

No matter how she looked at her situation, everything about it was difficult: a marriage she didn't want, a secret pregnancy she couldn't tell anyone about, a man who desired her who she didn't love, a boyfriend about to leave the country without giving her any consideration. As Salem talked nonstop, across the table from her sat Salem's two sisters, Huda and Salwa. They paid her no attention; they just whispered to each other and ate. Rose and her husband were seated next to her, their daughter Ouida on his lap. Rose was still sad because she'd recently lost a second child, who was just a few days old.

Layla got up and rushed to the bathroom and threw up the tiny bit of food she'd eaten. Rose followed her in, helped her wash her face and hands, and fixed her makeup. Layla explained that she couldn't handle the spices in the chicken that Hasmik had prepared, although Rose knew Layla well and gave her a look to let her know she knew she was lying. She hugged her close and said, "What's up with you? I know there's more to it than the spices in the chicken." But Layla avoided her gaze, muttering that it was only that. She hurried back to the dining room to avoid any further conversation.

Rose sat back down, a deep silence etched into her features. She contemplated her life. She thought about how she was an incomplete mother, with two children who'd passed away before she could even enjoy them. Layla felt for her. She wanted to hug her and tell her how life was nothing but an illusion, how distant their destinies were from what they'd dreamed they'd be. For a moment, she wanted to confide in her, woman to woman, to tell her she was pregnant. But she remembered what Shahira had whispered when she came into her bedroom to say goodnight: "Don't tell anyone your secret. Even me." Then she kissed her and walked out.

It was raining outside, and people were celebrating Lebanon's liberation from the French Mandate. The modern state had been launched, the winds of an allied victory were blowing over the Mediterranean Sea, and local newspapers reported on the joy of the entire nation. In Ksoura, however, many people felt no change. Their lives stayed as they always had been. Salem explained to Layla that the war had made it tricky for the newlyweds to spend their honeymoon abroad. Instead, he took her to a hotel in Dhour Choueir, where Nadim had booked a room for them. He'd spend a week there when he'd gotten married, and it was a lovely spot surrounded by stone pines.

Salem had promised Fayez that Layla could finish her final year of school and then go to university and study literature, but things changed after they were married. He let her finish the school year but then refused to allow her to continue her studies. His justification was that he was forty-three years old and wanted to waste no time in starting a family. If she went to university, it would be at least three more years until she could start bearing his children. When Layla complained to her uncle that Salem had gone back on his promise, he replied that she had to understand Salem's perspective and that he was aging.

Layla entered a life full of stress and new disappointments. Her quick marriage meant she didn't know what to say or how to act with the man who'd suddenly become her husband. She rubbed her belly, telling herself that her secret was safe. No one knew that she was carrying this secret on her wedding day. She was afraid nonetheless—afraid when she touched her belly, afraid when she tried to sleep.

It might have been a survival instinct, or it might have been a desire to die. But something pushed Layla to seduce Salem in the bedroom from their very first night together in the hotel. She came on to him every night afterward as well. Salem was overjoyed with how wild this young woman was. He'd originally believed her to be innocent and naïve. When they were on their way to the hotel after the wedding ceremony, he told her that she was too quiet, unlike any women he knew, and that he might need ten women like her to satisfy his desire. "You'll get used to how I talk," he told her with a cruel smile.

She wondered if he wanted her to get used to him being hurtful toward her. But she was already deeply wounded when she met him—she had been since birth. She was not only an orphan, but Yusuf had abandoned her, and now she was hiding a pregnancy from everyone. She only slept a few hours a night and had constant nightmares. In her sleep, she saw blood, running, mud, and rain. She saw herself carrying and then losing a baby, not knowing where to find her. She tried to convince herself that these dreams would surely stop after she gave birth. Reading novels was the only thing that continued to give Layla inner strength. As she started to show, she developed serious anxiety. But she managed to stay calm and finish her school year, with Salem thrilled at watching her belly grow bigger and rounder each day.

~

Asmahan was the first baby girl of her generation in Salem's family. She was a voracious child who woke every two hours to nurse and then fall back asleep. Layla got used to a light sleep. She started waking up whenever the baby did. When she was about a month old, Asmahan started sleeping through the night. Layla was so relieved. She'd refused Salem's sisters Salwa and Huda's offer to take care of Asmahan overnight. She never wanted to be separated from her.

But her nightmares wouldn't leave her be. One night she woke up with a start, as if someone had jolted her violently from her slumber. She sat up suddenly, rigid and worried, having woken from sheer anxiety. She still remembered the bad dream. She was in a house with no roof, rainwater pouring over her as if from an open gutter. To protect her baby, she had hold her and move from place to place without knowing where she could put her down. She was drowning in the heavy rain and freezing cold from the lashing wind. She went outside, still carrying the child. She found herself in front of Yusuf's building. She walked up the stairs and banged on the door, but no one answered. As she was leaving, she glanced up and spied him staring down at her from the balcony. She was still holding the baby in her arms. She tried to call his name, but her voice stuck in her throat. She was mute. He contemplated the two of them from his balcony, not moving a muscle.

She woke up gasping for air. She wanted to cry but couldn't. Her nightgown was damp, as if soaked from the rain in her nightmare. Somewhere between sleep and wakefulness, she asked herself how there could be cold wind and rain in the month of August. She got out of bed and tiptoed to her baby daughter's room. She bent over and rested her cheek near the infant's lips to be sure she was breathing. As she exhaled, she released a weight that had settled on her soul. She stood contemplating her daughter's face and noticed her resemblance to Yusuf. But she couldn't think about this now. Or go backward. She just wanted to forget the hurt. Nonetheless, she let her mind wander to the night of their last turbulent rendezvous and then to her hasty marriage. She thought about how she wasn't able see him and tell him she was pregnant before he left. She thought about how she'd given birth to Asmahan after being married only seven months. She changed out of her wet nightgown and tried to fall back to sleep. But no luck. And Salem still hadn't come back home yet.

Will she ever tell Asmahan whose daughter she is? Every time she looks at herself in the bathroom mirror this question flits by. She collects tap water into the cupped palms of her hands and throws it on her face. She washes and then she shakes her wet face violently side to side—as if repeating the word "no" or throwing the question back into the sink. She dries her face with a towel, shaking her head stubbornly, saying to no one but herself, "My daughter is mine alone, end of discussion."

Salem and Layla lived together as husband and wife. From a distance, they seemed like any couple living a regular life. Having a baby seven months after the wedding didn't seem strange to Salem. He knew that his sister Huda had been born seven months after his parents' marriage and the same was now true of his daughter. No sooner had Asmahan had her first birthday than a second baby was born. Layla was now a mother of two before she'd even turned nineteen.

Layla compensated for this by reading and writing about her life. She spent hours everyday reading in her room. She scribbled questions and impressions in the margins of her books. Writing notes was a habit she'd picked up right when she began to love reading. It might have even dated back to when she'd started writing her mother Yasmine's name in charcoal on the stone walls of the house. Sometimes she wrote in books, other times in her diary. She kept up a constant dialogue with the characters in novels or even with their authors. Sometimes she talked about these books with Rose, and they traded ones they'd already read. Unlike her, however, Rose found it difficult to finish even one book after she'd given birth to her daughter and son, Ouida and Nour.

Not long after Asmahan was born, Layla asked the administration at the English School in Ksoura if she could come back as a literature teacher. When she failed to convince Salem to let her go to university and continue studying, she felt she needed to get out of the house. But Asmahan wasn't even five months old when she fell pregnant with her second child. She never managed to work outside the house. At first, Salem's excuse was that Asmahan was too young. Then her brother Walid was born. Salem kept coming up with excuses until in the end he said firmly and directly, "No. You won't become a teacher. Stay home and take care of your children!" Salem didn't think this was strange at all—he hadn't changed. But Layla had changed. Returning to Ksoura after getting married, she was less curious; she lost the desire she had to explore things in the city. She never completed the experience of being a young woman in Beirut. That moment of joy remained on pause, missing and unfinished. She was never able express her deeply personal feeling of loss in the way she wanted.

Most days, Salem wasn't around. He worked in real estate and construction, and he dreamed of running for parliament. He would also go out for hours every night, and Layla had no idea where he was. He managed to hire a woman to help with housework and a man to work in the fields. He felt good about this, not because he loved Layla but because he didn't trust her. He also wanted to assert a certain social position for himself in relation to the people of Ksoura. Layla didn't have to do the domestic chores her late mother had to, or that her grandmother had done and still did. She totally lost her spirit of curiosity, though, and was semi-absent from her family and home life. She saw herself through the heroines of the novels she read and reread. The gap between her life as a student and her life as a married woman and mother was difficult for her to bridge.

There was a life out there that she couldn't live. This was a loss that nothing could make up for. She believed motherhood would fill in what was missing, but all motherhood did for her was widen that gap. She thought about this all the time but was too ashamed to say it. She was ashamed to tell anyone, even Rose or her cousin Mona. All these feelings were accompanied by a profound doubt that she could ever be a good mother. When she read books or wrote about something painful, a little voice would come out of nowhere and tell her she should be paying more attention to her children. Her constant feeling of guilt made her forget that Salem also had a responsibility to be a father to the children. She accepted that he was an absent father without complaint. She grew up used to absence. Her mother was permanently absent, her boyfriend left her, and then the man who became her husband acted like her own father who was always away.

Ghassan came back from Palestine early in the year 1948. Armed Zionist terrorist organizations—the Irgun and the Haganah—began targeting the British-owned railroad company where he worked. In that year the "state" of Israel was declared, expelling the Palestinians and occupying huge swaths of Palestinian land. When Ghassan finally returned to Lebanon, his daughter was already married and a mother of two. Ghassan never knew how to be a father to Layla after her mother passed away. He unconsciously held her responsible for Yasmine's death, perhaps to absolve himself of the weight of the guilt he carried with him. He couldn't handle the idea that the guilt was his alone. That's why he entrusted Layla to her grandma Shahira. He didn't know how to be a grandfather either, or how to interact with his grandchildren. He was like a stranger. Layla's younger uncle Tawfiq, who lived with Shahira and spent all of his time painting, was much closer to the children. He would invite them into his studio—the room he built for himself in the garden behind the house—and let them color on a big white sheet he kept there just for them. Or they'd draw on pieces of paper he'd torn out of a little notebook Fayez had brough him from a bookshop in Beirut.

Layla chose to raise her family on the ground floor of Salem's family house. Her choice harkened back to her attachment to animals and the garden that she filled with rows of fragrant sweet violets. She grew various other types of flowers as well, leaving the overgrown jasmine bushes as they were, their heavy branches spilling into the garden over its fence. Through the main gate of the building was a little dirt-filled area. Layla left it empty, with no plants, for her kitten Noosa and another cat who'd taken up residence with them. They used it to enjoy the warmth of the morning sun. One day, this little black cat had come and stood meowing at the door. Layla brought her inside, saying that she'd chosen them. She called her Mina. Salem complained that Layla was starting a collection of animals and that she liked to raise useless things. She should have been growing vegetables, parsley, and other herbs to make salads like tabbouleh

Layla and Salem each lived in their own world. Initially, this distance allowed Layla to enjoy her personal space. It meant she could read for hours on end and even do some writing. When she was reading, she carefully underlined every sentence that impacted her in pencil. She focused on words with new meanings that deeply touched her emotions and consciousness. But Layla's enjoyment of her privacy began to anger Salem. He felt his wife was behaving in a way he'd never seen in other women. He found her abnormal and her request for isolation and quiet unnatural, something no sane man would accept. He didn't keep his dissatisfaction to himself either. He started acting aggressive and hostile toward her. It began with constant criticism and then moved on to cursing and belittling her. This mostly happened when they were at home.

He cared about his image—how society and other people saw him. He always appeared welcoming, kind, sociable, and cheerful. But as soon as they were alone, he changed. That's when he showed a side of himself that she came to know all too well. Anything she did, any word she said, would give him cause to criticize and insult her. In the beginning, she tried to understand and find reasons for his anger that seemed to come from nowhere. But in the end, she found no explanation for his behavior.

She started to fear him, rushing to her room and locking herself in. She didn't come out to greet people visiting the house, or to see his sisters who'd married late. She didn't tell anyone what was happening between them when they were alone behind closed doors. She said nothing. Meanwhile, Salem continued to strip her of any shred of self-confidence. He described her to people as moody. Layla reached the point of self-loathing and fell into a deep depression.

"Our lives take unexpected paths. We search for hope, don't find it, and we discover that we've lost our way," Layla wrote in her diary. She still dreamed of traveling abroad and completing her studies. Or if she couldn't go far from home, at least to finish her degree in Beirut. But reality devoured her dreams whole. She corresponded with Helen less frequently. Their communication was predicated on the hope that they would meet again. But when Layla married at seventeen, this hope diminished.

Whenever Salem got home from the track, Layla would guess whether his horse had won or lost. If his horse lost the race, he would curse in English, muttering "fucking horse" over and over again to himself. She feared him coming home after a loss. His baseline bad mood would only get worse, and he'd be more violent towards her. But if his horse won, he'd open his arms out wide and start dancing around, laughing aloud. Then he'd put his hand in his pocket, pull out a wad of cash, and give it to Walid, who was a year younger than Asmahan. He'd walk around the garden overlooking the main village square, calling to his son to come sit with him. He'd sing a Frank Sinatra song that he'd learned in America, "You Lucky People, You." It was practically the only song he knew.

Asmahan disappeared when Salem started singing. She found herself at her friend Ouida's house, Walid having followed her. When they got there, they played with Ouida and little Nour. Halim Bou Tannous had built a wading pool for his children. Asmahan jumped in with all her clothes on. Ouida watched her and then jumped in too. They giggled and splashed around together in the pool. Walid followed and then so did one-year-old Nour. They played in the water, the strong sun warming it for them. Rose came out to scold the children, telling the girls that they'd gone mad. They must take better care of Walid and never let Nour go into the water alone. She handed the girls towels and told them to dry the little ones off, scolding them, saying they were naughtier than the boys.

Nour was actually a special case in comparison to other boys, as he'd been wearing girls' clothes since birth. There was a reason for this. Rose sought help after the death of her first child, and then a second one who she'd been pregnant with when Ouida was only five months old. One of Rose's neighbors took her to the Beqaa, where they'd heard there was a sheikh who could chase away evil spirits. The sheikh told her that there was a qarina in the house who would strangle any baby boy who was born there. To chase this spirit away, they'd have to trick it. They could protect the baby boy by dressing him in girls' clothes. When Rose was pregnant with Nour, she told herself she was going to have a girl and only bought pink clothes for the new baby. This way, if she did have a girl, everything would be ready, and if she had a boy then she could conceal this with the clothes. When she gave birth to a baby boy, she dressed him in pink and gave him a gender-neutral name: Nour. For the first six years of his life, Nour wore dresses and played only with girls. His father Halim Bou Tannous was never given the traditional nickname given to fathers of boys, and instead was called Abu Ouida, referring to his daughter. None of this was easy for Rose and Halim. Their steadfast commitment to his survival granted them the patience to wait until he was older to take him out of girls' clothes and treat him like a boy. But Nour had gotten used to his feminine identity during his short life, in the same way that the people of Ksoura had gotten used to calling his father Abu Ouida.

Asmahan sometimes spent full days at Ouida's in the summertime. Layla would come with her and sit a while with her friend Rose. "Rose has changed so much," Layla thought. "Her life is happy and well organized. It may be boring, but she has practically no stress."

~

Asmahan learned how to protect herself from a very young age. She would escape from Salem's moodiness and the toxic atmosphere at home. Her brother Walid was attached to her and imitated everything she did. They knew all too well that any time Salem seemed happy, it would inevitably be followed by his usual violence. They felt powerless to confront him or protect their mother from his violent behavior. They'd figured out that staying away from him was the best solution. Their mother remained on their minds, even as they distanced themselves from their home. This generated huge feelings of guilt that only grew with the passing of time. In later years, they'd think about Layla, knowing that she lived under the same roof as him, unable to escape.

When Layla heard Salem singing, she knew to withdraw. She'd go to her room and try to soothe herself by reading. A voice with no love, she thought. Even birds sleeping in their nests would be frightened and fly away when they heard his voice. When they moved into the big house Salem had bought when he returned from America, they seemed like a happy husband and wife at first. He told everyone that he'd bought it on the very same day he'd visited Layla's school with Fayez. He'd invented a whole story to tell guests—she was all grown up and he realized she wouldn't wait for him to build a whole new house. He didn't want her to fly away like a bird of paradise. He also said that he knew that how much she loved animals. "You know how Layla loves a garden full of dogs and cats!" he'd chuckle to the visitors.

Layla listened to how Salem spoke in front of guests, noting his hypocrisy and fakeness. She could hardly believe his nonstop lying. He made up stories out of the blue and people believed them. And he believed them himself. As she saw it, he lived inside a bubble of his own lies. She wrote on a page in one of her books, "He tells made-up stories about me. Our meeting at school was totally one-sided. I didn't choose it. The coincidence of it all is just an illusion, as is the time that I lived with him—that's an illusion too."

Layla remembered when her cat Noosa had her first litter of three kittens. When his friends and their wives came over to their place that Sunday, Salem told them about Layla's intense attachment to her pets. Then, after everyone left, he picked them up by their little paws, waved their legs around in the air, and tossed them one by one over the garden wall into the road like pebbles.

Layla almost fainted at the sight of him throwing the newborn kittens around like that.

Later that night, he came to bed as if nothing had happened. He told her that a wife had no right to refuse her husband sex if he wanted it. They fought. She resisted his advances and left the room to go sleep in the children's room. She needed to cry, but she couldn't. She couldn't bear being near him. This made Salem even more aggressive toward her. He forced himself on her, as if sex was his revenge. Violence defined their relationship, as she expressed in her diary:

> He chases away his fear of death with sex; I resist mine by writing. It's like he is fighting death with another kind of death. He always finds a way to justify his violence: my writing, my solitude, my silence. When I refuse to have sex with him, he's violent. Does feeling helpless breed violence? I know he has other women. Why me? I'm trapped. Am I such a bad omen that my mother died right after giving birth to me?

# The Dahli Family and Politics

Fayez spent most of his holidays in the village, playing dominos or backgammon with Salem and betting on the horses. On Saturday afternoons, they visited Ouida's father, Halim Bou Tannous, and talked politics. They spent whole days together; Fayez would come home at the end of the night only to sleep. He'd head back to his room on the second floor that Shahira would have asked Hajar to get ready for him by changing his bedsheets and tidying up.

He'd started building his own separate apartment atop the house years before but never finished it because he didn't have enough money. After he returned from America and became infatuated with Layla, he was able to finish it with Salem's financial help. Initially, this seemed like an innocent coincidence to Layla. But with time she understood how it all fit together. Her uncle's insistence on their marriage wasn't for her happiness, as he'd always claimed. Rather, it was to pay off his debt to Salem.

Fayez would arrive home in Ksoura in a Ford he'd bought—the village's first car. He liked to honk the horn repeatedly, as if making the car sing. Then he'd jump out with the engine still running.

His family members would spill out of the car, loaded down with sweets and other foods to store in the first-floor kitchen. His wife, Mufida, worked alongside Layla and Mona to prepare food for everyone while Fayez and Salem got a grill ready outside for the meat and potatoes. Shahira joined them. Since Nayif died, she and Tawfiq lived alone in the house. While the family gathered in the living room, Layla slipped away, wondering if Fayez's car was also a part of what he'd gotten out of Salem in the marriage deal.

Fayez and Salem had been friends before he'd married Layla. They were, of course, also relatives, as Salem was Grandma Shahira's distant cousin. Betting on racehorses, drinking arak, and playing backgammon all brought the two men together. But other things that they talked about had strengthened their bond as well. When he'd arrived from America, Salem showered Shahira's family with gifts, helping various people out, including financing Fayez's extension on the family house. He also helped Nadim with the cost of renewing the fields after the harsh winter's rains had washed away trees and destroyed the terrace walls. At first, everyone thought this was because Salem intended to marry his younger sister Huda to Naim, who was still a bachelor at the time. His interest lay elsewhere, though—on Layla, though she hadn't yet turned fourteen.

There were also things that Fayez and Salem did not have in common. Salem loved to go out and party in Beirut. But Fayez had become a follower of the Dahesh movement. Like everyone else, he followed the wars happening all over the word and believed that Lebanese independence was a first step toward building a modern nation. He engaged in conversations about the president of the newly independent republic, how the Lebanese people should demand his resignation as they believed he wasn't the right man for the job. After joining the Dahesh movement, Fayez still bet on the horses and followed the results of the races from time to time, but this was mostly just to please Salem.

The events happening in Lebanon, both large and small, always impacted the Dahli family. This was partly because family members held such diverse political views. Shahira carried memories of past wars with her, but she also brought the family together despite their different politics. The family lived through world wars, a major famine, and a faltering independence impeded by minefields from time to time.

Anyone who followed the family's news would have noticed that the execution of Anton Saadeh was a major turning point. Kamal emigrated to America and started a family, never to return. The events that later became known as the revolution of 1958 nearly drove Layla mad. The collapse of Intra Bank drove an irreparable rift between Salem and Fayez, totally changing what the family did and how they acted. Each of these events were stepping stones that altered the family's destiny. It was no secret to anyone in the family that Fayez changed after getting close to the Dahesh group. He started attending their spiritual events, bringing their literature home, and reading their writings.

Then Dahesh was stripped of his Lebanese citizenship, and President Bechara El Khoury issued a decree for his deportation. Many of his followers were also pursued by the authorities and some were thrown in prison. Fayez was afraid he might suffer from the same indignity and so he disappeared. He first settled his family into the newly built floor of their house in Ksoura. He then started sleeping in a hut Salem had built for him in the fields, where he delivered food to him for several weeks. This incident changed Fayez. He started reading a lot. He began meditating and peppering his conversations with spirituality. He grew increasingly angry with the politicians who'd taken power after Lebanese independence, especially after they'd imprisoned Dahesh's closest confidante, Mary Haddad, the president's sister-in-law. Her daughter Majida killed herself to protest the stripping of Dahesh's citizenship, as well as the accusations the Lebanese authorities kept hurling against him and his family.

"It's not OK, it's not allowed . . ." Fayez kept saying. "They oppressed this man, and other innocent people who had faith in him. The ink isn't even dry on the speeches and declarations they keep filling us full of. Where is the Constitution that they signed on to, which protects the personal freedoms and beliefs of every Lebanese citizen? Look at what they're doing to us." Obviously stressed, Fayez brought this issue up with everyone he encountered. He was on a kind of mission against the authorities. He would ask everyone around him, "Where is the judiciary? Why aren't they doing anything? Has it lost its independence? Is this now in the hands of executive power? Or in the hands of the president?" And he would carry on speaking as if he knew the answer already.

The first years of independence were disappointing to many Lebanese people. Lebanon had only been independent for six years when Anton Saadaeh was executed by a sham trial that was hardly a trial at all.

Thursday the seventh of July 1949. One week before Asmahan turned five, everyone was having lunch at Layla and Salem's house. Nadim took his mother Shahira home to get some rest and went to a meeting of his comrades at his house in Broummana.

Friday the eighth of July 1949. It was a hot day. That morning, Layla took her children over to Rose's house to swim in the pool with Ouida and Nour. She sat outside while the children swam and played noisily. Layla felt relaxed at Rose's house, in the warmth and comfort of family. Halim came home looking gloomy, bearing the news of Anton Saadeh's execution. He told Rose that Husni al-Zaim had betrayed Saadeh as part of a secret deal and handed him over to the Lebanese authorities the night before. He was executed by a firing squad in Ramlet al-Baida, after a show trial held under cover of darkness.

Everyone was sad and in a state of shock. Layla took her kids out of the pool, dressed them, and rushed back to her grandmother's house. She wanted to check on her uncles Nadim and Kamal. She knew what this would mean for them. She found Shahira still in bed. She looked sad and weak. She helped her out of bed so she could come to the living room, where family and neighbors had begun to gather. Hajar was serving coffee. Salem was already there, sitting near Nadim, listening to the news on the radio. She asked Nadim about Kamal. He told her that he was fine, and she shouldn't worry.

The atmosphere in the house felt funereal, as if people were coming to offer condolences after a death in the family. Extreme sorrow. In the silence, people's faces showed their shock. Tears filled eyes. Cigarette smoke filled the air. The news was broadcast. Major accusations against Anton Saadeh. "Lies! Slander and lies," Nadim protested angrily, interrupting the radio announcer. "Traitorous sons of bitches!"

Saadeh's picture was on the front page of every newspaper the next day. Many journalists protested what the Lebanese authorities had done. Some of them paid the price with harassment or imprisonment. Nadim got up and left in a hurry. That night security forces raided the homes of many party members. Some remained under surveillance, including Nadim, who was forced into hiding for several weeks. Two years later, the former Lebanese prime minister Riad El Solh paid for Saadeh's execution with his own life: he was assassinated by three party members while visiting King Abdullah of Jordan.

What happened to Dahesh—and all the incidents in Lebanon that followed from it—gradually brought Fayez closer to his brothers. They had previously argued about politics. Nadim was an enthusiastic member of the SSNP as a young man. He found his older brother Fayez was too prone to accept the status quo—he would benefit from it and improve his own situation without asking questions. Naim saw Fayez as somewhat opportunistic, but they rarely clashed. Ultimately, he was his older brother, and it was impossible to stand up to him or accuse him of anything. Nadim had never approved of his brother's relationship with Salem, from the time he first returned to Lebanon. He could see that Salem's ambition was to cement a place in politics and society no matter the cost. Kamal was quieter than Nadim. He preferred to remain silent about what his elder brother did or said. He was different from both of his brothers; he realized deep down that violence poisons society no matter which side it comes from.

Nadim celebrated what his comrades did in Jordan two years later, but Kamal had already taken a different path by then. He left Lebanon the year of the assassination, becoming the first Dahli family member to emigrate to America. Someone he knew helped him find a place to stay with a relative who worked at a printing press in New York City.

Kamal's decision to go to America saddened Shahira greatly. He was the child she was closest to. From the time he was tiny, a deep trust and complicity developed between them. He confided all his worries in her, and he helped her find solutions to all her problems with their land and harvests. Their only major disagreement arose just before Layla got married. He didn't think the marriage was a good idea. He told Shahira that supporting it was a betrayal of Yasmine and went against what she would have wanted.

On the night of his departure, Shahira couldn't get a wink of sleep. It felt like everything she'd built was slowly collapsing before her very eyes. As he bade her farewell, he promised her that he'd write as soon as he arrived. Fayez took him to the Beirut Port to board a ship heading for Malta, where he'd get on another that would go all the way across the Atlantic Ocean.

Shahira received a letter from Kamal five months later. He wrote that he'd arrived in New York and was staying with a Lebanese man on Atlantic Avenue. He was due to start work soon at a bilingual, Arabic-English printing press. He also shared how pleased he was that he was going to learn the trade, how to typeset and print.

His experience in the Dahesh movement helped Fayez see clearly what he called the lie of democracy and freedom of conscience in Lebanon. He came to believe that the biased politics of the newly formed republic were contrary to the constitution, as Nadim said. His family members reacted differently to these changes in Fayez. His son Majd left home because of the tense atmosphere and moved in with friends in an apartment near his university. When Fayez's friends came to visit, his wife Mufida made coffee for everyone and then went to her room and closed the door so she didn't have to listen to what she called "the same old broken record." His daughter Mona started to spend most of her time at the women's volleyball gym she'd opened.

The best thing that happened to the family was that Nadim and Fayez had stopped bickering about politics. They were in sync now. Political discussions with family and friends in Ksoura took a different turn. Fayez would suggest something, and Nadim would follow it up: "A republic that inaugurates itself by stripping a Lebanese person of his citizenship—can that be an independent republic? No! That's not an independent republic it's a dependent republic!" A critique of the presidency would follow: "We have no idea who's running the country . . . the president or his brother?" Nadim would then support Fayez, chiming in with his own biting commentary. "This republic's only achievement to date is the execution of a political intellectual with no justification and without a fair trial. They shot him, for fear his ideas would spread. What independence are they even talking about?" Fayez would interrupt, "This is only the tip of the iceberg. The republic won't last, it's already fallen." Suddenly Salem made his presence in the room known, saying, "Don't forget the republic under the Mandate, that was the best!"

"What do you know about politics? You were in America at the time, counting your wife's money before burying her. Don't talk to me about a "republic" under the Mandate. It wasn't a Lebanese republic, which means it wasn't a republic at all," Nadim retorted.

After his Dahesh phase, Fayez lived a simple life in the mountain house in Ksoura, looking after the land. Mufida and Mona stayed in Beirut, visiting him on weekends from time to time, and Majd went to America to continue his studies. Mufida kept on as she had been, selling stationery in the little shop next to their house.

Shahira couldn't decide if Fayez being at home made her happy or sad. She contemplated how many times she'd sat on the doorstep waiting for him to come home. Now her heart hurts when she sees him. "Kamal leaving shattered my heart into pieces, and Fayez's return couldn't put them back together again."

Fayez hadn't been back living in the mountains very long when Salem suggested they go into the real estate and construction business together—buying land and residential buildings, then renting out or selling apartments to families looking for housing around Beirut. Their partnership suited Salem since he was trying to strengthen his position in town by employing local people, including his father-in-law Ghassan. He thought the Dahli family's land would be good for building. The project helped Fayez break his isolation and slowly get active again. He began to meet up with Salem and his friends who were contractors. They established a real estate company together, which Salem ran. He registered the company's accounts in a new bank that had opened in Beirut and was encouraging new investors.

Life in Ksoura changed. More and more stone houses were being built with money sent by villagers who'd emigrated to America. Families came from remote areas that lacked schools and medical services, taking up residence alongside them. Wider roads were built for the constant automobile traffic. In the summertime, the little village became a destination for people who lived on the coast. None of Salem's brothers built a house in Ksoura though. His two sisters, Huda and Salwa, would visit from time to time and stay at Salem's house; it became a family gathering place with time.

All this happened against Layla's will. She was disorientated and emotionally detached from her surroundings. On the one hand there was Salem's complicated and difficult relationship with his family, and on the other, the townspeople were upset by the deforestation needed to mine rocks and minerals in quarries; they didn't like the destruction of the local natural landscape. Salem was working hard to polish his image in town because he wanted to become a member of parliament. He opened an electoral office and surrounded himself with assistants who worked with him and for him. They were the very same people who worked at his ever-expanding real estate company.

Salem's family's field was unlike others, as it was located at the top of the hill. You had to walk all the way up to the town square and then follow a footpath for about a half hour to reach it. They cultivated vineyards. Over the years, it was incorporated into a development plan that earmarked the area for building, meaning it was no longer zoned for agriculture. His company's relationship with lawmakers meant the agricultural land of Ksoura was being rezoned as residential, for apartment buildings and single-family homes. Real estate prices soared. Local people realized that it was more profitable to build apartment buildings and rent them to vacationers than it was to tend to the land and work so hard every harvest season. Agricultural land gradually transformed into residential areas, meaning cement jungles crept right into the heart of the village in less than two decades.

The Dahli family largely resisted these changes in land use and rezoning. Salem's brother Hamed joined them. He believed that what was happening in Ksoura was killing the soul and spirit of the place. Kamal had given his elder brother power-of-attorney before he'd emigrated. This eventually gave Salem control of decisions about his share of the land as well as Fayez's.

Salem had a complicated relationship with his sisters, Huda and Salwa. He found Huda more problematic because she lived in Ksoura and he saw her all the time. Salwa was more distant geographically, as she lived with her husband in a frontline village in South Lebanon and only visited Ksoura a few times a year. She was always fearful and anxious during wartime, as her daily life was threatened by constant Israeli attacks. She often postponed her visits for fear that she wouldn't be able to make it back home to the South with her family if war broke out when she was away.

Salem always believed that his brothers-in-law didn't like him and that they were always pushing his sisters get him to sell off their shares of the family land. In his opinion, his brothers-in-law wanted to sell, collect the money, and squander their wives' inheritances. This is why he refused to follow the normal inheritance procedures for settling the estate after their father died. At least, this is how Salem narrated his version of the problems between them. It wasn't entirely clear if this was true or came from his own relentless desire to monopolize his sisters' share of the family inheritance.

Though his relationship with his sisters was up and down, they did continue to spend time with him. He often said to their faces that they must be going senile, it was the only way he could understand how they could give in to their husbands' pressure to sell their shares of the family landholdings. This didn't mean that Salem was being honest, or that he had a similar position to the Dahli family about how their land should be used. In fact, he was waiting for the opportunity to be the sole buyer of his sisters' shares and get them at the lowest possible price.

Amidst all this, Hamed remained distant from the family dramas about the inheritance, his brother's politics as well as his real estate dealings. He came up to the village in the summertime to spend time with his family. His kids would tumble out of the car, looking for Asmahan and Walid so they could go to Ouida's house. They looked forward to fetching water from the natural spring above the family house and taking it down to the wading pool Halim had set up for the children.

Layla left her room to welcome her sister-in-law who, was already sitting in the garden drinking coffee. Layla remained silent as Hasmik told the story of how she and her family had fled Türkiye for Anjar, where they took refuge with relatives. Though she knew all the details by heart, Layla listened to her family's story each time as if it were the first time. Hasmik's eyes filled with tears, and Layla encouraged her to keep telling the tale she'd heard so many times. She listened as if she were reading a novel, and pleaded, "Please write this all down, Hasmik, write your story."

Hasmik didn't write. But she wanted to talk and endlessly retold her story, always afraid she might leave out some minor detail.

Fayez got there just before lunch. Hamed stayed quiet as there was no love lost between the two men. Salem suggested that Hamed come with the two of them to visit the plot of land their real estate company had recently transformed into a quarry. He walked into the garden and invited Layla and Hasmik to come along as well.

The quarry was needed to support the construction of the stone houses that were so popular with people who'd emigrated. They extracted boulders from the land, cut them into stones, and polished them so they could be used as building materials. Plots of the land all around town had been transformed into such quarries. From a distance, they looked like the entrails of dismembered corpses. Ancient forests of trees were cut down to their trunks for these construction projects.

Salem's siblings were annoyed by Fayez's constant presence in their brother's life. He was closer to Fayez than he was to any of the rest of them. This is partly why Hamed was reluctant to stay in Ksoura for more than a day. He spent Saturdays at Salem's house, and then he'd set off for Anjar with his wife as the sun was setting. They'd visit his mother-in-law and spend the night there. Their two sons preferred to stay in Ksoura when their parents went to Anjar. They played with Asmahan and went out into the fields during long summer days.

Even though she complained that Fayez was always there, Huda kept up her visits to her brother Salem. But Salwa rarely came. When she did manage a visit from the South, she'd stay for many days, her family taking up the entire first floor.

The first floor of Salem's family house in Ksoura stayed empty for a while after Huda and Salwa got married. He later rented it out to a series of schoolteachers who'd come with their families from far away to work in Ksoura and neighboring villages. These families would stay only temporarily and then move when they found larger houses. He added another floor to his house and rented rooms out to British people who taught in the three English-language schools in the region. He also rented to their families during the summer before they found better places than Ksoura for holidays. They liked his place because he spoke English and could understand what they were saying. He provided them with furniture and other things that they needed but local renters wouldn't ask for. Later on, he built rooms right at the end of his property, far from the main house for local day laborers from distant mountain villages, as well as the Beqaa and Syria.

Layla swapped books, magazines, and stories with their women renters. But she never really formed deep relationships with them. She preferred her solitude, her happy isolation. Books were her only companions. Layla had no real relationship with other women in the family, and her daughter Asmahan had no idea why. She'd welcome them into her home, drink coffee together, and then just leave abruptly. This was her pattern. She'd go back to her room, sit there for a while, and then go back out to be with them. But when the women gathered around drinking coffee and eating sweets, she'd say she was tired and close herself back in her room for good.

Shahira would bail her out and play the role of lady of the house, regaling the guests with stories about wars, famine, and families in the mountains. Grandma Shahira's topics of conversation always fascinated Asmahan, who would sit right beside her, hanging on her every word. Shahira would say goodbye to everyone and apologize for Layla, who would still be locked in her room, claiming that she'd come down with a sudden headache.

Asmhan would go to her room and find her mother lying on the bed reading. Or she'd be writing—either in her notebook or on the pages of a book, underlining words and sentences. When Asmahan asked her why she'd left the visitors, she'd complain of a migraine. She might also add that so many people talking at once exhausted her. She could only handle being with one or two people at a time in her condition.

Growing up, Asmahan knew deep down that her mother was fragile and weak. She was like a flower planted in the garden that wilted in the cold winter wind. She thought of her mother and father as Beauty and the Beast. She loved to read that story at night before bed. But in their case, Salem always remained the Beast—her mother couldn't bring out the Beauty in him. This may have been due to her constant silence. She hardly spoke. She was locked in her own world and Asmahan didn't know what went on there.

Layla's silence also made Asmahan feel that she had to be protected against something, even if logically a mother should worry about her daughter, not the other way around. Even when she was a little girl, though, Asmahan had been a mother to Layla. She'd lie in her room at night, waiting for Layla to read her a bedtime story. But Layla would often get lost in one of her novels and forget. Asmahan would lie in bed, eventually get bored of waiting, and just fall asleep.

Zeina's arrival disturbed Layla's silence and isolation. This visitor took Layla back to her short-lived years as a teenager in Ksoura, before she'd moved to Beirut. Zeina was a Bedouin woman who visited her family in town twice a year, in autumn and springtime like a migratory bird. She used to come by the house to see Shahira when Layla was a girl. No one knew her family name or her real first name. Shahira called her Zeina because she thought it suited her. Whenever she flew from one place to another, she stopped by Salem's place to sit in the garden and have long conversations with Layla, who always served her food and drink and passed on her old shoes and clothes.

One day when Zeina was not yet fifty, she came to visit with a girl who was around eight years old. She told Layla that this girl's father, her son-in law, had killed his daughter—the girl's mother. He was in prison and Zeina had to raise her granddaughter alone. She now brought her along with her everywhere she went.

Zeina was wearing a black dress and a bright orange scarf tied tightly around her forehead that day. She had traveled for many long hot days to reach Salem's house, and body odor wafted from her clothes. Layla got her set up in one of the rooms at the end of the garden. She gave her everything she needed—soap, water, clothes, toiletries, and a towel. Zeina's visits were like a holiday for Asmahan because they were some of the few times that she'd seen her mother chatty and seemingly happy. But this angered Salem. Zeina's presence angered him. He forbade Layla from welcoming her inside the house. Layla waited for Salem to leave and then showed Zeina to her garden room.

When Salem came back and saw Zeina, he grew frustrated and enraged. But Layla turned her back and walked away from him with no reply. Salem feared his wife's seasonal transformations. She'd change from being an absent, silent woman to one who laughed and talked loudly, ignoring her husband. He was generally contented with her silence and likewise preferred there to be silence in the house during his frequent absences. Whenever Zeina came, he'd start mocking Layla, saying that her homeless Bedouin friend had come to visit and squeeze everything she could out of their relationship. At those moments, she'd choke out in a low mumble, "You're the ugliest creature on the face of this earth." But she never told him directly what she really thought about him.

Asmahan didn't understand Layla's silence in the face of Salem's verbal abuse and emotional violence. Initially she was deeply angry at Layla, even blaming her for the tense atmosphere in the family. When she was younger, she didn't understand that Layla wasn't responsible for any of this. Salem was violent by nature. As Asmahan matured into a young woman, she started to understand the psychological and emotional toll this abuse had on her mother.

One Sunday morning, Asmahan didn't find Layla when she woke up. But she could hear sounds of far-off laughter. She walked outside toward the room at the very end of the garden. She found her mom there still wearing pajamas, sitting on a mattress next to Zeina. She was holding a notebook in which she'd written the letters of the alphabet. She had a wooden box filled with all kinds of colored pencils that Tawfiq had once given to her. Layla had drawn a picture next to each letter. She was teaching Zeina how to read and write. They giggled every time Zeina mispronounced a letter. Asmahan stood at the door looking at the two of them, surprised. But she soon succumbed to their infectious laughter. She found her mother radiant and contented, the morning light reflected in her eyes.

~

Fayez's relationship with Salem remained strong, despite the silent sadness and lack of joy he noticed on Layla's face. He tried to convince himself that he was mistaken. Layla never said a word to him about her private life with Salem.

One day, Salem convinced Fayez that Intra Bank should manage the income from the buildings their company was constructing. He said that they'd reap the benefits. Fayez signed an agreement he didn't understand or agree with, whereby the bank would become the guardian of the company's assets. It didn't bother him too much since the company started to yield annual dividends. According to Salem, the bank knew how to manage money.

Fayez and Salem's relationship led to Hamed growing more distant from both his brother and Ksoura. It could be because he was jealous, but that's not what he confided in Nadim. Hamed knew that Nadim was different from Fayez. He also understood that this relationship had a negative impact on the entire family, especially in relation to work and construction. After Kamal left Lebanon, Nadim no longer saw Salem as much—only at family occasions. One day, he told Fayez that he didn't want his land to be used for construction projects managed by Salem. He preferred to be a teacher and live modestly, rather than participating in Salem's schemes. Tawfiq kept himself totally out of politics and pursued his interest in art. He worked as an art teacher in local schools and displayed his paintings at village fairs during the summer, when local vacationers as well as those who lived and worked outside Lebanon came to Ksoura. He bought new canvasses and art supplies with the money he earned selling his paintings.

When Salem registered as a candidate in the ministerial elections, he started making the rounds of the region, visiting as many people as he could. He withdrew huge sums money from the company's accounts, distributing it to people who came to his office. Sometimes people wanted to resolve issues with other people. Some were asking about road improvements. When the elections came around, he was not elected as a member of the ninth parliament of the independent state of Greater Lebanon.

Salem used his candidacy to convince a few Ksoura locals about the benefits of changing the way they used their land and rezoning it for building. He continued his real estate projects apace, dividing up plots of land. He uprooted, destroyed, and cut down trees. He even cut down stone pines to build new roads connecting his new four-story buildings to the main road.

His electoral adventure lost Salem a lot of money. The bank stopped granting him business loans, so his projects remained unfinished. He couldn't sell anything that year.

Not long after the elections in the summer of 1958, rising local and international tensions gave rise to several scattered violent incidents. Gamal Abdel Nasser's rise to power in Egypt affected Lebanon, and people working against him there tried to include the country in the Baghdad Pact.

That year greatly impacted the Dahli family. Layla's life that summer changed completely, as did the rest of her family's. Her mental and physical health both began to deteriorate. She imagined that she'd lost her son Walid in the ongoing local violence and had a nervous breakdown. Salem became more violent toward her following his loss in the elections and this only increased her fragile state of mind. The lost election not only made Salem more violent toward Layla, but also led to major financial disputes between him and his business partner friend. Fayez accused Salem of mismanaging the company's savings by using it for his election campaign.

The relationship between the two men soured. Fayez no longer went right over to Salem's house when he got to Ksoura. In fact, he ignored him and didn't even pause as he passed by the house, though he knew on warm summer days everyone would be sitting under the pergola in the garden looking out at the road.

Fayez felt his neck and shoulders cramp up as his car approached Salem's house. They lived near each other, their houses separated by only a little road and the square with the Greek Orthodox church. In her final years, Shahira reminded people again and again that his small sliver of land encroached onto theirs and Nayif had originally given it to the town. Despite the road cutting into their property, Shahira's house still had a garden encircled by an iron fence. Their jasmine bushes were as tall as trees, branches spilling over the sides the gate.

Word of their quarrel spread through town. Salem's siblings' jealousy turned into silent gloating. The two men grew increasingly distant. Fayez rarely saw Layla, only if she happened to be around when he was visiting Shahira.

Several years after their conflict began, Intra Bank—where Salem had deposited all the company's money—went bankrupt. The founder and owner left Lebanon and never returned.

# Layla's Illness, Summer 1958

The revolution of 1958 in Lebanon—what people referred to as "the events"—did not pass unnoticed by the Dahli family. On the contrary, it significantly exacerbated their political differences. What made matters worse was that these differences had to do with money. But most important of all was that Layla's illness started that summer when someone wrongly informed her that her son Walid had been killed. On that day, she suffered a nervous breakdown that sent her into a spiral from which she didn't emerge until her sudden disappearance in the spring of 1963.

Tensions between political powers in Lebanon reached a fever pitch in 1958. Political differences turned into a quasi-civil war between the parties opposed to the government and those supporting it. Camille Chamoun, Lebanese president at the time, asked the US Sixth Fleet, located off the coast of Beirut, for help. One of their units had already landed and positioned itself on the hills overlooking vital coastal facilities—the airport, the port, and the main highway leading to Syria. Because of its geographical position, Ksoura was also contained within this area of American deployment, which President Chamoun had called for to rescue his local political position and counter the rising tide of Nasserism in Lebanon.

One afternoon that summer, Hamed's two sons Salah and Emad went out to the family's most distant field. After the rezoning of the land in the area, the path right next to it had been totally transformed. It was now a public road open to car traffic. The two young men were both wearing straw hats to protect themselves against the blazing sun. They walked through terraces with a row of fig trees growing down the center and green grapes crawling up metal trellises that Salem had installed next to the fence surrounding the field. A section of this terraced land was devoted to growing seasonal vegetables.

It had been two weeks since anyone from their family had gone to the fields, because of the tension in the area that reverberated with the constant sound of machine gun fire and rifle shots. It was a calm day. When the young men arrived, they filled two baskets with vegetables—tomatoes, squash, and cucumbers. They then walked over to the climbing vines and picked a few bunches for Asmahan, who really loved green grapes. They noticed a long piece of black electrical wire that had been stuck along the edge of the terraces, some of which was now covered by vine leaves. They followed the wire to discover where it led and what it was far. They walked all the way to the end of the field and found that it kept going right into other plots of land. They stopped walking.

"What's this?" Salah asked, as Emad patted the wire. "Why is it here?" He bent down to examine it further. He suggested to his brother assuredly, "Let's cut it." Salah thought it was a good idea and encouraged him. Emad yanked off part of the wire, sticking it against the wall, while Salah picked up a big rock and started banging the wire with it until he cut it completely. Emad climbed up into a tree with ripe figs, picked some, and put them in a basket he hung on a tree branch. Salah was trapping colorful cicadas in empty matchboxes he'd brought from home for this purpose.

Less than half an hour had passed when an American military jeep rolled up, quickly followed by a second one. A solider clambered out of the front seat of the first jeep, and then another from the second. The soldiers strode together over to the terraces. One of them was carrying a tool to find where the damage was. They struggled with the wire, chatting in English. They went into the field where the Salah and Emad were and found the broken off bit of the wire. One of soldiers went up to them and asked them loudly in English what they were doing there and why they'd cut the wire.

Emad jumped down out of the fig tree right away when he saw the soldiers. He wanted to ask them the same question: "We're on our land—what are *you* doing here?" But, they stayed silent.

One of the soldiers suddenly burst out laughing. The other followed suit. "They're just kids. No one sent them," the one said, while the other started placing more wire to reconnect the wire. They communicated with the soldiers back at base with a walkie-talkie-type device to confirm that everything was back to normal. From the few words he'd picked up from their conversation about the wire, Emad figured out that it was an electricity link that lit the American base from a hilltop village overlooking Beirut Airport.

Before returning to the vehicle, one of the soldiers patted Emad on the shoulder. The other put his hand in his pocket and took out a little flashlight. He gave it to Salah, saying, "You can have this flashlight as a present, take it. But don't touch that wire again!" Holding the flashlight, Salah stopped and stared at the two military vehicles heading back up the hill on the dirt path through the field. He stood silently staring until Emad broke the spell. "What's wrong with you? You look drunk, yellah it's getting dark." They carried the baskets of vegetables and figs and headed home. The sun was dipping into the sea, the day's heavy heat had begun to dissipate with a breeze rising from the valley.

Emad knew who the soldiers he'd met in the field were and why they came to Lebanon. He'd heard about them many times at Asmahan's house. He was nonetheless still surprised that he and his brother had encountered them that day. He told his classmates that he'd spoken to American soldiers, but no one believed him.

The boys grew up and changed year after year, but the intense family conversations never stopped. Sometimes Asmahan and her cousin Emad would stand and just stare at all the people in their big family who'd gotten together and were debating furiously. They'd fight and then turn their backs on each other in anger. The two of them made fun of the disagreements that had cost them and the younger generations of the Dahli family the best years of their lives. The biggest countries in the world were fighting, and it caused tension in one family located in their tiny country that was almost invisible on the world map.

"Don't talk politics, for the love of God! May He keep all politics and bad people from you and your families," Shahira said. "The people in charge do nothing. If they had any good in them at all, they wouldn't have made it to the top." Shahira was anti-authoritarian by nature. She repeated her request to stop talking politics, but by then the debate between the SSNP-backer Nadim and Mona, who was Nasserite to the core, had gotten heated. Her view was that Chamoun was betraying Arabism. She argued with her uncle, telling him that the SSNP's support for Chamoun was a big mistake that they'd all pay the price for one day. "Look, it's because of you all that the country's divided. The imperialists don't want us strong. They don't want us to be independent. They just need us to remain submissive. That's why they all united and bombed Egypt. Everyone participated in this attack, even the Arab traitors!"

Nadim cut her off, accusing her of being brainwashed. "I must correct you here; everything you're saying is wrong. The establishment of the State of Israel and its voracious desire for our nation of greater Syria is the real reason for all this tension. Don't distract us with other issues and conflicts!"

"It's unbelievable! The Americans asked their ally Chamoun not to renew his term to absorb the anger on the streets. They knew what they were doing. Everything here is a failure. Our country is built on miscalculations: Ottoman miscalculations, Turkish miscalculations, French miscalculations, Maronite miscalculations about independence. Political parties have made miscalculations, so have the leaders of the republic. Tell me, whose calculations have been correct? You people?" Mona asked her uncle Nadim provocatively. She then answered her own question. "Nope! You've also miscalculated; Shihab's state-building project failed, though you all were deluded when he came in and thought it would be easy to take over."

Following along, Fayez intervened to cool things down. He could see that their positions weren't at odds fundamentally. "Guys! Everything you're all saying is correct. Where's the disagreement? From the time Israel was created, there's been constant devastation day and night. Our regimes are complicit and lacking in imagination. Otherwise, they would have found a solution for Jews and Arabs to live together in peace."

"Maybe I don't understand politics," thought Fayez to himself, "but these family arguments are unproductive." Even though he'd joined the Dahesh movement when it first got active in Lebanon, and had resented the government and rule of Bechara El Khoury, with time he forgot about Khoury's wrongdoings, or tried to forget them at least.

When autumn came, Emad still remembered his family's heated political debates from that summer. It was like watching a film when you're not sure who to side with—the good guy or the bad guy. Revising for his exams, he wondered, with a dash of cynicism and irony, which was better for his own academic success and happiness—a Syrian nation? Or a united Arab nation?

~

After his dispute with Fayez, Salem became more violent toward Layla. She felt increasingly frustrated and trapped. Whether the men agreed or disagreed didn't matter to her; either way she paid the price.

Salem came home and didn't find Layla. It was a Friday. She was having lunch with Rose at Shahira's house and reading Kamal's letters to her grandmother. She and Rose later stopped by her uncle Tawfiq's studio to look at his new paintings to choose one to hang in Ouida's room.

Layla came home carrying a painting that Tawfiq had gifted her. She took down an old painting that was displayed in the entryway to the house, rested it on the table, and hung the new one in its place. Tawfiq had done a portrait of her sitting on the sofa holding an open book. She stood back and contemplated it, then tilted it slightly to one side, adjusting it on the wall.

Salem suddenly appeared in the doorway. He'd stumbled out of the living room, holding a glass of whisky. He watched her hang the portrait. As soon as she'd finishing centering it and stood back a little, he walked right up close to the wall, a deep growl emanating from his throat forming garbled words. All she could understand was, "TAKE IT DOWN, take it down now." He ripped the painting off the wall and threw it on the floor. "Put the old picture back up where it belongs," he demanded. "This is my house! You can't do anything here without asking me first." The stench of whiskey hung heavily on his breath. Layla stepped back without answering. She padded into the living room, sat on the sofa near the heater, and retrieved a book from her handbag.

He followed her, ripped the book from her hand, tore pages out of it, and threw them into the fire. "When I speak, you'll answer, and do what you're told." Watching the fire consume the pages of her book, Layla shouted, "Leave me alone, that's enough. Stop it!" He whipped around and started smacking her face and head. "You don't even look like a woman—you're basically a man. I curse the day I met you." Every word he shouted further aroused his anger and fueled his fists. She started screaming, "Leave me alone, I'm not a punching bag." But he didn't leave her alone. He kicked her and pulled her hair, punched her in the face. He pushed her so hard she fell on the floor moaning.

Cursing and swearing, he left her there and went back to his room, slamming the door behind him. She struggled to get up. She grabbed the edge of the sofa with both hands and lifted herself up slowly. She made it onto the sofa, shoulders hunched. She was a distressed lump, grunting and crying. She didn't know how much time passed before she could raise her trembling hand to feel her bruised face and head. She started wiping the blood off her forehead, cheeks, and upper lip with the hem of her dress.

She was still a heap on the sofa when her daughter Asmahan got home from school. She was terrified by the sight of her mother's bloodied face—she looked like she'd been thrown out with the trash. Asmahan rushed over, hugged her close, and started sobbing silently. She knew who'd done it. She stifled her sobs, afraid that if she made a peep, he'd hear her and beat her up too. She knew that Salem was violent, but this was the first time she'd seen her mother in such a state.

She held her mother close for a long time, without a sound. They believed that silence was the price they had to pay for survival. Quite a while passed before anyone knew that their house harbored a monster. At her tender age, Asmahan didn't realize that there was a way out. She couldn't see any bright spot in this brutal world that could save her mother—and her as well. She worried that her mother's fate might become her own. She knew she had to escape.

When Walid got home, the blood was still visible on Layla's face. He knelt down next to where she was sitting on the sofa. He started stroking her face and hair gently. Pain radiated from his eyes.

"I'll show him," he choked out.

The anguish visible on his face turned into cruelty. It became a part of him and lingered throughout his life whenever he thought of his father. He massaged his mother's shoulders and squeezed them gently. Then he walked over to the closet in the little room next to the kitchen where he kept his hunting rifle. He loaded it, turned around, and pushed the door open with the muzzle of the gun. He strode over to the room where his father was taking his afternoon nap. Layla sensed what he was up to and hoarsely called his name, pleading with him to just walk away. She didn't want her son to spend the rest of his life in prison on her account. Despite everything, Layla still felt this was all her fault.

Walid walked right up to his father, who was now half-awake. He shook him harshly and pointed his rifle at him, voice trembling. "If you ever touch her again, I'll pull the trigger and be done with you. I'll shoot you and give my mother some rest. I swear, not one person will be allowed to walk in your funeral procession and you'll be buried like the animal you are." Walid's hand was shaking. His voice turned to a howl; he was on the verge of collapse. Salem never expected that his son Walid—who he'd looked after and played with as a child—would stick a hunting rifle in his face and threaten to kill him. Such a thing had never ever occurred to him, not even in theory. But clever and manipulative, he flipped the script of this drama and cast blame on his son, as he often did with his family. He lowered his head and began to cry. He lamented fate for taking his late wife Barbara from him and for his marriage to Layla, with whom he'd never had one day of happiness. Even though she was there, it was as if she wasn't, it was as if he lived alone.

He began wailing about losing his money because he went into business with partners who'd cheated him. He'd been forced to sell the land that he'd bought in Beirut for dirt cheap. Or so he claimed. He raised his head slightly and continued with feigned humiliation, "I'm your father—you're all I have. And you want to kill me? I love you. You're my son. Could you actually kill me?"

He buried his face in his hands, his sobs echoing throughout the room. Not knowing what to say or do, Walid retreated. His eyes were fixed on his father's face. His trigger finger and his body relaxed at the same moment. His heart was broken, bleeding in two places, and he didn't know which wound to attend to first. This may not have been the first time that he'd seen his mother abused, but it was the first time he'd seen his father break down and cry like a child.

Layla asked Asmahan for a cold, damp towel. She took it, balled it up, and pressed it against the wound on her head. Stories of Salem's violence had started to spread throughout Ksoura, but people there believed that no one had a right to interfere in things that didn't concern them, especially domestic matters to do with wives and children. After all, there was such a thing as the sanctity of home at the end of the day. Who has the right to interfere in the sanctity of a man's home?

According to Salem's sister Huda, surely everything was down to Layla's behavior. She found it easy to spread this rumor. She said private domestic matters pushed Salem to the brink. As Huda reported it, Layla wasn't good to her dear brother, whom everyone else valued so much. She asserted that everything was Layla's fault, she was always doing things wrong. Salem didn't want to hurt her, but she made him lose his temper. The three words, "lose his temper," became Huda's favorite expression. She made him "lose his temper" every time he walked into his house. He "lost his temper" if he came back and didn't find her; he "lost his temper" every time his food was salty; he "lost his temper" if he couldn't find a pair of clean shoes . . . or if she answered back . . . or if she didn't answer him . . . or if a deal didn't go through. And, of course, he "lost his temper" if he came back from his weekly trip to the racetrack and his horse had lost.

That day had already been eventful for Asmahan. When she was on the playground, she'd noticed drops of blood running down her leg. Terrified, she raced over to the teacher on duty and told her what had happened. She was sure she was dying and would never see her mother, brother, or Ouida ever again. The teacher smiled and gave her a thin sanitary pad to put inside her underwear until she got home. "Tell your mom," the teacher said kindly. But Asmahan didn't tell her mother. She was left totally speechless when she got home and found her.

Layla finally got herself together and stood up. She walked like an old woman, though she hadn't yet turned forty. Asmahan walked behind her like a shadow. Layla turned around and asked her to bring some clean clothes. She went into her daughter's room, sat down on the bed, and stared into space. Asmahan came in carrying clean clothes and handed them to Layla who was still staring blankly, even though Asmahan was speaking to her, saying, "Mom, get up and change your clothes." Tears streamed down her face as she spoke; Asmahan was frightened and confused. She felt time had stopped and there was no tomorrow, nothing except hopelessness and despair.

At that moment, Asmahan felt that she could have cursed their father, told him how much she hated him or even beaten him up. But she just stood there next to Layla and helped her take off her blood-stained clothes. Layla put on clean clothes and went into to the kitchen, which opened out on the back garden. She walked across the garden, where the soil was moist with rain. She headed toward her grandmother's, passing in front of the Orthodox church in the center of the town square, surrounded by cypress and thorn apple trees.

She couldn't make it all the way to her father's house. He'd finally returned from Palestine years ago and settled down in the village. She slowed down as she passed by her grandmother's house and hesitated before knocking on the big iron gate. She wavered, wondering if she should go back home. At that moment, she heard her uncle Tawfiq calling her name from the second-floor balcony. He was opening the gutters to drain the rainwater that had pooled on the balcony.

He rushed down to open the gate. Shocked to see her in such a state, he asked, "What's wrong?" From the way he was looking at her, she could tell that there were still traces of blood on her face. He hugged her and stepped aside so that she could enter. She sat in the room where they always gathered in the winter.

Voice quivering, Layla began to speak. Tawfiq listened and hugged her again. He remained totally silent though the bruises on her face and blood on her forehead really upset him. When

Shahira came out of her room, Layla scrambled over and buried her head in her grandmother's arms. She said shakily, "I can't go on like this. It's too much. I'm too tired." Shahira stroked her head and gently told her to calm down. "He was going to kill me and take my son down with him," she choked out. "He's our dear relative. What can we possibly do?" Tawfiq asked his mother, his tone dripping with sarcasm.

Shahira shot him a look that told him to stop. Then she sent Hajar to go ask Ghassan to come over. Layla was in the kitchen when he got there. She was paralyzed by the thought of facing her father; she was too sad to know what to say or do. Shahira explained him what had happened. He listened calmly, took a short pause, and then called his daughter over to hug her. He sat down right beside her, saying, "I'll speak to him, my girl. He won't dare touch a hair on your head ever again." Then he went silent.

After he finished his cup of coffee, he said, "Get up and go back home. You belong at home." Layla stared back into his eyes, hardly believing what he was asking her to do. "Go back home?" she sputtered weakly, patting herself where she was in pain from the beating. Ghassan repeated, "Do as I say. I have to work with him. I'm asking you to treat your husband well; don't make him mad." He couldn't look his daughter in the eye when these words came out of his mouth. Nor could he meet the gaze of Shahira or that of his cousin Tawfiq. His head was bowed, his body tilted forward, he was staring at the carpet on the floor in front of him. This posture was familiar to his daughter; she didn't know him any other way.

Shahira always said that he'd become indecisive since Yasmine's death. He'd given his daughter to Shahira and entrusted her education to Fayez. Layla knew this all too well. But how could he not react to this? She couldn't understand. Did he feel helpless? The only words he could blurt out expressed fear and resignation. He suddenly jolted upright, as if he could tell what she was thinking from how she was looking at him. He followed up by saying that there must be a logical reason for a man to lose his temper.

It seemed to Layla that he was saying the same thing Huda had been saying. She began to doubt herself. Was she the one in the wrong? Her father was right there with her, and she wanted to believe him. She replayed everything; all the scenes of their life together flipped through her mind silently. Going back through it all, she tried to find something she might have forgotten she'd done that could have made him so angry. But she couldn't. There was nothing.

She felt as if she were surrounded by high walls—no light coming in, no way out, with no one to help her escape. Whenever he was violent with her, she always wondered what she'd done to make him angry. She kept wondering; he stayed violent. Living like this, she started to hate him. She avoided the bedroom on evenings when he was still awake. She'd pay close attention to the rhythm of his breathing and wait for him to fall into a deep sleep. Then she'd tiptoe in and crawl into bed, leaving as much space as possible between them. And she'd try to sleep.

She was a prisoner tricking the prison system by spying a sliver of light sneaking in through the window. She was totally alienated—from her married life, her own room, her own bed. Her feeling of estrangement intensified when her father told her to go back home, as if her grandmother's house was no longer her home and she had no place there. It's true that she didn't love Salem. It had been an arranged marriage and had nothing to do with love or desire.

But over time, she'd gotten used to having him around. After she had children, she was more willing to accept this marriage and a life she hadn't chosen. She wanted to be a good mother and shower her children with all the affection she'd missed out on because of her mother's death. Shahira's voice shook her from her reverie. She was addressing Ghassan. "No. She will not go back. We do not allow our daughters in this family to be beaten up." She welcomed Layla back into her old room with a wave of her hand.

It had been some time since Layla had been all alone in her childhood room. She used to bring her kids and let them play there, rifling through family photo albums and children's books. She perched on the edge of her old bed. The day's remaining sunlight was seeping through the window. Suddenly, she felt the cold pierce her bones, as if ice water was sliding down her back. She feared being in this room; she felt she was a stranger who'd snuck in. The place was freezing cold and smelled musty like places that have been shut up for a long time. She turned on the lamp on the bedside table. Some of her old toys were in a basket in the corner. Though her own children had broken most of them, Shahira kept them where they were. When Salem arrived late that night to beg Layla to come home, Shahira stopped him from entering the house and slammed the door in his face.

Asmahan arrived in the morning, followed by Walid. They'd waited for Salem to leave and then sneaked over to be with Layla. Their arrival coincided with Nadim's. He started cursing Salem and calling him a beast. Walid listened stone silent. He was angry and confused. He didn't know what to say or do. He was terrified of his father's violence toward his mother, but at the same time this man was his father. When his mother's family cursed his father, it was like they were cursing him as well. Asmahan cried. She didn't want her mother to go back home. She begged Shahira, "Don't let her go home. There's a monster in the house. He might not let me even see her."

Layla stayed at her grandparents' house for more than a week.

Huda visited her at Salem's request. She came with invented excuses and stories about her brother's financial situation. He'd lost all his money and was in bad shape emotionally when what happened, happened. Things like this go on in every home and it's a wife's duty to support her husband no matter what.

Shahira started escorting her out before she'd stood up to leave, saying, "Go back home, goodbye, be well."

Layla hardly slept more than a few hours on those nights at Shahira's house. She was worried about her children. "Don't worry," her grandmother told her, "he won't touch a hair on their heads. He's learned his lesson, you'll see."

One Sunday morning, Shahira waited for her children to all come over for lunch. After they ate, she asked Fayez to bring Salem over. Initially he refused, but then he realized that it might be a good opportunity to intervene and help the couple make peace with each other. His own financial disputes with Salem had not been resolved; perhaps intervening between the couple might help them solve this too. It wasn't easy for Fayez to see Layla. He had to face up to her reality, which he always tried to ignore, especially as he was the one who pushed for their marriage.

When he got to Salem's house, he found Asmahan and Walid in the garden. They rushed over to him, asking for news of Layla. Asmahan whispered to them quietly that Salem had learned his lesson and that it would be better if their mother stayed away for a while. Walid looked at Asmahan, surprised. Fayez called out to Salem, who was inside, "Come on out, let's see how we can solve this problem." Salem stayed quiet, not knowing what to say.

The two of them arrived together at Shahira's house. Salem walked in behind Fayez like a child who didn't know where to put his feet. Shahira didn't welcome them in or respond to their greetings. He sat, staring at the ground, fidgeting, not knowing what to say. Shahira told him that she'd asked her sons to be there as witnesses. "Divorce Layla," she said. "We don't want her to be married to you anymore. Give her an uncontested divorce, or else we'll take you to court."

No one in the family—or even Salem himself—expected to hear this. Salem started spluttering out his apologies, embarrassed again. Layla was in her room trying catch some sleep when Salem arrived, but she could hear what was being said in the living room. She started to wonder what she really wanted—a divorce or just to go back home. What about her children? What would happen to them?

But it seemed Shahira hadn't finished her scolding, which she carried on right there in front of everyone, except Layla, "Listen, cousin. Your mother, God rest her soul, told me everything before she died. I know how your American wife died. I know better than anyone else here. And you know that I know. Despite this, I covered for you; I didn't tell anyone in the family. I gave you the most precious person to me. I thought that maybe we could make things right and you could start a new life here. But you're no good."

"You married me off to a woman who's more like a man. All she does is read novels," Salem retorted, clearing his throat and looking down at his feet. His words came out choppy. "Even so, please can't you cover for me, for what I've done wrong? Forgive me, give me a chance. If not for me, then for our children."

From inside her room, Layla listened as if none of this had to do with her and Salem was speaking about another woman. She got out of bed and gazed into the mirror hanging on the wall. The questions constantly running through her mind started to stress her. How did his first wife die? Would she die the same way? He told everyone that she'd died after falling off a horse. He used to cry telling the story. But Shahira knew otherwise. Why did her grandmother agree to their marriage if she knew things she wasn't telling anyone?

She stood there in front of the mirror, staring back at her own face, into her anxious, fearful eyes. She hardly recognized herself. She tried to think back over her own life, if only for a few moments. But she couldn't. It was as if her past had been forgotten, as if her memories no longer had a place in her life.

Layla went back home for her son's sake. He'd asked her to. She explained this to Rose, who'd encouraged her not to go back, to stay at Shahira's. When Walid visited her the last time, he said, "Come home, and I promise you, if he lays a hand on you, I'll kill him. I promise. He knows this now." Asmahan wasn't happy about her mother's decision. She knew deep down that her father wouldn't change. All that would change was the kind of violence he'd use against her.

That was the last time that Salem beat Layla. No one knew exactly why. Was it because of the family's intervention—leaving home and staying a few days at Shahira's? Was it because of how her son got involved and threatened him? Was it because of what Shahira said to Salem about keeping the secret of how his first wife Barbara died? He quickly settled into a routine of verbal abuse, which made it difficult for others to detect as it left no physical marks on the body. He got even more emotionally violent after Layla's illness. He began mocking her for her absentmindedness and constantly forgetting things. He'd chide her for small mistakes, like adding too much salt while cooking or forgetting she'd turned on the stove. And he started cursing God for his lot in life.

# Disappearance

The Dahli family was growing, and Shahira was aging. Her house was no longer the gathering place for the family on weekends. They all had their own families and lives outside of Ksoura. As the children married and had their own children, new families were added to the family.

Layla began to feel that winter weekends were lonely in Ksoura. Asmahan and Walid had their own lives. Asmahan spent all her time with Ouida. She read her the poetry and observations that she'd written in her notebook. Walid went to Broummana to spend the weekends with Nadim's son Bassem. Layla knew that they were escaping the deathly atmosphere at home, as well as Salem's constant verbal abuse.

Summertime reigned supreme in the hearts of all people from Ksoura. They liked to head out a bit before sunset and walk in the fields just outside town. They'd stroll along for an hour or more and then retrace their path back when the sun began to dip behind the sea in the horizon. When the sun is totally gone, darkness slowly descends on the hills around the city. It transforms into dark shadows out of which they liked to invent characters and sing to them. Those magical moments between light and darkness were permanently imprinted on Asmahan's memory, sharpening her imagination as a writer.

New Year's Day 1962. Emad came to Layla's house that evening and told everyone that her uncle Nadim had been arrested. Security forces had barged into his house the night before and searched the beds, wardrobes, and even the pantry. They threw the children's toys outside. After the SSNP's failed New Year's Eve coup attempt, they'd received a tip that Nadim's house was a weapons storage depot. Searching the house, they found a brown box under the bed that Nadim's daughter had lost months ago. Initially they thought it was a bomb. He was detained for a month. When he was released at the end of January, he didn't speak to anyone about what his imprisonment had been like.

Layla had a second nervous breakdown when she heard this. She was terrified that something horrible might happen to Walid, as he'd begun participating in party-led youth camps during school holidays. He only had two years left in school before university. She wrote to her uncle Kamal in New York, pleading with him to help her send Walid to America. "I beg you, take him today. Let him live with you and go to school there. I'll die if anything happens to him."

Layla started avoiding being alone with Salem. She no longer slept in her own bedroom. She moved to Ashman's room and stayed there until he left. She only left the room if she had to. Her mental health worsened after the coup attempt. She couldn't shake her memories of 1958. Asmahan would come into her room and find her mother talking to herself as if she were speaking to one of them. Layla's happiness was refreshed whenever Rose visited. They'd sit together and she'd tell her about Yusuf. Rose would encourage her to get dressed so they could have a walk together into town. They'd stop by to see Shahira, who'd aged and rarely left home.

Layla prepared for her son Walid to go abroad in the summer of 1962. Once his travel was organized, she took to her bed. Her condition worsened and she no longer wanted to go out at all. Days passed before she even moved. But one day out the blue she got up and announced that she wanted to visit Rose.

After Walid left at the end of the summer of 1962, the family moved to Beirut. This made Asmahan happy. She thought that moving to Beirut might revive Layla's desire to leave the house. But they had only lived in Beirut for a short while when Layla disappeared. It was the spring of 1963.

Even before Layla's disappearance, Salem was afflicted with a sort of depression. The Dahli family had asked him to stop building on their land. He'd lost the election, his family had stopped visiting him, and then he had his financial dispute with Fayez. All this made him feel extremely isolated. His dispute with Fayez was almost like a divorce because it wasn't just between the two of them, but also the two families, even if it was hard to know who belonged to which. Salem received blow after blow. The Dahli family leveled all kinds of accusations against him. They believed that his constant abuse and violent mistreatment of his wife were the main cause of her illness and eventual disappearance.

Salem lost all his savings when Intra Bank crashed in 1966. This was a devastating blow for a man like him, who'd built his dreams on the misery of others. He started drinking heavily when others were still at work or out in the fields. He stayed home, consuming alcohol in place of water and hardly eating during the day. He started selling off plots of land whenever he needed money. He'd gotten used to a certain lifestyle and found it difficult to adapt. His horses began aging as well.

He no longer wanted to leave the house. He began asking friends to come to his place and sleep over on weekends. He was lonely, especially once Asmahan stopped coming to Ksoura every weekend. She'd started saying in the girls' dorms at university after Salem vacated their rented apartment in Beirut. Longer and longer periods of time passed between her visits. Each time, she promised herself she'd never go back home again, despite her longing for Ksoura, her love for her friends, and nostalgia for her old childhood haunts.

Whenever she did visit, she'd spend hours with Shahira, recording her stories and memories. It was heart-wrenching to listen to Shahira talk about Layla; her eyes would well up with tears and she'd have difficulty breathing. She'd take Shahira's hand and walk her out to the garden, which was all but abandoned since she'd stopped tending to it. Asmahan turned on her tape recorder and let Shahira speak naturally. She recorded everything, adding in her own descriptions of her grandmother and the place. Shahira talked about Ajmat too, at times mixing up the two towns—she'd say Ksoura but mean Ajmat. Her tales could get confused, and Asmahan would have to repeat the question. Whenever Asmahan asked her to sing, her eyes would light up and she'd recall songs from her childhood in Ajmat. She'd begin by repeating the opening lyrics of a song several times: "Reem al-Falla, Beauty of Beauties." Asmahan would lend her voice to Shahira's as she tried to remember the rest of the song:

> Delight of lovers, past and present
> If only you and me were alone
> We would enjoy the melodies of the rebaba

She could recall distant memories more easily than recent ones. She told Asmahan about the First World War, and then the Second, as if they'd just started and were still ongoing. "Wars don't end, my dear. Nothing ends, sweetie," she said, sitting in front of the house, warming herself in the spring sunshine exactly as Nayif had done in his final days.

"Nothing ends," Shahira repeated over and over when she spoke to Asmahan months before her death, after the outbreak of the civil wars in Lebanon.

Shahira no longer cared about her jasmine bushes or the other plants still alive near the house. She left the planting around the house to Hajar, the woman who'd come with her husband from the Beqaa to work years ago. She'd settled down in Ksoura, where she'd given birth to her children and was raising them. Shahira didn't like to sit outside much, except when the weather was nice. Most days she wore heavy, warm clothes and kept repeating that the cold was hurting her limbs. She'd sit right in the sun and stretch out her hands, trying to wiggle her fingers now gnarled by chronic arthritis.

She nonetheless repeatedly refused Fayez's offers to come and live with them in Beirut. "I won't leave my home," she told him. "If I'm going to die, I may as well die in my own bed. The clothes I want to be buried in are in my closet. I have all my things here." She never gotten along with Fayez's wife Mufida particularly well. She called her "the Beiruti" when she was mad at her and said she was "a nag and a complainer who causes people to lose their livelihood."

After Layla disappeared, Shahira stayed shut in most of the time. She'd go outside and sit in front of her house for only a few minutes at a time. She'd wait there, imagining that Layla might return for a visit. When she caught a cold, she took to her bed for a whole week. One morning she hobbled outside on her crutch to catch some sunlight. She heard the faraway sounds of workers and machines in the forest. Hajar brought her coffee. She sat alone, sipping it slowly. She didn't usually enjoy drinking coffee alone. Often Anahid, who'd stopped sewing when her eyesight weakened, came over to sit and talk, going home after a short visit.

One day, Shahira stood up and ambled over to the garden entrance. She exited the iron gate and continued out to the forest where she once was able to see the treetops stretching out before her like a green carpet. But no longer. There was just a vast open space that, from a distance, looked just empty. The forest was now surrounded by construction projects.

For a moment, Shahira thought her eyesight was betraying her. She blamed the damned medications that Mona and Asmahan had convinced Hajar to force her to take. But no! It was the same forest that she knew down to the last tree, where pine cones fell to the ground year after year, season after season, harvest after harvest. She'd inhaled the scents of that forest and they were stored deep inside her. Once upon a time, that absence had been filled with the scents of Ajmat. Shahira wondered why this was now just a memory and felt an enormous anxiety pressing down on her.

Yasmine passed away. Then Layla disappeared. And now the forest. Perhaps it would abandon her too. She turned to the garden gate to go back into the house, feeling totally spent. She grabbed the sides of the gate with both hands, no longer able to make out what was in front of her. She saw the world through a thin film. She felt the earth spinning around her like she was a sheaf of wheat blowing in the breeze. And then she collapsed. Hajar found her lying on the ground in front of the house, unconscious. Her body was resting against the gate, her head bowed.

She woke up in the hospital the next morning. Everything around her was white. Bright lights shone in her eyes. She spied Asmahan sitting beside her, her face pale and yellow, holding her hand. Shahira asked about Layla. "Is she okay?" She knew that Layla had disappeared without a word and that it had been a massive shock to Asmahan. But Shahira felt close to her anyway. From the time she disappeared, Layla kept appearing in her dreams, waving to her and then leaving.

Though she was still exhausted, Shahira didn't wish to stay in the hospital more than one day. Majd took her back to Ksoura, after pleading with her to stay with them in Beirut. But to no avail. He told her about his plans to travel to America and complete his studies. He said his parents would be less lonely if she stayed in Beirut with them. But Shahira was stubborn. She wanted to be at home.

Asmahan and Mona came to stay with her in Ksoura for a few days. Mona tried to help her get to the bathroom to wash up. But she refused. She said she could do it alone, despite the doctor's warning that her medications could cause dizziness. She went alone. Worry visible on her face, Mona said, "I'm standing outside the door. If you want anything, please tell me." She wasn't used to seeing her grandmother weak.

Shahira stood naked in the middle of the bathroom. She stared at her body. It looked strange, ancient, unexpectedly not a part of her. With a heavy heart, she played back in her mind so many images from the past. Memories popped up, but she didn't let them all in. She didn't have space in her heart for all of them. Her grief took over and rejected many. She thought about how loss dominated everything, even things she deemed unimportant or that no longer had a place in her life—enjoying a walk in the forest, inhaling the scent of wheat in the spring, listening to wheat sheaves blowing in the breeze, rejoicing at seeing spring swallows building their nests in the cracks of the wall, or waiting and watching their babies emerge from the nest and fly.

She could no longer experience the intimacy she'd neglected—she failed to touch her body, to caress it, to close her eyes and conjure up her desires, even with the man she didn't choose. She could have done this, allowed time for love. She loved life in a different way, but life didn't allow her to express love. Neither to Yasmine, nor to Layla. If she had been able to express her true desires to her daughter, perhaps Yasmine might have held herself together. Or she might have been stronger and fought off death. If she had conveyed the desires she'd denied herself to Layla, her granddaughter might have broken out of her imaginary bubble and changed her reality.

Shahira felt she could no longer stand up. She swallowed her saliva and sat down on a wooden bench they kept in the bathroom. She shook out her hair and then wet it with hot water, scrubbing her head with soap. The hot water mixed with salty tears on her cheeks. It was the first time she'd cried. Her soul wept, every part of her being joined in. She asked herself why she was only crying now that she was nearing the last days of her life on earth.

Fear spread across Lebanon once again—or rather time and time again. The people of Ksoura don't rest, they start over. But they're tired. They're tired of starting over because new beginnings are impossible. There is such a thing as time. Time is real, not an illusion. Only Layla—who disappeared—saw time as an illusion, because she didn't want to see it at all. People deluded themselves, believing that they'd be able to rest. They said that surely this time they'd be able to rest. But then a new civil war started up right away.

# Asmahan 1982

I'll write about myself in the first person. I don't know how to write about myself in the third person, like I wrote about Shahira, Yasmine, and Layla. My writing will thus come full circle. I started sharing stories about my family in a letter I wrote to Ouida. But I'll end here with some longer stories, larger than the dreams of the women in my family. This story won't end, though I wish it would. I'm sick of the past. I'm sick of disappointments, despair, and false hope. I'm also tired of repetition: violence, hope, war, violence again. It's a loop—an endless loop—that we can never escape. I don't want to stop questioning and asking why. Because I'm afraid of dying. I'm afraid to die feeling that I've not yet been born. I was born, though. I was born in 1944, on an ordinary July morning.

I was meant to be born at the end of August, they said. But I was born in July, premature. Shahira claimed that this explained my impatience, bad sense of direction, and lack of spatial awareness. Salem wasn't home when I was born. When they told him I'd arrived in the world, he didn't come. He was out gambling, betting on a new horse. The night before I was born, he'd decided his baby would be named after his next winning horse. It's a good thing that his horse lost that day or else I would've been named Lightning.

They named me Asmahan instead. It's the name my mother wanted. But being named for the singer was perhaps a bad omen, as my namesake died in a tragic car accident only two weeks later. I grew up always hearing the women in my family say that my name was a mistake, and none of this would have happened if Layla had given me another name. I internalized what they said and believed it, until the day my mother disappeared when I was nineteen years old.

Layla's disappearance helped me learn the truth about my birth. I read her diaries and letters and found out about everything. After she was gone, Rose handed all of her papers over to me. Her absence from my life made me rethink everything I'd ever heard, believed, and repeated like a parrot. I wasn't born premature. And even more importantly, I wasn't Salem's daughter. I'd waited years to learn the truth. My mother made many sacrifices for her unfulfilled love. But her disappearance was the greatest sacrifice.

Neither my mother nor I had ever known my grandmother Yasmine. She'd passed down her olive-green eyes and lush brown, honey-hued hair to me through my mother. I cut my hair super short after my mother disappeared.

I spent my whole childhood and most of my teen years in Ksoura. I knew its roads and fields by heart. I loved spring and summer there. I grew up playing with my male cousins and relatives from our big, extended family. When Ouida was away traveling with her family, I was the only girl around. The age difference between me and Uncle Hamed and Aunt Huda's children didn't affect our relationship. They spent summers at our house, which Salem had bought from a family who'd emigrated to America.

They were distant relatives who he'd become friendly with in Chicago. He bought the house from them for the amount they needed to settle there and open a restaurant they called Beirut-Chicago Grill. When his American wife Barbara died, he returned to Lebanon and renovated the house, adding an additional floor with more rooms.

Salem told everyone in town that his wife had died in a horse-back riding accident and that he'd inherited her estate because they had no children and she herself had been an only child. That's all he said. His violence toward my mother, however, made me start to doubt the credibility of his American story.

I understood early in life that happiness exists only outside the home, not inside it. I believed this to be the nature of families. A father is almost always absent, and he's violent when he's there. I believed that violence was triggered by coming home. If you want to be happy and live a peaceful life—you need to stay out of the house. Though Salem was moody and abused my mother, I felt that I had everything I needed to amuse myself and pass the time. This is also because I had Ouida. I had my extended family too, especially Hamed's children, who spent their holidays at our house. When I was younger, I blamed the tension at home on my mother. I thought she'd find happiness and peace if she went out more, like my father did.

But there could never be total happiness in Ksoura—a bit of happiness would always be tainted by some kind of news or event related to politics in Lebanon. I felt this chasm in my life intensely. I would live with it for days at a time, listening to grown-up conversations between Grandma Shahira and her brothers.

Over the years, I started to understand my mother's isolation as her way of shielding herself from Salem's violence. I had to accept what was happening around me. Either that or go mad.

Later, I found a balanced way to feel better. I began asserting that total happiness is an illusion—there's no such thing as happiness without something missing.

My mother often told me that she'd wanted to go abroad after she finished school. She'd planned to follow Miss Helen to the UK, where she'd returned after gifting my mom much of her personal library. She moved all those books with her when she got married to my father. She brought her dog Baroud and her cat Noosa too. That's all she took from Shahira's house.

Her books were scattered all over our house like talismans when I was growing up. They lined every shelf and were piled up in every corner of every room. She carried them around like children. In my earliest memories, I can't separate my mother from her books. All the books in the house were hers. Newspapers, horse racing bulletins, and a few pamphlets about the Dahesh movement that Fayez had given to Salem. I knew he never read them, but he held on to them nonetheless.

My mother would pick out her favorite poems from Walt Whitman's *Leaves of Grass* and then read and reread them out loud while sitting next to me on my bed. I'd be hoping she'd tell me the tales of Sleeping Beauty or Shater Hasan the Hero. But she'd forget about those stories and lose herself in the poetry as she recited it. I didn't understand anything she was saying, but I loved listening to her voice. She incanted these poems as if humming a lullaby. Though I longed for her to tell me a story, I was content just to have her there. Even at such a young age, I understood that I should let her have this little bit of joy.

I'd cuddle up next to her, hug her close, nuzzle my face in her neck, and inhale her fragrant skin. I'd stay silent, mesmerized by the rhythm of her heartbeat and her deep, warm voice. I was so contented in those moments; I needed nothing more. They were everything to me. I could feel the warmth of her body and see the sparkle in her eyes as she recited poetry. Being so close to her satisfied me. I cherished those times together. They allowed me to enjoy touching her skin, feeling her breath on me. Whenever I think of her, I still can conjure up her fragrant scent.

My mother was happy so rarely, usually only with her books in her bedroom. Her eyes would sparkle and her voice would soften as she read. That's when I knew I had to be silent. I had to allow her voice and my silence to merge and flow through the room like a gentle stream. I derived my happiness from my mother's, and I learned early on to be quiet in her presence. I may have been the only one who saw this side of my mother. I saw her as more of a woman than a mother when she was in touch with her true soul—immersed in *Anna Karenina, The Hunchback of Notre Dame*, or *Gone with the Wind.*

She read *Gone with the Wind* many times. Whenever she got to the part where Scarlett O'Hara visits Rhett Butler in prison, she'd sigh deeply, because that's when Rhett realizes Scarlett is lying to him. Her calloused hands alerted him that she was visiting him not because she was in love but because she was in dire straits and needed money. My mother would pause and daydream for a bit, then put the novel to one side and walk over to the gramophone that my father had brought back from America. She'd turn it on and play a record by Asmahan. My mother adored the late singer so much she'd named me after her. Asmahan's voice would fill the room:

> I intended to mask my suffering,
> conceal my grief and tears
> and to tell of my sorrow and my love
> only to myself, and to the shadow of my beloved

Her face would soften and relax as she whispered the words to the song along with Asmahan.

My mother surely identified with the women in the novels she read. She repeated the first line of Tolstoy's *Anna Karenina* over and over again: "Happy families are all alike, every unhappy family is unhappy in its own way." She couldn't live the love she carried in her heart. Not only love for the man she dreamed of, but she could never fully express her love for me—her own daughter—or for my brother either.

Did being unable to express or fight for love wear her out? Maybe I'm putting too much weight on the reasons for her departure, and it was simply too much for her to bear. Or perhaps she just wanted to disappear and reinvent herself in a place of her own choosing. Maybe she wanted to declare that mothers deserve lives free of violence.

No one knows how my mother ended her life. No. Actually I'm not even sure if my mother is dead.

To this day, we don't know if she died or if she wanted to flee the life imposed upon her, leave behind the burden of being a wife and mother. Perhaps she didn't want to be the wife of that beast of a man who hated himself for it. Perhaps she didn't want to be a mother at all.

No one ever asked her what she wanted to be. No one listened when she spoke about her dream of traveling and discovering the world. They married her off to a man her father's age before she'd even turned seventeen. They chose him because he was distantly related to her grandmother Shahira and knew her maternal uncles. Her father was abroad and had no say. They just married her off to this man who later became my father. It took me a long time to forgive my mother. And to fully understand that she was as tormented as I was by her love for me—that I never felt.

When she looked at my brother, her eyes danced. She picked him up and kissed him and sat him on her lap. I'd stand near the two of them and wish she'd pull me up there beside him. I'd speak to her, but she wouldn't reply—it was as if she didn't see or hear me. Or maybe she answered in a voice so soft and helpless it was inaudible. You would have thought my brother was her only child and she'd simply found me on the doorstep in a basket.

Though her eyes danced when she looked at my brother, she still rarely exchanged more than a few words with him. She'd shower him with scattered kind and loving words and then stop. Motherhood exhausted her. She'd let him run off out to play in the back garden and head back to her bedroom, where her books and notebooks were strewn all over her desk waiting for her.

I'd follow her in, open my schoolbag, and start studying. I was convinced that this might bring us closer—she'd see the difference between me and my brother. He just liked to play and only did his schoolwork after a great deal of nagging.

Motherhood for her was shrouded in silence. Was this another reason she felt so alone? That's what I ask myself today. Did that one day in the summer of 1958 make her lose her mind? My brother Walid had started going to political meetings with my mother's uncle Nadim. He'd also started training with the scouts and going on camping trips organized by the SSNP. That day, someone came to our house to inform my mother that my brother had suffered a chest wound. A passerby had found him lying on the ground in the middle of a nearby town, covered in blood. It was the first time I saw my mother lose her cool and display a full range of emotions. She started shouting, screaming my brother's name, slapping her face, and banging her head against the wall. Blood oozed from her forehead as she collapsed to the ground, unconscious.

In the end, it wasn't my brother who'd been injured but a different boy from another town. He was taken in for treatment and he didn't die. They reassured her that my brother was fine, but my mother didn't believe them. She was delirious all night long. She was in another world, and the doctor eventually decided to admit her to the Dayr al-Salib hospital. It was the first time she'd stepped foot in a hospital, and she stayed a few nights. Being in Dayr al-Salib didn't completely cure her. She came back medicated, with lots of pills. She'd become even more fragile and totally silent. When she disappeared, she was thirty-seven years old. And she was beautiful.

~

After the attempted SSNP coup on New Year's Eve 1961, my mother had another nervous breakdown, similar to her first one three years before. Though she was still unwell in the new year, she managed to correspond with my uncle Kamal. She wrote him letters asking for his help, imploring him to help my brother Walid travel to America. She did this without Salem knowing, as he'd never liked Kamal. Kamal had a similarly bad opinion of Salem and his marriage to my mother. In her letters, she begged him to extract Walid from the tense political atmosphere in Lebanon. It was like she was organizing her own eventual disappearance by first easing her anxiety about Walid. That's how my brother went to the States. He lived at Kamal's place while finishing his last two years of school, and then enrolled in medical school. My brother wasn't in Lebanon when my mother disappeared. In her last letter to him, she wrote that they would meet again. But she didn't say when.

I do also remember that Salem took her back to Dayr Salib for several short stays that year. When she returned home afterward, she was usually sad and aggressive when she spoke. She'd start off with an insult, interspersed with a curse or two. She'd begin with her lost love, Yusuf, who'd gone to Moscow and never replied to her letters. She'd gotten his address from his friend Talal. She kept writing letters, asking Rose to post them. Rose always kept her secrets. But Rose herself got angry at his lack of response so she eventually stopped mailing them. She collected them all in a cardboard box atop her wardrobe. The last time I visited Rose, she passed my mother's letters on to me. In one, I found a picture of myself on my first birthday that she intended to send to Yusuf—my father, who I hate and never ever want to see.

My mother's health deteriorated after my brother left. She lost her appetite. She suffered from nervous fits from time to time, though she regularly went to the clinic to see Dr. Haddad, newly arrived from the States. Her cousin Mona took her to her appointments at the AUH, and she came back sad and confused. After taking her pills, she'd quickly calm down and sleep deeply. Despite this, she carried on cursing my father in a low whisper. She also cursed her uncle Fayez and the whole family. It wasn't in fact so much cursing as making illogical and incomprehensible accusations. Like she'd say that Fayez had lowered her into a deep well and wouldn't help her get out. Or that her uncle Nadim could no longer see her because politics had gnawed away at his eyes. She said that Salem was missing in a sky that she could see underground.

Salem would never tell her where he was going. When he came home, he'd say that he'd been at the construction site on new land he'd bought to rezone, turning agricultural land into a concrete jungle, on the advice of friends who'd immigrated. Or he might justify his absence by saying that he was with his friends watching the horses. His relationships with other women were a part of his life that remained shrouded in mystery. He never spoke of this with Fayez, who had heard about his many extra-marital affairs from friends but never broached the topic, even though

Salem was married to his niece. He should have shown greater concern because of their familial relationship. But Fayez believed that a man had the right to amuse himself however he wanted, so long as he provided for his family and didn't leave them in need. Thus, despite everything that Salem did to my mother, including his worryingly long absences from home, Fayez remained Salem's closest friend and staunchest defender—until they parted ways over a fight about money. The only people spared Layla's anger were me and my younger brother Walid.

~

We were visiting my grandma Shahira in Ksoura the day my mother disappeared. A few months earlier, we'd moved to Beirut so that I could get ready for university. We were staying in a small apartment on Caracas Road just near the incline. It was the same place that Salem used to rent whenever he was Beirut and away for days at a time. I didn't understand back then why he'd decided to move the whole family into this little apartment. Perhaps it was because of how bad his relationship with the Dahli family had gotten. Or maybe it was to be closer to his friends, who were always the reason he was away from us in the first place. But he justified his decision by saying that I was going to university, and it would be better for the family to live where I was studying. Despite everything, I was happy with this move. I thought that my mom going back to Beirut might bring joy back to her heart. None of the Dahlis were left in Ksoura except my mother's youngest uncle Tawfiq, who had transformed practically the whole top floor of the house into an art studio for him to paint in.

On the day my mother disappeared, we'd come to Ksoura to see Grandma Shahira. After having fallen in the fields, she had to rest for weeks and could no longer walk easily. She started using a cane to help get around. It was true that she'd really aged, but she didn't need much help from her children. She lived with Tawfiq and refused Fayez's invitation to move into his house. Winter was over and spring had begun to reveal everything that nature had been hiding. But in the early evening, the weather changed, so Hajar lit the stoves in the living room and Shahira's bedroom.

My grandfather Ghassan was at Shahira's house. So was one of my two paternal aunts who lived in the mountain house with my parents before she married. My mother didn't come with us to Ksoura that day. She said that she was going to see a film with her cousin Mona and that Fayez would drive them up to Ksoura later that night.

Tuesday, April 3, 1963. I will never forget that evening. My mother insisted on staying in Beirut. Fayez suggested that he could drive them to Ksoura after his meeting with the other Dahesh followers. Mona would pass by to pick up my mom, then they'd walk from Raouche to Sahat al-Burj in downtown Beirut. They planned to wait for Fayez in a café near the cinema after the film finished. Fayez's meeting was at Dahesh's house, which wasn't far from the Serail downtown.

The weather started to change that evening, and the temperature dropped quickly. No one expected the cold weather to return on that spring evening, no one foresaw that snow would blanket Beirut overnight. Fayez arrived a little bit late and found neither of them in the café. He went into the cinema and the person at the ticket window informed him that the film had ended more than a half hour before. The next screening was about to start. He looked all around and couldn't find them anywhere. The streets had begun to empty.

Out of breath, Mona finally appeared. Her features were full of worry, fear visible in her eyes. She told her father that she'd passed by Layla's to pick her up as planned and that they'd gotten to Sahat al-Burj early. They had to wait for the movie to start. Layla asked Mona to wait for her while she popped into the pharmacy to pick up some medicine. She came out a few minutes later holding a little paper bag. Mona didn't know which medicine she'd gotten. She wondered if it might be what Dr. Haddad had prescribed, but she wasn't sure. They walked together toward al-Lazariah, window shopping along the way.

Layla initially stayed silent when Mona asked her which of the two films showing she wanted to watch—an Indian movie or Sabah's *The Rebel*. She proposed Sabah's film because of the title, saying, "Let's see what it's about." They got to the Rivoli Cinema. Layla stopped to look at the film posters, walking right up close and reading what was written on them while Mona bought the tickets. They went in and sat down in the dark theater. Not long before the end of the film, Layla whispered that she had to use the restroom.

Mona stayed watching the film and didn't notice that Layla hadn't returned. But the film ended, and she still hadn't come back. The lights came on, and Mona stayed seated as everyone started to leave. The room emptied and Mona still waited for Layla to return. A worker came in to clean up before the next showing and asked her why she was still sitting there. He told her that he'd just cleaned the restroom—no one was there.

Mona figured that maybe Layla was waiting for her outside. She walked out and didn't find her there either. She looked everywhere she could think of, calling her name out loud. She went in the shop next door to the theater—maybe she stopped inside to buy something. Then she carried on looking for her outside. The big public square was starting to empty of people and cars, and she called out her name again, as loudly as she could.

"Might she have gotten into a taxi and headed back to Ksoura by herself?" Fayez asked Mona. "No, she didn't want to," Mona sobbed in reply, adding that Layla had wanted to stay in Beirut and not go to Ksoura at all. She'd learned that Salem would be up in the mountains that evening. "She told me that she hates herself and the people around her when she's with Salem. She says that when they're home alone, he turns into a monster."

I remember what my mother told me the day she came back from Dr. Haddad's clinic. Before the appointment, Salem had verbally abused her in an unbelievable way. She said, "I wish I were a grain of salt and could dissolve in a glass of water, so no one could see me." My mother eventually did dissolve and I wept.

Layla disappeared before nightfall on that snowy day. I was in my grandmother's room, studying to prepare for my AUB entrance examination. The next day was a school holiday, May Day. I remember that my grandmother had taken the painkillers for her swollen leg and was fast asleep when Uncle Fayez and his daughter, Auntie Mona, told me that my mother had gone missing. At first, I wasn't alarmed. I started thinking of plausible reasons for her absence, a disappearance that would surely end soon. I thought that she might have gone to the bus station and gotten on a bus for Damascus intending to get off at Ksoura. Maybe she fell asleep, missed the Ksoura stop, and ended up all the way in Damascus instead.

But Fayez replied that there were no buses that evening. I said that maybe she hadn't found Mona and started searching for a taxi to take her home. I also thought that this could perhaps be one of her short fits. It would soon pass. She'd regain her balance and come back to us. I was already sort of used to her not being there. Sometimes I'd search for her at home and not find her, then she'd come out of a room and be right in front of me. Her silence was like a cloak of invisibility. Perhaps this was just another version of the same thing. Of course, my father was also missing, as usual. He'd be gone for days and then come back with excuses—one of his horses was sick in the Beqaa or he was visiting one of his friends who he hadn't seen since he'd come back to Lebanon.

Why did my mother decide to disappear? I ask this, but I pretty much know the answer. Repeating the question has become an exercise in forgiveness and dealing with loss. I always thought that what drove her to disappear was a deep sadness that she could no longer bear alone. My mother was lonely. Her marriage to the man they call my father gave her no comfort or ease. She was all alone in a new family, none of whom ever loved her—Salem didn't love her, nor did his sisters or brother. His brother in fact spent his life jealous of my mother's uncles, especially Fayez, whom Salem bought off by paying his debts.

I can hardly begin to explain the huge change in Salem after my mother's disappearance. I can't deny that for about two years, one of his projects after the other collapsed. Almost everything that he'd ever dreamed of fell apart. His relationship with the Dahli family deteriorated, and he lost all his money. On top of this, he also suffered a stroke, which left him paralyzed for a time. He aged quickly after that. The stroke didn't kill him, but his left leg remained partially paralyzed. He started moving again slowly, always relying on a crutch. From that time onward, he needed someone to look after him at home.

He used to repeat that life is just a game of chance—you often lose your bets. He insisted that my mother's disappearance wasn't intentional; something had happened to her by chance. When they'd moved to Beirut, she liked to walk on the corniche alongside the rock at Raouche. Perhaps that evening, she went for a walk and the snowstorm took her by surprise. Maybe she was swept out to sea. He'd say this, sigh, his mind would drift off, and he'd fall asleep in his chair in front of the house.

When Layla disappeared, Salem returned to Ksoura, leaving the Beirut apartment empty. He only visited the city occasionally —for a doctor's appointment or the like. In that small town, it was easy for him to make up stories and spread the rumor that my mother had died. For example, he claimed that women's clothes were found washed up on the store and that they were presumed to be hers. Everyone who visited him listened to the stories and nodded their heads, as if they agreed with what he was saying. Their feigned assent, however, was nothing more than silent resentment that the people of Ksoura kept suppressed.

He organized the funeral ceremony alone and received condolence visits alone. Walid was already in the States by then. Neither he nor I believed his story about her clothes being found. We didn't want to believe it.

It occurred to me that Salem didn't love anyone. His life was mainly filled with gambling, horse racing, and women for entertainment. He didn't love my mom the way she wanted him to love her. He saw her as the mother of his children—Walid and me. And like me, he was unaware of the fact that he wasn't actually my father. When I found out, I didn't care. If he found out the truth now after my mother's disappearance, I don't know if he would care either. Especially with her no longer there to take revenge on.

Besides, he'd aged a lot and was too old to take revenge.

~

Fortunately, or unfortunately, Salem didn't live to see what happened to his horse in the summer of 1982. He died before his horse did. I risked my life, as well as my daughter's, crossing the horseracing track to reach the other side of the city. I saw the horse there, alone and forgotten. Or perhaps no one could get to her after the month-long continuous Israeli bombardment of Beirut. She looked like those men who give up hope after fighting as hard as they could.

I crossed the city square to get to East Beirut and take a taxi to the Port in Jounieh. I walked across the whole empty square. The horses were groaning, trembling from fear, and then surrendering, falling to the ground unable to get back up. This is the last image in my mind from Lebanon. I can still picture that horse, lying on the racetrack, staring up at me. I can see that horse's eyelids fluttering when I close my own eyes. The horse was exhausted and let out a human-sounding moan. I don't know how long it had been out there lying in the sun, while people were suffering the brunt of the Israeli violence being meted out upon Beirut by land, sea, and air.

We got out and we survived. But what does surviving mean? What survival? I drift off and I can't sleep properly. I still miss my mother. This is a loss that didn't just start with her leaving. From the moment I was aware of this world, it was impossible to feel she was a mother. When she disappeared, I started noticing that we'd never done much together. There were many things I would have liked to have done with her—going shopping to buy nice clothes, like a dress or a skirt for Eid. Normal mother-daughter things. When we were young, my aunt Huda bought my brother and me clothes for the holidays.

Sometimes I thought that it was a good thing my mother disappeared before the civil war, before my grandma died, before my only friend Rose was devastated by her son Nour, who was the light of her life, like his name. C'est la vie. War became a part of our life. Is it possible to imagine life in Lebanon without violence, disappearance, and loss?

After we got to New York, I found the handful of soil I'd brought from the pot where my mother had planted her gardenia seedlings. It had turned to ash. The soil was now as light as dust and its color had changed. Does loss transform soil's complexion in the same way that people's complexions change? No, I'm not trying to write poetry; this is our reality. I saw soil turn to ash the color of the Beirut sky on Christmas Eve 1981. There were no Christmas bells that December, the sounds of bombs and explosions filled the sky instead. Civil wars and local battles erupted like volcanos and then calmed down only to blow up once again. I didn't know that would be my last Christmas in Beirut.

I try to imagine what Ouida would have said if I'd told her the story of the soil face-to-face. She'd have smiled, sarcastically shaking her head, and said, "Enough with all the drama, Asmahan! You have to just bury it all, along with the past, and cover it with fresh soil." She'd conclude decisively, "You're in New York now. You're going to start a new life with Lama!"

~

I truly loved Ouida. She was my childhood best friend. Our friendship was a lot like Layla and Rose's. The first thing I loved about her was her name. In Arabic the sounds were strange, they felt incomplete and unformed, but all the vowels came together to create an entirely feminine name.

Ouida's only a few months older than me. Anyone who saw us together though would have presumed that she'd experienced much more of life than I had. I was amazed at many stories she told me, things that she'd done at school with older boys. She told me about secret messages flying back and forth between them, furtive kisses exchanged in the corners of the playground. I wondered how this was possible. Even though we were in the same class at the same school, I didn't really know. Ouida was the school's keeper of secrets and held the keys to the school's underground life. Stories of love and betrayal, who cried, who was expelled from school and why, and even more important, the secrets of the boys and girls who came from other Arab countries and attended the school as boarders. Those people had the strangest stories of all.

There were many days when we slept in the same room in the same bed. We spent time together on our holidays and a special complicity developed between us. When she got love letters from Naaman—the tall, blond boy in his final year of school—I was indescribably jealous. It wasn't a girl's jealousy of another girl; I felt left out. Every morning, Ouida would find a love letter from Naaman propped up on her desk in the classroom, full of colorful words, hearts, and poems. I found him thick and unbearable and wished that he would get sick and disappear so I'd never have to see him again. But every morning when I got to school, I saw him there, waiting for Ouida.

One spring morning Ouida and I walked together to the fields silently. When we got there, we started picking green almonds and eating them with salt. I found myself blurting out, "I wish he'd just die!" Ouida laughed. She didn't need to ask; she knew who I meant. She climbed a nearby acidinia tree, saying that her love for him would fade away as quickly as almond blossoms, which bloom only for a short time, then wither and die.

One Friday afternoon, Naaman left school early with the excuse that he was sick. When class ended, Ouida took my hand and said, "Come with me!" I asked, "Where are we going?" and she replied, "Just come on." We walked to the main road where I saw Naaman parking a red Mini Cooper on the sidewalk, waiting for us. We crossed the street, and Ouida told me to get into the backseat. She sat next to Naaman and kissed him furtively, spinning her head around to check that no one had noticed. I stood there hesitating but then got in, because Ouida insisted. I found a small young man already sitting in the back seat. "This is my friend Grigor," Naaman said by way of introduction.

Ouida was relaxed. She laughed and sang, waving a brightly colored silk scarf out the window as Naaman drove away. I didn't know how to act. This was the first time I'd been in a car with a boy I didn't know. I felt confused and upset. Ouida hugged Naaman. They whispered incomprehensible words to each other and giggled together for a long time. Ouida looked back to where I was sitting silently next to Grigor, who also seemed confused and didn't know where to put his hands. Flirtatious and full of confidence, she told us, "Go on, have fun, life is short."

At my tender age, it wasn't easy for me to hear that "Life is short" or that "Love is as timeless as an almond blossom." These expressions meant little to me; they came from a life I'd not experienced. I grew up with a mother who lived her life inside the pages of novels, their characters keeping her company; one grandmother I never knew; and another who was everyone's grandma and had devoted her entire life to the family's welfare. Even the house she lived in her whole life was referred to as Shahira's house rather than Nayif's house!

What I enjoyed doing was spending time with Ouida in the pool at her place. Or writing alone in my room. Or reading a book. I also liked taking walks around Ksoura on the weekends with Imad and Saleh; sometimes Walid and Nour would join us too.

My life felt impoverished compared to Ouida's. She was precocious in so many things—she had modern clothes and haircuts; she wore high heels before any of the other girls. She brought a colorful portable radio with her on school trips, dancing to its tunes on the bus. She ate strange canned food that I'd never seen before even though we grew up in the same town. The only area where I felt superior to Ouida was school. If she hadn't paid attention in class, she used me to help her with her homework and exams. She asked me, "Why should we both waste our time? You study, so you can help me on the test. I'll tell you everything I did at my auntie's house in Beirut, and you can write about it in your stories."

Ouida used to visit her auntie on the weekends, coming back every Sunday evening. She told me about movies she'd watched at the cinema and the boy who lived in the apartment across the hall. He bought her ice cream, took her to Horsh Beirut, and asked her for a photograph of herself. Though she stayed in Ksoura in the summertime, she traveled all around Lebanon with her family. She'd come back and describe the beaches in the North and in Byblos. Another time she told me about their day trip to Baalbak.

At that time, I hadn't left Ksoura all summer except to go to the seaside, which was less than ten kilometers from our town. Our families had very different ideas about vacations and entertainment. My friend was living a full life, lacking nothing but the boredom that I felt during summer holidays with my silent mother, missing brother, and cousins. When they came though, I could hardly contain my emotions! We started big projects; we'd go down to the seaside or we'd make a campfire and stay up late near the olive press. They still made olive oil there, though they'd lost some of their clients with the construction of big, new, faster automated oil presses. I remember the nights that Ouida and I spent in the attic of the house in Ksoura. I'd read to her, and she'd interrupt, giggling, "No . . . no . . . what are you even saying?" She'd comment wryly that no one but us should ever read what I was writing.

Two events in our lives marked a crossroads for us. The first was my mother's disappearance on the night of the April 30, 1963. The second was her brother Nour's suicide, which happened five years after my mother disappeared.

We parted ways when we went to university. I moved to Beirut, and she won a scholarship to study in Montreal. We spoke a lot about the future and our plans, what we'd do together after graduation. We stayed in close contact for the first few months, and then our relationship started to alternate between periods of connection and disconnection. Time apart led to gaps in the relationship. Then we stopped hearing from each other. Before her first trip, we stayed up all night planning a big project. We were going to open a bookshop/cultural center/café in Beirut, focused on children's literature. This was in fact my dream project. Ouida assented to it without much enthusiasm. On the way to the airport to drop her off, we discussed the project, her studies in Montreal, and our eventual return.

The last time Ouida came to Beirut was on the eve of a war that would drag on for years. We didn't know when it would end. I'd started working at a news agency and moved into an apartment near the museum with Mazen. One night, we all stayed up late at our place with our group of friends. Ouida was smoking a lot of hash, like the others. After dinner, everyone left and only Ouida was left with Mazen and me. She smoked heavily, as if in a race against time. She spoke a lot about her desire to return to Lebanon, how she was unable to adapt to life in Montreal, and how hard it was to wake up every morning and go to work. She also spoke about how lonely she felt there and her difficulty in making real friends.

She seemed like a different woman, so far removed from that girl who loved life, laughed, and told crazy stories. She started speaking in numbers and calculations. After doing one such simple calculation, she reckoned that it would be better to sleep at her auntie's house that was so far away she had to take a taxi to get there, rather than her other aunt's house that was closer. Ouida had a key to this closer apartment, right behind the museum, a few meters from where I was staying. This old house belonged to an aunt who lived in Saudi Arabia; her husband had inherited it from his family. Ouida told us that she was scared to sleep there because her aunt believed in spirits and expelling negative energy from the body. Ouida's aunt had confided in her that her husband's paternal grandmother had accidentally killed a child a very long time ago and that when she—the aunt—was in bed, she could hear noises she believed to be the soul of the murdered boy calling out for revenge on the person who killed him, who herself had died long before. Ouida's fabulous stories had fascinated me since we were schoolgirls. Whenever I would read her what I had written, Ouida would add strange and unimaginable details.

That night, I couldn't understand what she was saying. I felt like she was making things up or that she was delirious from the amount of alcohol and hashish she'd consumed.

As soon as she finished telling the story about her aunt, she walked over to Mazen—hash-filled joint in hand—and suggested that they go into the bedroom together. She said that she needed to have sex to fall asleep. Though shocked, I didn't react. Mazen just stared at me, unsure of what to say or do. A sudden silence descended on the three of us. Ouida looked at me as if this silence had jolted her into realizing what she'd just said. "Why aren't you talking? Say something!" she ordered me and fell silent again. Then she completed her thought. "Nothing we do means anything, except the emptiness that consumes us all. And we shouldn't let it. What I asked Mazen to do is only about that empty feeling.

Believe me, it's nothing else."

The joint she was holding in her fingers was burnt down to the end. She stretched out on the sofa where she'd been sitting and dozed off, snoring softly. Mazen looked at me, shaking his head, and said in a whisper, "She's a crazy one . . . totally mad. For sure, your friend is crazy."

What happened that night led to another rift between me and Ouida.

I wrote to her again when I heard the shocking news about her brother's suicide. Nour could no longer live a life torn between a mother who feared even a mere breeze might harm him and a father who taunted him about his masculinity. He spent his childhood wearing girls' dresses and playing with his sister's dolls, on the advice of a sheikh. When he entered puberty, it was difficult for him to just switch from femininity to masculinity. He had to learn to wear boy's clothes, play like a boy, and act like other boys do around girls.

At his father's insistence, he applied to the military academy to do an officer's course. He was rejected twice. His peculiar childhood remained stuck in the minds of everyone who knew him. People compared everything he did to his feminine behavior before puberty. He was forced to become tough and hyper-masculine so that people would forget how he was before. But in Ksoura no one really forgets. People's gossip reached the corridors of the military academy. When he was rejected for the second time, Halim lost his temper and said things that were beyond Nour's capacity to bear. At that moment, his father laid the burden of the entire family's history on his son, making him responsible—both for their failure to produce a male heir and for failing to raise him like every other boy in town. He told his son, "Of course they won't accept you. At least try to act like a man at home, so people start to believe you are one."

After this fight with his father, Nour went into the bedroom, picked up a gun, put it in his mouth, and pulled the trigger. It only took a few seconds. His death was the unbearable price the entire family paid to preserve their narrow-minded town's image of masculinity.

Ouida and I reconnected over this, but only for a bit. At the time, I wrote to her, saying, "My mother's disappearance and Nour's suicide both left holes as big as craters in our relationship. These wounds remind us of the pain of loss every day."

~

In the final years I spent in Lebanon before I left, my soul was numb. I needed to pour my heart out to Ouida about everything I was going through. Our lack of regular communication made me wither away. Each time we were cut off, I felt like a part of my soul died. Time passed and I didn't buy a new notebook. I wrote on scraps of paper I found here and there—edges of old newspapers, discarded envelopes that recently held letters, at times even arriving empty or with torn edges. They were like incantations whose impact and influence on my world I could hardly believe. Without Ouida, there was no one to read my writing to. Everything changed in Beirut and we got used to the changes. We got used to the insatiable beast that gnawed away at our souls.

Every time I met Ouida, I saw she'd changed too. She would come and go. Each time, I found the things that had once bound us together had become increasingly fragile. That last night at my house in Beirut with her shattered my heart. She was a different person. I had to get to know her all over again. She never stopped speaking once that whole evening. She told many stories of her reckless adventures. I wasn't sure if all these things had really happened or if she was speaking in some kind of nocturnal delirium.

I asked her to lower her voice because the family next-door weren't known for their kindness and understanding. But she didn't listen. I told myself it was fine—I'd just wait for her to stop talking. Perhaps she's really upset and needs to vent, so it's better to listen to her. We'll just forget everything in the morning: words spoken at night can be wiped away by the light of day.

But I had a lesson still to learn, after she'd finished smoking the hash she'd brought and drinking all the wine we had in the house. It was simply one more in a long line of lessons she'd delivered to me on many different occasions. I knew that she was no longer the same person and that we no longer shared the same hopes and dreams. I don't know how I knew, but I knew. And I was still attached to our shared hopes and dreams. I was waiting for her to come back so that we could start on our project: a café with a lending library in it, open to everyone. It would have lots of children's books, and we'd make sweets at home for the children to enjoy while they sat and read. I was waiting for Ouida to come back from Montreal so we could make it happen.

I wonder if she remembers when we decided we wouldn't leave Lebanon. We said we'd stay and make our dreams come true together. But she decided to remain in Canada, and she pursued our project over there alone—without telling me first or even sending me a picture to let me know she was thinking about me. Canada became her country. I was left behind in Lebanon, in the morass of war after war.

Though I started working as a journalist, I never let go of the dream of the café-library, and the all-natural homemade sweets we planned to make with dried fruit instead of processed sugar. We'd spoken about this dream every time we'd met for many years. That night at my house when she stood in the middle of the living room like a fool, waiting for Mazen to go to bed with her, I could finally grasp how much we'd grown apart, how she was living in a totally different world.

~

I'd met Mazen after I graduated in 1969, during a short period when I was working at the university. We were introuced at a student meeting in Beirut. At the time, Mazen was a student activist in his last year of an engineering degree. The city was at the boiling point. Lebanon was on the verge of political and security threats that would last for a long time: student demonstrations, clashes between the army and protesters, work stoppages, the Palestinian armed movement entering Lebanon and gaining legitimacy with the Cairo Agreement, constant industrial actions—labor strikes and student strikes. The war was gearing up to insert itself into our lives, our daily routines, and our dreams, which were soon to turn into nightmares.

We moved in together just before our wedding in 1973. We got married in Lebanon and didn't travel to register a civil marriage as we'd originally planned. We had a simple ceremony presided over by a sheikh who was a relative of Mazen's and could sign the marriage contract. We laughed when the sheikh asked us about the details of the dower payments—the first one, the muqaddam, and the deferred one, the mu'akhar. What did I want? Mazen and I had never even thought about such things. Putting an abrupt end to any discussion, I said, "Nothing for the muqaddam and one pound for the mu'akhar." Mazen agreed.

That's how we signed a marriage contract that was more of a joke than a reality to Mazen and me. We dreamed of changing the world! How could an outdated, traditional custom like a marriage contract be of any importance to us?

Marriage was the last thing I'd ever wanted. But sometimes

things seem to happen on their own, as if the paths that life open up lead us to predetermined destinies.

My joy at becoming a mother was perhaps the most important thing that had ever happened to me. But the births of Lama and Karim came at time when they couldn't bring me pure joy. The Ain El Remmaneh bus incident happened when I was in the delivery room in the spring of 1975. That's when the war started. It wasn't easy caring for twin babies, especially as I'd recently started working at a western news agency and rarely got home before seven in the evening. Mona used to come over at the beginning, and then Imm Zeyad started working at our place to help me with housework and babysitting. At that time, Mazen was launching his career as an independent architect.

Mazen went to the Emirates to find work because of the war. It was extremely difficult for him at first, and we were able to keep our love alive through phone calls and letters. He came back twice a year. As he started getting more work, he had to stay away for longer periods. Eventually, he only came back to visit us during spring break.

Mazen wasn't really a part of our daily life, and I got used to that. At first, I found it exhausting. I'd wait for him to come to celebrate the twins' birthday.

~

It was the children's fifth birthday. We'd agreed that he'd spend two weeks with us as a family. I took time off from work as well, so we'd all feel freer. It was springtime, and I'd been dreaming of spending time together. He called me one day before he was meant to arrive to tell me that he couldn't come—it would be better to postpone celebrating the children's birthday. I was surprised by his decision since it was also Ramadan, and I knew it was difficult for him to find work at that time of the year. I went back to work after a few days, reassuring myself that I'd take another vacation when Mazen came.

Coincidence can sometimes destroy one life and prop up another. A colleague of mine who worked at the agency as a photographer ran into him by chance. My colleague was on a week's holiday with his family in Cyprus. He saw Mazen at a beach resort in Limassol. He was sitting with a woman next to the pool, playing with a little boy who was with them.

This colleague of mine told me about this several days after I'd been back at work. He said it spontaneously, assuming that I'd been in Cyprus with my husband. I didn't want to speak to my colleague any longer than I had to, so I didn't ask him anything else.

When Mazen eventually came, I confronted him with what my colleague had told me. He didn't deny it. He'd started a relationship with a woman whose husband had died and who had a young child. He said in the driest possible way, as if punishing me. He reminded me that he'd asked me to quit my job and join him in the Emirates with the twins. But I'd refused. He couldn't live all alone over there; he needed a woman with him. He then added that though he'd married her, it was only a marriage on paper—so that they'd be allowed to live together. His marriage to her was simply a mutually beneficial agreement between them. He informed me of all this as if what he'd done was totally normal and natural. As if I should simply understand.

This came as a total shock. Enraged, I told him, "No. It's not natural or normal for you to cheat on me, even if we are far apart. What about me? Look at me! Did I start a relationship with another man while you were away?" He stared at me, seemingly astonished, as if what I was saying made no sense at all to him. He didn't respond.

I asked him for a divorce. He refused. I had to go to court to ask for a divorce. I discovered that the marriage I'd gotten into was filled with all kinds of complicated twists and turns that I knew nothing about and whose details I did not understand. He had to agree to the divorce for it to happen. If he didn't want to agree, he could make impossible demands—asking me to "show him the stars at noon," as my lawyer so colorfully put it—before he signed the divorce papers. It turned out that showing him the stars at noon in this case meant that he would ask me to immediately give up custody of the children. Then he'd agree to the divorce. Otherwise, I could keep my children and wait for him to decide if he would divorce me or not.

I chose the lesser of two evils. I remained Mazen's wife for another year, with him in the Emirates and me in Beirut. The only thing that he agreed to, after pressure from the lawyer, was that I could stay in the house, and he would stay elsewhere when he visited Lebanon. On his visits, he'd come over to see Lama and Karim and take them out.

On the day of the divorce judgment—initiated by Mazen this time—he strode into the house using his own key. It was a Sunday at noon. He shook the divorce papers in my face. "Here you go! You better hope your feminism helps you." He threw the papers on the table and left, taking his house key with him. I didn't understand why he still had the key. This was the first time he'd used it since I'd asked for the divorce. I went to sleep afraid, imagining that he could come back at any moment, unlock the door, and just come in.

My pride was wounded. He'd gone ahead and gotten the divorce through the courts without even informing me. He wanted to prove that he could control my life and destiny whether I liked it or not. But in some ways, I was happy—happy and free.

A year after our divorce, on the twins' seventh birthday, Mazen came to the house and took Karim. Mazen had been a militant and a student activist. He used to lecture other students, calling on them to eliminate all traces of sectarianism from their identity. And now here he was applying the sharia personal status laws to the letter. I begged him to let our son stay with us, even just for the day so he could celebrate his birthday with his twin sister Lama. But he swept him up and marched out, leaving a copy of the Sharia court's decision granting him full custody on the table.

I can't just go and see my son anymore. Mazen took Karim with him back to the Gulf. He told me that I could visit him in the summers at his grandfather's house in Saida. Or I could come to the Emirates. Otherwise, I'll just have to wait until Karim is old enough to travel to London on his own for university. He'll be far away from me for many years before he's at university in the UK. When I called him about a month ago, Karim told me he wasn't doing well. He blamed me for not joining his father in the Emirates when he'd asked me to, adding that everything that had gone wrong was my fault. It was all my fault and mine alone. I listened to my son's voice down the phone line. He'd just turned eight years old and lived far away. He parroted the words his father had taught him.

How can love turn to hate and resentment? How could Mazen fill his son's head with such nonsense? I couldn't understand it. I held my head in my hands and started sobbing.

Karim's toys are still lying around his bedroom and his clothes are still hanging in his closet. They must be too small for him now. But I left them where they were. Maybe he'll go back home while I'm away. I'm going to miss him, for sure, and Lama will miss him too. Mazen couldn't take her. There's still some time left before I'll be deprived of her too. Many things made me decide to leave

Lebanon. The most important is that I didn't want my daughter to suffer the same fate as her brother. Nonetheless I still had to get permission from Mazen to take her with me on a trip outside Lebanon.

I thought about it a lot. In the end, I only managed to tell him half the truth. I said that she'd been psychologically devastated by her brother leaving and by the Israeli invasion of Lebanon, which destroyed a large part of her school. Her friends had all left the country and we wanted to get away to Cyprus just for a little while. We'd meet my brother, her uncle Walid, there. He was now a doctor in Los Angeles and would spend a week with us in Cyprus. I didn't tell Mazen that Walid had organized our travel to the States. Of course I didn't tell him. I didn't say that I'd sent all the papers to apply for an immigration visa for Lama and myself a year ago. He didn't know any of this and he wasn't going to. At least not for now. I still couldn't believe that Mazen agreed. He sent me a signed, written letter of consent allowing me to take Lama with me to Cyprus.

I won't tell him anything. He can stay tangled up in his lies and delusions between Beirut and the Emirates. I'm the one who will leave. I'm going to leave to free myself of delusions; I'll find another place in the sun for Lama and me.

---

Mona didn't want to leave Beirut. But, in the end, she left in her own way, while remaining in the same place. She lost her memory. Memory loss is a kind of a journey. She found a solution for herself. Something I couldn't do. Some doctors diagnosed her illness as Alzheimer's disease, others said she had early-onset dementia. They called it "early-onset" because she wasn't even sixty when it began affecting her. To be honest, I didn't know the difference between the two. Early-onset dementia and Alzheimer's disease are two of a few kinds of escapes we might use to cope with life in Beirut. When the friends we had left would get together, we'd list them off: yoga, whiskey, tranquilizers, madness, Alzheimer's, suicide . . .

I no longer see my friends—male or female. I don't know if the last of them left Lebanon or stayed, making their own lists of escapes to cope. I don't know. What I do know is that Mona forgot my name. She was the one who'd helped me collect stories about my mother and the other women in my family. Shortly before she was diagnosed, she told me all about the most important moments in her life. She described her total shock when she heard that Gamal Abdel Nasser had died. She left home barefoot, wandered through the streets, and lost her way back. Nasserite Mona then kept to her room for days, drinking only water and refusing to eat. She cried all day. "If Nasser were still alive, would we be where we are today?" Mona asked. Layla's disappearance gave another major shock. She said no one she loved was left now that Nasser had died and Layla was gone. When Umm Kulthum died, Mona was unaffected. She loved the great singer and listened to every one of her monthly concerts on the radio. But her death came on the eve of the Lebanese Civil War, when Mona was deeply involved in volunteer work in the Palestinian refugee camps.

Every time I went to see her, I found her looking through pictures of herself playing volleyball. She'd been the driving force behind the first girls' high school volleyball team in Lebanon and later opened a gym in Beirut. One day I interrupted her leafing through a photo album. She raised her head and gazed at me with the derisive half-smile I'd known so well from my earliest childhood. It was as if she didn't believe in anything, as if her life passed like a dream. "How terrible the world has become," she muttered incomprehensibly before growing silent once again. A delicate thread of tears silently slid down her cheek, but quickly dried. Mona stared off into space once again.

Two days before I left Beirut, I passed by the agency to collect some papers I'd left in my desk. The office was empty. Everyone had moved to the Commodore Hotel, which had become a fortress of news agencies, cameras, and tape recorders, with dozens of cars parked outside, waiting for journalists. Then I visited Mona to bid her farewell. I stayed with her until late that evening. I didn't leave until she started to look sleepy. I kissed her and told her that I was going away with Lama. We shared a moment of serenity that evening, and Mona was the person I knew once again. "Why are you upset?" she asked. From a deep reverie, her voice emerged strong and clear. "Do you miss Layla? Are you still searching for her?"

She still remembered my mother, her cousin who'd disappeared in the spring of 1963. She'd dissolved like a grain of salt in the sea. Mona could remember her name. They'd been together at the cinema in Sahat al-Burj just before her disappearance. In that moment of clarity we shared, surely Mona could tell that my emotional distress was not just caused by the loss of my mother, but countless others as well. My son had been taken from me by his father on his seventh birthday. And there was also Ouida's permanent absence from my life—I missed her every day.

Sometimes when Mona talked, she seemed totally normal, as if she'd gotten her memory back. It felt like it was possible she might again talk to me like she did in the old days. But these flashes of logic would soon fade, and she'd go back to her silent absentmindedness.

I left Mona just before midnight and walked back to my flat in Mar Elias. We'd moved there after the war intensified and it became impossible to stay in our old place near the museum. The night was pitch-black, only a few dim lights in militia offices and military checkpoints lit the way. The long summer of the Israeli siege, its destruction of the city's roads and buildings, had emptied Beirut of its people. The city bade the Palestinians farewell when they left. At the time, Beirut felt fragmented and paralyzed. I hadn't seen any of our neighbors for more than two months. The faces of the men guarding the checkpoint right near our building kept changing. They knew me by name. I still don't know how they recognized us and knew our names. They got used to seeing me come home from work in Ras Beirut at night, crossing the narrow street to reach my building.

I climbed the stairs to the fourth floor. The elevator had been broken for two years. Half of the residents had left Beirut; the other half were refusing to pay their building fees, so it never got repaired. When I got home, the electricity had been cut. Lama was asleep and so was Imm Zeyad, the woman who'd helped look after my twins since they were young. She stayed with them until I came home from work. Ever since Mazen took Karim, she only looked after Lama. I searched around for the candle that I kept near the door since I knew the building's generator went off at 11 pm. Unable to see in the dark, I felt my way around with my hands, a move I'd mastered from living with no electricity.

I fumbled around until I found the candle on the table in the entry way. I lit it and used it to light another candle so that I could finish packing. I'd already collected all the papers I needed to take with me. I gathered all my writing about my mother and the other women in our family—the interviews and stories I'd recorded; my recollections of my struggles in Ksoura and Beirut; my mother's notebooks and papers, as well as my notes about everything she'd said that had stayed stuck in my head.

"My whole life is in this suitcase now," I muttered to myself, zipping it up and resting it by the door.

I couldn't sleep on that last night in Lebanon. There was hardly any time to sleep anyway. When I went into my room, I found Lama fast asleep on my bed, as she always was when I got home late. After Mazen had taken her brother from us, she once told me innocently that my bed was magic because it helped her fall asleep faster. I snuggled up next to her and put my ear close to her mouth. The rhythm of her breathing made me feel—even if only slightly—reassured.

I'd totally lost that feeling of reassurance the very moment Mazen abducted my son. Yes, he stole him from me. And he did it using the law. The day he came took him was a catastrophe. It was a Tuesday. Lama cried and cried, begging her father to leave him with us a few days so they could have their birthday party together at the end of the week. But to no avail. I silently packed Karim's things in a suitcase and asked him to call me when he got to his grandma's house in Saida. But he never called.

Shutting the bedroom door behind me, I walked back into the living room. I stretched out on the sofa and settled down under a woollen blanket. Staring at the candle as it melted and disappeared, I waited for dawn to begin to light the living room. Dark thoughts ate away at my mind like fire consumes a candle. It flickers and dances, throwing light on images and faces, then fades and disappears.

There is something that unites us. Something like my life. My life melted like a candle. There was nothing happy about my youth. First, my mother disappeared. Then, I moved into the university dormitories and lived alone. And then I found out that Salem was not my father. Everything I did was a kind of revenge that I took on her silence, her absence, and my loneliness. Imm Zeyad woke up and started to chastise me, as she always did after I'd gotten home late from work. "You should be kinder to yourself, and to your daughter."

She worked as a cleaner at the news agency early every morning, before she came to my place. She said she'd waited for me so that we could eat dinner together and that if I kept living my life like this, I'd die young.

She was such a strong woman, I thought, especially after everything that had happened to her. She'd lost her two sons in the civil war, one after the other, and she still could smile, laugh, make jokes, and care for her loved ones. She lost her eldest, Zeyad, on Black Saturday when he got into a shared taxi from Aley to Beirut and never returned. Her younger son was a military man who'd joined Fatah and was killed in the battle of Tell al-Zaatar. They both passed away in a period of less than a year. She rarely failed to mention them in conversation. She'd always tell me about the foods Zeyad used to like and the stories his brother used to tell. She'd take a deep drag on her cigarette, exhale, and pronounce in her raspy voice, "Life is short, Asmahan. All we can do in life is keep the memories of our loved ones alive in our hearts." She said this over and over, pounding her chest with her fist and bursting into a fit of sobs.

In the morning, I left my keys with Imm Zeyad and crossed over to East Beirut to get to the Port in Jounieh, so we could take the ferry to Larnaca.

—

On the plane from Larnaca to New York, Lama rested her head on my lap and fell asleep. I stroked her chestnut hair, contemplating how we were going to manage to live in the States. How would I pay her school fees? Or buy her things? Mazen would never send us a single cent if we didn't go back to Lebanon. Maybe I wouldn't find work quickly, maybe the university I'd been in contact with wouldn't hire me to teach Arabic after all.

I knew that no one would be there waiting for me; I'd never been to this city before. But that's OK. As long as I still have my memory and my memoir-in-progress tucked away in my bag, I'll be fine. The flight attendant passed by my seat, smiling. She asked if I'd like a cup of coffee, adding that it was 8 am New York time and that we'd be landing in two hours. I still remember her smile. It allowed me to take a deep breath, exhale, and say to myself, "It's going to be OK. We're here now, and Walid won't be far away."

I'm remembering all this today while Lama is sleeping peacefully in our new house. The exhausting little details of life can overpower us. I hardly recall my dreams here. I just keep on remembering the hurt. I used to see myself flying in my dreams. I no longer see myself flying, or even running. I wake up and try to rid my mind of my demons so I can start my day normally.

One morning after arriving in New York, I woke up with an overwhelming desire to cry. Remnants of a fragmented dream lingered but were still fuzzy in my mind. I saw Mazen with another woman and they were having sex on a bed in a place I couldn't identify. But it was somewhat familiar to me. The scene quickly went foggy, and I could see empty space stretched out in front of me. In the dream, I started searching for that place, but I couldn't find it. I was overcome by a powerful feeling of loss; it filled me with despair. I woke up still feeling it. I hadn't seen Mazen in a dream for a long time, as if he'd evaporated. I hardly even remembered the shape of his face. I don't know how he suddenly appeared to me in this way. What saddened me wasn't that he visited me in a dream, but that I'd lost a place that I used to know and couldn't remember how to find it.

That same morning, I started thinking about my mother. I'd rarely seen her with her family, except with her grandma Shahira, who'd raised her. I never saw her with my grandpa—her father, that is—nor with either her maternal or paternal uncles. It was as if she were all alone, with practically no family, no one to ask after her, no one to support her. And her husband Salem abused her. For various reasons, her father and her uncles left her to face her marital fate alone.

My mother always kept a journal, but she wrote in it less often after the events of 1958. I reread what she wrote one month before she disappeared:

> Walid has left Lebanon and gone to the States. Asmahan will go to university here. I wish she'd left with him. Salem is away. When he comes back, he'll unleash his violence on my body. I wish I had an invisibility cloak like in the fairy tales, so he wouldn't be able to see me. But there's no such thing as an invisibility cloak, and I don't want to wait until life becomes less painful.

I don't know if my mother found happiness wherever she went. In the three pictures I have of her, I see no signs of happiness in her eyes. Whenever she found photos of herself, she'd rip them up and throw them into our back garden. One day she was out there, tearing up one picture after another and throwing the pieces up in the air. They fluttered down around her, and her eyes shone with sorrow. When I ran over and hugged her, she pointed at the garden wall, telling me without batting an eyelid that this was the very place that Salem had thrown the newborn kittens, while their mother Noosa stood at his feet and wailed in distress like a bereaved woman.

One of the three pictures was of her and Salem after he'd pitched a tent for us on the roof. The second picture was of the day Miss Helen left, when my mother was still a student in Beirut.

The third was of her in front of Shahira's house: Walid was on her lap, her arms wrapped tightly around him. I was sitting in a chair next to them. She was clutching him like a drowning person holds a life preserver. It was as if I were far away, or she didn't even see me at all.

My head is so full right now it feels like it might explode. Tonight, I have to forget everything. I need to shake off all the stories—my own as well as those of the women in my family. I need to sleep, if only for a few hours. Tomorrow, after I put the manuscript in the envelope and post it to Ouida in Montreal, I'll take Lama out to buy her a warm winter coat. Then I'll call Walid in California and let him know that we're coming to see him in a couple of days to spend the Christmas holiday with him.

Right now, I feel very sleepy.

# Translator's Note

During the final stages of finishing the translation of *Songs for Darkness*, I narrowed down a list of specific things to discuss with the author, Iman Humaydan. I was hoping that this would help me decide what would be included in this short translator's note. We'd been having regular Zoom and WhatsApp calls, leading to many interesting discussions. In the spring of 2025, we were able to follow these up with more satisfying in-person conversations in Beirut. My narrow list was soon replaced by wide-ranging discussions of many different topics and questions—some related to specific elements of this novel, and others that more broadly inform the worldview of this work and its sweeping view of history.

Even in this translator's note, I hesitate to label *Songs for Darkness* a historical novel. Iman had told me when I first started the translation that this wasn't the right term for the book. She felt the weight and detail it implies was not quite right. In refusing the terminology, she emphasized that this is a novel by, of, and for women. As such, "history" must be thought of in particular ways. We therefore amended our working definition of the novel by unpacking what history and histories this novel recounts—as well as how they are told.

Perhaps history here is curvy like the bodies of women, as Iman suggested—like the kind of body that Shahira's mother and auntie Ikhlas call the devil's work when they are preparing her for her wedding day. Iman proposed that when a history is less linear, rounder, and more circular, that's when it can be a history of women and for women. I felt that this rethinking of history, derived from our conversation, could be a useful framing of it for the English-language reader of this novel. Below are others, distilled from the scribbled notes I took in Beirut several things that she and I felt should be conveyed directly to the English-language readership of *Songs for Darkness*.

The first detail we decided might ease the reader's journey through the text is that the villages that animate it—Ksoura and Ajmat—are not real, though the contours of village life depicted here are very close to real, lived experiences. Ksoura is based on Mount Lebanon villages, and Ajmat on villages in the Western Beqaa. All of the details, characters, and families depicted here are also fictional, except in the case of well-known political and historical figures.

Iman emphasized to me several times that the stories and characters depicted here are inspired by real life, but they are not real stories, even if certain deeper truths about life in the time and place they are set emerges from them. From Iman's perspective, the stories told in *Songs for Darkness* gain legitimacy from how they are embedded within the history of Lebanon. She crafted them through extensive research on this history, including digging deeply into the role of women, and their many roles, in the country over time. The novel pays particular attention to women's roles in the movement for independence, political change over a century, and the creation of the nation. This novel depicts in detail their impact on ordinary women.

Though the women whose stories are told in this novel are not real women, they do reflect a real truth of women in Lebanon. In my own reading of *Songs for Darkness* as a translator, one of the most important elements is how powerfully the novel depicts different challenges that women face differently over time. There is no linear sense of progress that shows women being more liberated as time marches forward. The difficulties that women of later generations face are no more easily faced than those of their foremothers. We do not see daughters and granddaughters living lives that are more free compared to their elders. The conditions of freedom and unfreedom are shown to be different.

The novel depicts the hardships women face across different communities in Lebanon both directly and subtly. The family at the center of the novel is never identified in communitarian or sectarian terms, but indirect hints allow the reader to understand they are Druze. Many of the other characters in the novel belong to Christian communities, reflecting the demographic realities of Mount Lebanon. The women from these backgrounds have in common that they live in a patriarchal society that limits their choices and opportunities. Thus, we see Layla and Rose coming to terms with similar kinds of lives as they reach adulthood. Both are married off as teenagers, for example, and though their choice of husbands means their womanhood is shaped differently, their destinies are both not so different and bound together.

Iman emphasized this to me many times. How mountain-based communities eat, how they wear their clothes, how they raise their children—their customs and traditions—are only very subtly differentiated. The religious/sectarian differences between Druze and Christian communities in the novel are not the main, defining features of women's lives. This is part of the reason that Iman chose not to name these communities or focus on their differences, and to rather emphasize how they share more than what separates them, culturally speaking. With the decision not to name the Druze community in particular, Iman remains aware of the importance of eliding difference in the name of some kind of national unity. The novel is deeply researched historically, politically, and culturally, and the details she does use in the text are important to its texture. They add nuance to the plot and character development. The intertwined familial and individual relationships—not only between Rose and Layla, but also generationally between Ouida and Asmahan—are highlighted.

It is not only interpersonal details of mountain life that Iman attends to in the novel. We see, for example, the importance of agriculture to Druze communities in the Western Beqaa and Mount Lebanon, and how they depended on this historically. Moreover, the economic changes over time impact the al-Dahli family. Ouida's family leaves the village to work in the port, showing the shift from agricultural work in an era of rapid urbanization. We also see how Christian families often were impacted by these shifts roughly one generation before Druze families in the same region, with Asmahan's family members working in agriculture longer than Ouida's and only joining the "modern" economy later.

We also see cultural and historical details that impact all communities in Mount Lebanon. The role of mission schools is underlined with the character of Miss Helen, for example, and her relationships with local women. Grandma Shahira's intense commitment to educating her children, no matter the cost, shows how people used these schools to achieve social mobility for their children as a way to propel entire families to different kind of lives.

A final cultural feature of this novel—reflected in its title and epigraph by Brecht—is songs and singing. Many of the songs come from Soueida in Southern Syria, emphasizing the regional connections and intermarriages between Druze communities in this region, Mount Lebanon, and the Western Beqaa. These songs that punctuate the text and emphasize key moments are crucial to understanding it. Songs, which are after all poems, are among the most challenging elements of a text to translate, with layers of meaning difficult to convey; wordplay, rhymes, and rhythms are notoriously difficult, if not impossible, to render across language. In the process of translation, I spent a great deal of time on the songs and how to render them in English, as well as thinking through how moments of singing impacted the narrative structure. The novel itself offers a kind of song about dark times, in our own dark times.

—Michelle Hartman, Montreal, 2025

## ABOUT THE AUTHOR

Iman Humaydan is a Lebanese novelist, creative writing teacher, editor, and freelance journalist. Her novels received wide international acclaim and were translated into English, French, Italian, Dutch, German, Armenian, Polish, and Georgian. She is the author of five novels, including *B as in Beirut, Wild Mulberries, Other Lives,* and *The Weight of Paradise*, all published in English by Interlink. She is also the editor of the collection of short stories *Beirut Noir*. She is the president of the Lebanese chapter of PEN, and splits her time between Beirut and Paris.

## ABOUT THE TRANSLATOR

Michelle Hartman is a literary translator and professor of Arabic literature at McGill University. She has translated more than a dozen novels from Arabic to English including three other novels by Iman Humaydan, *The Weight of Paradise*, *Other Lives*, and *Wild Mulberries*. Her latest translation is *A Long Walk from Gaza* (Interlink, 2024). She has also written on Lebanese women and the Civil War in two co-authored volumes (with Malek Abisaab), *Women's War Stories: The Lebanese Civil War, Women's Labor and the Creative Arts* (Syracuse UP, 2022) and *What the War Left Behind: Women's Stories of Resistance and Struggle in Lebanon* (Syracuse UP, 2024).